LIST

THUNDER AND LIGHT
MARIE-CLAIRE BLAIS

TRANSLATED BY NIGEL SPENCER

LIST

First published in French in 2001 as *Dans la foudre et la lumière* by Les Éditions du Boréal.
First published in English in 2001 by House of Anansi Press Ltd.
This edition published in Canada in 2019 and the USA in 2019 by House of Anansi Press Inc.
www.houseofanansi.com

House of Anansi Press is committed to protecting our natural environment. As part of our
efforts, this book is made of material from well-managed FSC®-certified forests, recycled
materials, and other controlled sources.

23 22 21 20 19   1 2 3 4 5

Library and Archives Canada Cataloguing in Publication

Title: Thunder and light / Marie-Claire Blais ; translated by Nigel Spencer.
Other titles: Dans la foudre et la lumière. English
Names: Blais, Marie-Claire, 1939- author. | Spencer, Nigel, 1945- translator.
Description: Translation of: Dans la foudre et la lumière. | Reprint. Originally published:
Toronto: House of Anansi Press, 2001.
Identifiers: Canadiana (print) 20190056487 | Canadiana (ebook) 20190056517 |
ISBN 9781487004255 (softcover) | ISBN 9781487004262 (EPUB) | ISBN 9781487004279
(Kindle)
Classification: LCC PS8503.L33 D2913 2019 | DDC C843/.54—dc23

Library of Congress Control Number: 2019931304

Series design: Brian Morgan
Cover artwork: *Mondrian Electric Storm* by Julianne Gladstone
Typesetting: Sara Loos

*We acknowledge for their financial support of our publishing program
the Canada Council for the Arts, the Ontario Arts Council, and the Government of Canada.*

Printed and bound in Canada

INTRODUCTION
by Noah Richler

WHAT DOES THE NOVELIST DO? Engages, entertains, disrupts — and, for present and future readers, is a witness to the times — to "events," yes, but as much to our hopes, dreams, and aspirations, our anxieties and fears. Writers, even seemingly frivolous ones, express what we may not yet know is occupying our minds. For the writer is a conduit, a medium, travelling the middle ground and providing shape and voice to stories residing there, stories evolving in that realm in between the world as it is and the sense we eventually make of it. The middle space is the crowded agora of our lives, a den of memory and — its corollary — the projecting imagination. It is a place where present and future and past are one, and Time is a stock, not a measure. It is a place of constants: of eternal mysteries, not verities (how to explain the beautiful and the good, but also "Wrath"?); a place of quantities and of *thirsts*.

Marie-Claire Blais knows this space. She, like so many of the characters she peoples her novels with — the writer Daniel, his sons Augustino and Samuel, the poets Adrien, Jean-Mathieu, and Rodrigo, the photographer Caroline, and others — is an artist and, as such, a force guiding us through the maelstrom of the world. Just as she writes of Dylan Thomas, though it could as easily describe any of the artist-heroes to whom she pays impassioned homage (Balzac, Dickens, Stendahl, Beethoven, Paganini, Schubert), she is "chained to [her] torment, as though harnessed to a tree and the far-spreading roots of a nightmare carried a long time within." Blais's characters wrestle almost rapturously with questions of how to be, so intense and demanding is their engagement, though, rather than any particular lucidity, it is her artists' capacity for *feeling* — their painful sensitivity to all the inexplicable chaos, cruelty, and pathos of humanity — that illuminates the cyclonic world. Thus, at the centre of Blais's Cycle of Thirsts — for justice, love, kindness, though also evil, says the author — is the nonplussed and melancholic father and writer Daniel, melancholy and bafflement being the most rational of existential states.

Blais, born to a working-class Quebec family, was raised a Catholic and taught by nuns. She quit school at the age of fifteen to work and to write, but the weighty edifice of the church remains. Her pastors, when they are not pilferers or pederasts, are radicals, and the author's own fury is biblical — a rage against not the dying, but the perfidy of light. So, then, street gangs, floundering boats carrying refugees, the long shadow of Hiroshima, the massacre of tourists at Luxor, the penury and valour of the downtrodden — the grief-driven suicide of Kevin Carter, the Pulitzer Prize–winning photographer of a starving Sudanese infant with vulture in attendance ("it is to the great photographic journalists," thinks Caroline, "that we owe the world's collective memory") — are a portion of her terrible real. Virtue, there is that too, derives from the naked exposition of vulnerable souls without which there is no art; in our not forgetting, in our not conceding to the complacency, akin to sin, that privilege extends to the few.

There lives in Blais — she likes this thought, that the spirit of artists is ineffable and lives on in others who come after — something of Giotto and Hieronymus Bosch. If she helps us navigate the pool of our being, it is because she presents it to us as a mostly (but not completely) acrid Garden, where all things happen all the time. Her impulse, says her French-Canadian editor Jean Bernier, is less for the novel to be like Stendahl's mirror walking along the road than "an exhortation to see, and to enter in communion with the characters she exhibits to us." To be aware is a first, necessary step to some kind of choosing. The journey is dizzying and uncertain, and her characters are imbued not so much with purpose as a momentum that cannot be halted — the very momentum of existence. The ground shifts underfoot, and the destination determined by humankind's headlong rush toward conflagration would be ineluctable were it not for the chance of recognition that our thirsts provide.

Blais entertains, disrupts, and engages but is witness, most of all, to what she has described as "the haunting of the present." It is as if the formidable array of characters these pages have room for move through her unimpeded — and were there room enough, then all our stories would be told. Hers — and the uninterrupted flow of sentences, the "stream of consciousness" aspects of her text, reflect this — is an interconnected world in which relatives, friends, and strangers, the living, the dead, and those not yet born are inextricably tied by a flawed, often defeated but always incandescent humanity. Still, it is misleading, if not a mistake, to compare Blais's style, as some have done, to William Faulkner's, James Joyce's, or Virginia Woolf's, for the life she has breathed into the characters woven into her quilt, more than tapestry, is a stream of *consciousnesses* and not a single consciousness; a chorus of simultaneity rather than an aria of the interior life in which, despite the tumult, the players remain distinct and the reader is never left behind. This is also Blais's genius, that in the Babel of her agitated, impassioned, and so often desperate world, there is little reliance on the cleaving and distinction that a full stop or a paragraph break confers. We know in whose company we are and, besides, this is not how we live. We are connected, through memory and that projecting imagination, to the sum of lives underfoot, beside, and in front of us — to everyone we know and everyone we shall never meet. To enter into Blais's onstreaming is to give ourselves up to dreams, nightmares, and the ad infinitum of our connection — to the whole of our being. Blais demands that we succumb, as she herself does in her own navigation of the middle space, to great swelling waves of our parallel lives and, ultimately, our equivalence. For despite her being the author, the Grand Designer; despite the agonies of Daniel and Augustino and Caroline and Rodrigo the poet from Brazil, who occupy the main stage of her cycle; despite their insatiable thirsts — for justice, for beauty and the good — there are no principal parts. The world Blais is channelling is one in which rival presences and quantities co-exist, no matter their jostling, because there is no other true way.

"Let the waves take you. Don't try to touch bottom and you won't hit the rocks," was the advice of Blais's translator Nigel Spencer to the Montreal writer Marianne Ackerman and, through her, to readers. And yet we live more fully for knowing the rocks are there and touching them once in a while. Blais's contagious empathy has plumbed the depths and tells us so. Be aware. Read the signs.

NOAH RICHLER is an editor, a journalist, and a cultural critic. He was born and raised in Montreal and is the author of *This Is My Country, What's Yours?: A Literary Atlas of Canada*. He has won the BC Award for Canadian Non-Fiction and has been a finalist for the Governor General's Literary Award, the Shaughnessy Cohen Prize for Political Writing, and the Stephen Leacock Medal for Humour.

For Michèle and for Julie Mailhot

Source of tears and cries, with what brilliant apparel you have honoured and laden us. Anguish and love, as mourning and joy, are equally celebrated, engraved as landscapes in our faces.

ANNE HÉBERT, *ÈVE*

THUNDER AND LIGHT

Polly brushed her head against Carlos's feet, their soles pink and curved in rubber sandals, for these were her refuge from danger, flailing the air and sand on the beach that was damp from ocean and salt, as well as the dust from the streets, with the robustness of his body and the speed of his step, what unfamiliar noises, shouts, and rumblings hung suspended around Polly and Carlos as they ran side by side, Polly knew the cruelty of unavoidable destiny, an arrow strung to the life of every living creature, Bahama Street, Esmeralda Street, her faith in life was instinctive, she proudly bared her teeth for Carlos, greedy they were too, and her tongue, with which she licked the undersides of his feet, Carlos her refuge, her lair, he raised an angry face skyward, that Lazaro, I'll get him one of these days, Polly, he shouted, so you're going to follow me everywhere, are you, Polly, and Polly saw those large hands of his, yesterday so supple and ready to caress, now tightening into fists, and where were they headed anyway, running like this under a scorching sun, Lazaro's watch, he murmured, that Egyptian, that Muslim immigrant on Bahama, always smothered by his mother in gifts she got from Cairo, he wants me to give it back to him, him with his bicycle, his digital watch, and that King Tut fetish he wears round his neck, but no, he's

3

got to have his Adidas watch back, and every night he lies in wait to get it from me, Polly heard him go on bitterly between clenched teeth, and if he doesn't let up, I'll lean on him, scare him with one of those Cuban guns but no bullets, Lazaro the Egyptian, you'd better not follow me there, Polly, and where on earth were they going in this leaden heat before the storm, the tempest, wasn't it time to be tackling the waves, this dream of water throbbed through Polly's sweat-covered temples as she heard other dogs barking in the distance, still she followed Carlos, panting and glued to the pink underside of his feet, Carlos her refuge, her shelter from danger and annihilation because anything, however savage, could befall her in a second on Bahama or Esmeralda Street when rival gangs fought it out, Carlos and Lazaro the Egyptian, inseparable only yesterday, Carlos, Lazaro, and Venus with her iguana on a yellow leash, staring at the ocean, feverish from the burning air, no, thought Venus, the Captain her husband wouldn't be home tonight, the huge bed covered in silk cushions would be deprived of that unbridled lust of his for a long time yet, his late-blooming love so often haunted by the thought of death, the green iguana and the affectionate dachshund, now without a master, went everywhere with Venus, when she wandered all alone through the cedarwood house, opening cupboards that held Captain Williams's things laid out on the shelves, possessions dear to him that Venus left in untroubled silence, his extensive collection of seamen's caps, pipes of exotic shapes from which she could still smell the contaminated odour of islands ruined by the White man's passing, she slid along the hallways of the house, its walls covered with the Captain's lascivious paintings, the painter-musician-adventurer who had sometimes asked Venus to pose for them with an obscenity so candid it moved them both to laughter, liberated from Pastor Jeremy's sermons, Venus could still hear the powerful voice of her father remonstrating that he never would set foot in Venus's house, one where as a young female escort from the Club Mix, only fifteen years old, she had consummated her marriage to a man easily forty years older, a phoney, sixty-year-old captain with such a shady reputation that even his disappearance at sea was suspect, Mama just didn't know if she could forgive Venus for all these foul-ups, after all, didn't she have enough to worry about with Carlos and the gang fights on Bahama and Esmeralda; since that Egyptian Lazaro had come on the scene, he was always getting himself into fights, Carlos her baby, in some no-good outfit, Venus perched the green iguana like a scaly crown on top of her head, its paws overlapping her forehead, no predator's going to catch you by the tail up there, she said laughing, although the voice of Pastor Jeremy still sounded in her ears, echoing as it used to do around the Temple of the City of Coral, if the serpent was the tempting devil of the Scriptures, as her father preached in his sermons, why mightn't Captain Williams, the man Venus had chosen over everyone else at the Club Mix, and of all those in the jungle whose snakes and iguanas she tamed, why mightn't he be the serpent she had charmed with the sweet airs of her voice, seduced in fact, the pastor said, because long before this she had been seducing men, and the Captain was tough, not tender, she thought to herself, but what could a zealous father know of a free-living man who lavished the flame of his passion and the jumble of his riches on a Black girl, a cedarwood house Venus thought she would never escape from, cared for by Richard the estate manager, this house and its works of art, libidinous bits of wreckage salvaged from the varied stops the Captain had made in every port of the islands, why did this man, a man with some charitable principles, thought Venus, why did he have to wind up like all the others, captains whose bodies the crews had to bring home some morning under a fluttering black flag, on board his own ship and headed for the tepid waters of the canal, lined with arborescent vines, grasses, and ferns, the kingdom of iguanas and watersnakes, Mama and her eight children, after all, didn't they live

5

crammed into a single room when Venus would have preferred to put them all up in her villa, but, no, the Pastor had repeated, never will we enter Venus's house, so long alone Venus had waited for the return of a ghost whose voice she still heard in fragments, wouldn't he just step out of the mangrove mists one day, this Captain of hers, the way drunken, dope-dealing sailors sometimes did when they slid onto shore in their tipsy boats, soon his home, its terrain being gradually swallowed up by the waters, would play host to a charity party, Venus was thinking, a bazaar for the kids who had to go off to school on Bahama Street with no food in their stomachs and no smallpox, meningitis, or any other kinds of shot, all the town's bigwigs would be her guests, all those who had looked down on her when she'd accompanied Uncle Cornelius, singing in taverns and dingy cabarets, Venus was the wife of a hero who, so he said, and she knew he wasn't lying, would never hesitate to kill a dangerous rival in order to defend her honour, and who knows, maybe that's how he'd lost his life, maybe he had killed for her or been struck himself some stormy night and drowned in the swollen waters, everyone had envied their happinees, their lush paradise where birds ate from Venus's hand, sparrows and hummingbirds taking the fleshy fruit, pink melon with sweet juice trickling through her fingers, but better not think about it, the picture of Venus's honour being defended by a crime out on the ocean, no, she said to the green iguana crawling through her hair, and to the dachshund sniffing the wild scents on her tattooed ankles, no, here no predator would come, and the dachshund, feeling playful all of a sudden, jumped at her feet, focused on the clicking sound made by her anklets as she walked toward the beach, the Captain's boat tied up in the waves, nervous before the rain, the iguana, which seemed to have fallen asleep in her hair, opened its large, bulbous eyes and looked all around from behind wrinkles made by long-ago apprehensions and from under the rough, leathered skin of its eyelids, the iguana on its yellow leash listened to Venus's laughing voice as she said, no predator can reach you, a voice that echoed in its heart, under its armour, like the call of freedom in the heart of a prisoner, the captive iguana heard the rustling of water, of insects, of marshes where reeds and climbing plants criss-crossed, far off the time when the iguana crawled on its short legs and belly toward the world of men or over beaches, no, she had been tamed to decorate their rock gardens and poolsides, here no predator could come, Venus said, the lizard, the iguana, and the crocodile lived alone in the thick scrub of the savannahs and forests, in the giant grasses of the hot and humid brushlands. The bus was tearing along, deep into the high regions of the Pyrenees, when Mother said to Mélanie, who had reached the age for her First Communion and was done up for the trip, as they all were, in a white dress and crinoline, don't turn around, Mélanie. Don't look back at the string of cars by the side of the road, one of them has been hit, a fine-scaled butterfly caught by a passing car, and wasn't it because of the dress and crinoline, that white armour mothers dress their daughters in for their First Communions, that the little girl was killed that day, Mélanie thought later, and the negligence of a drunk driver, a disaster conceived and inflicted by heaven on that radiant afternoon in the hollows of these snowy mountains and glaciers, and now a butterfly caught in the trap of joy, Mother had said to Mélanie, for one moment, these children were singing and humming, the next, the sun seemed to grow pale, and the mountains trembled with fear, Mélanie hearing all around her nothing but the silence of glaciers, and the bus careering up the spiralled mountain roads, and so quickly the communicants were scattered in a broken chain of brilliant white along the highway, no, don't look back, Mélanie, her mother had said, and Mélanie pronounced these words, there's nothing we can do, it's a crime, Mama, what can we do, a little girl sliding along the icy path on the day of her First Communion, the fatal winding of a spindle, the lace from a crinoline on a car wheel that

Mélanie was spared the sorrow of seeing, though now, many years later, the pain was still frightful, Mélanie thought about the son from whom she would soon be separated, still an hour to think before Samuel leaves for New York, that day in the Pyrenees, a crime had been committed, and soon Samuel would be gone, Samuel, without knowing that his mother was watching him, perched on the terrace of a Moorish-style hotel with a view of the town, pink blocks of houses overlooking the sea, Samuel knew his mother's sobriety, often touching only water, he wouldn't have liked knowing she was so near, Mélanie thought, on a terrace, sober amid these flaccid, shambling, cocktail-soaked tourists, and watching, always watching him, Samuel, who hated that very thing, Mélanie thought about her mother telling her not to turn around, because in an hour Samuel would be stepping up to his convertible, an extravagance for a seventeen-year-old, Daniel and Mélanie would never change, Mère used to say too, when they're seventeen, they just leave, Samuel has to keep on training as a dancer, but it would be better if he set his sights on going to a prestigious university, though his dyslexia might set him back, her mother's allusions had brought back to Mélanie the weight of the Pyrenees and their glaciers; from the lofty terrace, Mélanie glimpsed every movement Samuel made, why swim in a public pool, why say goodbye to his friends there, when he could have invited them up to the house, and those fries they were all eating with drinks that would ruin their health, yet all so relaxed, leaning on the wooden railing of the restaurant and bar with its roof open to the burning sun, a few steps away from the sea, Samuel enjoyed this low-end place, where the loudspeakers blared their raucous music all over town, even to this peaceful terrace, an outrage, Mélanie's mother had said, notes from a Beethoven concerto amputated and scattered into a howling cacophony and further chopped and telescoped into a repetitive rap rhythm, a whining din from the naked, sunning youth on the docks; palm trees and flags waved in the wind, what anxiousness filled this time of day, thought Mélanie, these girls and boys, really too healthy, couldn't they hear the rumbling of the waves, then and there, all of a sudden she saw him stand out from the others, Samuel, back straight, neck a little too thick of late, windblown hair, pulling his clothes from a lounge chair and putting them on, chatting with some young woman, soft and slow and sensual these instants were for them, as Mélanie saw his car door close, it'll be only a few months, Mama, proudly at the wheel of his car, she would watch the red convertible slip away among criss-crossed streets and avenues, soft and slow and sensual these instants were for them, as Mélanie had studied her son, young and vibrant, an hour before his departure, and she would think about mounting an exhibit of photographs from recent decades kept by African Americans as a memorial against the indifference of the millennium, this would be one of Mélanie's projects for the year, but would the signs of a slavery as recent as the Second World War register on senators and representatives, how would they react to these pictures draped in mourning of what was only recently called the Colored City, a sated city of living skeletons barefoot in winter, of Negro servants, of people living day to day in degradation, Mélanie could not get out of her mind the worn faces of fruit pickers, bike messengers in the cold, old women who had washed White people's laundry, and the virulent image of lobbyists for the poor, very dignified in black and grey suits, confronting their oppressors through the bars of a presidential palace or at the doors of an administrative capital, though dating only from 1944, these photographs had already been forgotten, and exploring craters on the moon could not salve the fresh blood of wounds in a tunnel-city where Black servants had lived, but Samuel would remember, thought Mélanie, young and vibrant, for him the future would not be an immaculate discovery, how much he would have disliked his mother's being so close by as she refreshed herself with ice water on a terrace and watched his every move, kissing a woman, putting his arms around a friend's shoulders, and *shhht! shhht!* said Carlos, go home to the mothers that had you stoned on cocaine or crack the minute you were born, he yelled, leave the cocks alone, you freaks, stop grabbing them up in your traps and nets, you creeps, he continued howling as he crossed Bahama Street, Polly panting and nipping at his calves as she followed him, you and them dagger tattoos on your arms, I know you're in with the Bad Nigger Gang, *shhht! shhht!* Cock thieves, feather pluckers, you all oughta be locked up, the two thieves, their bicycles lying beside them in the middle of the asphalt, scooped up their baskets and hopped the fence into the garden of the desolately flapping, squawking cocks, seven-year-old assassins, yelled Carlos, you're not gonna make them fight and tear each other apart, you scumbags, maybe because of his furious voice, the cock thieves flattened themselves in the grass under the bougainvillea branches, and the violet-purple flowers stuck to their clothes, and the brown cocks fled on thin straw-coloured feet, cackling with fright, scuzzballs, Carlos started up again, eight of you raped the school shrink who came to detox you, you're rotten right down to your genes, go on back to your mamas, he noticed they were lying flat in the grass with their empty baskets, listening, and he felt disgusted by those rolling, dilated eyes under caps pulled down low, but as he cursed them, his voice was drowned out by another coming from the open doors of the church, it was Pastor Ezekiel calling from the meeting house, a woman's voice, thought Carlos, yet still able to draw a crowd, while Pastor Jeremy's church often lay empty, still it was rare for Pastor Ezekiel to be praying in her church since she travelled around the country so much, moving toward the church, he tried to give Polly a shove and missed, go on home he said angrily between clenched teeth, you can't go in there with me, those cock thieves might get you in their nets and wring your neck like the hens, they're wreckers, vandals, thieves, Carlos could hear Pastor Ezekiel singing, it was a set of chanted, modulated calls for the faithful to come and pray in a church that was open to all, and he thought no woman could be as close to God as Pastor Jeremy, his father, after all, didn't he say that only men could share God's secrets, and now this lush woman, this Ezekiel, strode to and fro under the wooden vaulting of her church, the milk white folds of her tunic covering massive but agile feet, quick to move her body into dance, into fusion with God, come here, little fellow, tell me what's wrong, she asked one of her flock whose hands covered his tear-stained face, what is it, my little chick, come closer, sick, you said, but you're healed, didn't you know that, I could hold your skinny neck between two fingers, because Jesus loves you, say it with me, son, simply, calmly, I bear you in my heart's faith, my pale little man, my little chick, may bitterness and pain be far from your soul, my little spotty-face, you must learn to smile and to love, all of you who feel abandoned, come to me, now practise taking the hand of the person to the left in yours, the same thing to the right, and let's all sing together a hymn to joy and healing for your White brother, the scrawny chick, so he needn't feel all these nasty things tugging at him, stand up straight, O man beloved of Jesus, don't stoop like that, laugh and sing, dry your tears, we love you, and Jesus does too, sick, oh no, not you, come here by me, no, don't stiffen like that when you pray, dance and pray at the same time, listen to me, now isn't that a smile I see starting on your pale-born face, why yes, it is a smile, you say no one will touch you because you're full of sores, well, come here and let me hold and comfort you, sweetie, you'll be better by Christmas because here you've got all of us praying for you, and every one of us has faith in Jesus, so take heart, my frail little guy, isn't there someone at home for whom you're pre-cious, because love will heal you, come on, all you lonely ones, you two, suffering just as much as this little one, this little chick, whoever says you're misunderstood, whoever says you're hated and despised is pathetic, Ezekiel, whose name my parents gave me, was a Hebrew

11

prophet who called out the destruction of Jerusalem, but I'm here calling out hope, joy, love, and don't you listen to those nighttime preachers in the churches, don't you listen to them when they preach discrimination against this one and that one, they're just crazy spirits, oftentimes corrupt, they even work their way into politicians' speeches, they are hatred and evil and fraud, and they'll destroy humble folks, so don't you listen to them and their talk of flooded continents, and their talk of shadows and the destruction of Jerusalem, why, they might take over your lives and your future, what else do they foresee, earthquakes in California and South America, raining fire and ice right through the walls of your houses, no, you just go on shining in the light like the lilies of the fields, ah, little man, what's eating you is fear, and you the child of Jesus, and while the dance of Pastor Ezekiel charmed all the faithful so that they filled the church with their songs and supplications, Carlos saw the cock thieves clamber up, stunned looking, and climb onto their bikes, with not a cock in their nets, and yelling back at him from the distance, calling him a nobody-sellout to the White folks, bad nigger yourself, and Carlos thought that if Pastor Ezekiel, who said she could see into people's souls, could see his, she would know about the dark designs in his heart, guiltier than the cock thieves, training fighting-cocks was no crime, thirty-five dollars, that's what a good cockfight brought in, dreaming up some new disaster for Lazaro, that Muslim, that Egyptian, that immigrant on Bahama Street, Lazaro's watch, he's waiting for me every night to try to get it back, I'll shoot an empty gun at his legs, that'll scare him, better watch out for the cop who might be in front of Trinity College counting everyone who went by with a knife or a chain, and that other cop on guard in front of Trinity Baptist Church, what if he saw or heard us, he would say, carrying weapons again, eh, boys, what are your dads, all gunrunners? Noon, that's when it would happen this day of vengeance, noon, just Lazaro and me, and the police officer would say, all pompous with his hand on his hip where he holstered a gun, I'm telling you, you're going to grow up and die in state prison, because you don't just live out your life, eating every day and getting fat and strong as a horse, no sir, you die in those places, at noon, with the planes droning overhead, Lazaro's voice will be dry and feeble, come on Carlos, give me that watch, my mother gave it to me; I'll have a case or a binder under my arm with the unloaded gun in it, you're going to be in C Block, the officer will say, we're through playing nursemaid, you'll get old in a grave with bars, barbs, and razor wire all around; with life for murder you'll be a hundred, yeah, thought Carlos, they're going to need dogs to dig up this gun, we've got 6,100 of you in jail, the cop will say, and more every day, remember last spring, Crazy, the sixteen-year-old who killed Black Madness the Episcopalian minister, he's doing life in the coal valleys in Houtzdale, Pennsylvania, oh, he's got religion, they all do, crosses and crucifixes everywhere, in their cells, on their chests, some of them, the young ones, learn to read while they're inside the coal pits and steel fences doing time, Crazy had $20,000 from a holdup stashed away in a shoebox, now he says he's Christ, a nasty, sneaky piece of work the Houtzdale Christ, you'll wind up hanging in a cell four metres square, he'll die longing for his grandma's grilled chicken and broccoli and lasagna, but they aren't going to get me like Crazy, they'll take eight or ten shots at my back and miss every time, Carlos remembered Graduation Day, when Mama had bought a red silk outfit, a real extravagance that red silk suit and tie, there's nothing that can't be undone or taken back, sang Pastor Ezekiel in her church, don't listen when they say a blood red moon is going to rise some January first, remember these words, the just shall inherit the earth and live in it forever, and death will be no more, nor grief, nor crying, nor lamentations, so straighten up, little pale man, there's nothing that can't be done over again, put those nights of convulsing fear behind you, haven't you got faith? The cock poachers and their bikes disappeared in a thick, hot cloud of dust, bring Lazaro on, oh, just let him get here, Carlos thought, I'm ready for him, his bare sandalled feet whipped the street air, and the sidewalk cracks filled with roasted insects, Polly craned her neck up toward his sky-turned, angry face, a bike, a digital watch, and he's got the guts to ask for them back, he kept repeating, where exactly were they headed like this, Carlos and Polly; as for Lazaro, he was walking calm and determined under the heat of the sun, on his way to confront Carlos right in front of Trinity Church, if there were no cops hanging around, actually he did not really feel like fighting, in fact he remembered the time, back when his parents had moved there, Carlos and he had been inseparable, boxing one another in the gym over the gutted restaurant, in some improvised stadium in the streets, or in the faded gardens along Bahama Street, amid the rotting smells from garbage cans, with Carlos's mean kicks, although he had always been more agile than Lazaro, those times were dead and gone since Carlos had betrayed Lazaro, a digital watch and a bike, a thief, that's all, Lazaro passed a hockey game, both teams on in-line skates, each trying to stickhandle the puck into the other's net, he felt like joining in with the Black kids all dressed in black, but they were too noisy, he thought, cats darted lightning-quick between car wheels, and Lazaro worried they would get killed, too bad he had to meet Carlos today, it would have been a good day for fishing; in the backyards at daycare, children waited for their mothers, mourning doves sipped from stone baths, lifting pink throats and shaking the drops from their beaks, yes, and why did he have to fight today anyway, when his mother had told him not to, they had fled a land of damnation where Lazaro's cousins and uncles were all going to die like martyrs, his mother told him, militants or terror-ists, they had attacked innocent people in the temples, young boys stoned them, women spat in contempt at the sight of them, they van-dalized the temples at Luxor, killed tourists, and swore to spill yet more blood, as they prayed by the hundreds in their mosques, their leaders called on them to die with honour for Islam, Caridad, Carlos's mother, had broken a law by refusing to be one of those women covered from head to toe, even wearing gloves to be more fully concealed, no, Caridad would not be one of those getting tea and coffee ready for the men in their committees or meetings where they urged hatred, women could not take part in these, no, they were allowed only to serve coffee, dry cakes, and fruit, then withdraw immediately, the uncles and cousins would be swept up by the Egyptian police, convicted, and imprisoned unjustly, and dogs would howl during the torture sessions, women would berate walls with their lamentations, mothers to all these young men, and God is great, the militants would intone, and incense sticks would be lit as they died, having already bid farewell to this land of martyrs, and Lazaro cast a disdainful smile over a group of uniformed blonde schoolgirls with their teacher, in England or in North America, his uncles and cousins had told him, these girls would be on their way to hell, falling quickly into the sinful temptations of sex and drugs, for Islam alone offered the purity for salvation, too bad about having to meet Carlos at noon, where's the good in fighting, his mother had said, when every country is awash in the blood of war, but Lazaro, proud of his Egyptian heritage, strutted, showing off the King Tut fetish around his neck, it was noon when he saw Carlos roughly push the dog aside and rush toward him, Polly was surprised and pulled back onto her hind paws before bolting, go on home I told you, yelled Carlos, there was nothing but uproar and shouting all around them, the droning of commercial aircraft as they landed on the tarmac beside the sea drowned out Lazaro's voice, which demanded that Carlos give back the watch, my Adidas watch, I want it back, Lazaro could no longer be heard because of a shot that leadened the calm air, so it wasn't an imitation .38 with nothing in it, thought Carlos, his forehead feverish from the sun, and no one seemed to hear Lazaro's yell as he fell to the sidewalk, hugging his wounded leg to him, it just grazed him, thought Carlos, just a scratch to his right leg, come on, get up, Lazaro, he ordered, the Cuban cook told me it was just a toy he kept in the kitchen for protection, but Lazaro flopped heavily and tipped back his head on the cement as though dead, as Carlos's large shadow leaned over him, boy, what an actor, he thought, but then Carlos saw blood on the sidewalk, and now Lazaro was stretched out under the tree with fresh-fallen orange hibiscus flowers, and yes, he was breathing, calling for help, and soon the cop would be here with the hue and cry, Carlos had taken off, but the high-pitched wail of Lazaro followed him, and Lazaro was telling the officer it was Carlos, he's the one that's killed me. Soft and slow and sensual were these instants for Samuel at the wheel of his car, hair flying as his red convertible tore along, bathed in intoxicating perfumes, a profusion of smells, the ocean scent exuding from his skin after hours of drifting on his sailboard, or jet skiing over the waves, or skin diving, these were things he always did on the island, and the perfumes wafting from the tall trees that decorated the doorways of the wooden houses, but soon there would be the whirlwind of his new life in New York, thought Samuel, he would have to do without seeing the faces of his younger brothers and sister, of a mother, adoring though frequently absent, who tonight would be leaving for Washington, just a furtive stroke of her son's cheek and she would be gone, and what had she said as she held him tight, listen to your father, he's right, training as a dancer's going to be good for you, his grandmother had volunteered the fact that his dyslexia would be a severe handicap at university, everyone in the family said he loved only music and dance, why couldn't he just have been that simple Papageno so taken with the music of bells, the song of birds, the trills of the human voice, the piping and singing of birds coming through his earphones, the sound of water at his feet as he dozed on a beach, goodbye to lazy afternoons with girls, lazy lyrics too, of course, these

Papagenos and Papagenas in love with love, the sun, and the sea, the crazy happiness of doing nothing at all, like that idle Papageno, singing, dancing, dreaming, the Black teacher Arnie Graal, renowned as a choreographer, would transform Samuel into a disciplined artist, said Daniel, and this way his spoiled son would stop lolling about in the water and on the beaches, staying out all night with the young islanders in those noisy discotheques, and they would no longer indulge his son's whims, Daniel said, Arnie Graal would put some rigorous discipline into the boy, Samuel had danced in public on the holidays, he had sung in the churches and synagogues, his voice had broken just as snakes shed their skins, animals, oh, if only he could still be this animal, Samuel thought, flowing beneath the silken plumage of a fresh new skin, each blond hair glinting in the sun, his mother worried about his love life, what was this liberalism of his parents that was so quick to take things badly, or was it the grandmother's influence, Samuel's dyslexia bothered them as much as his precocious sexuality, well, at last he was leaving, acting like a man, escaping from the anguish of puberty, swiftly the frangipanis spread their heady-scented flowers over the sidewalks, and the royal poinciana their red blooms, and the rain lilies whose poisonous bulbs Mère liked to gather grew in the garden, Daniel and Mélanie had admitted to Samuel, after all, that they too, when they were fourteen or fifteen, had known these voluptuous pleasures of evening and night perfumes, but soon, in a few years, they would be forty, their senses would be dulled and atrophied, thought Samuel racing along, racing through life, in his red convertible, leaving the seashore behind him, he thought he heard a wild white parakeet call from its nest; now was when dogs would be out for their walk along the Boulevard of the Atlantic, in the pines the orphan parakeet sang its desolation to all around, people in the neighbourhood had called the three parakeets the angels of the pines, two had been hunted down by vandalizing children, and a passerby had

17

gathered up the handful of mangled feathers, now the sole white survivor flew off into the evening sky, gliding over the pines, the mango trees, calling out for its lost ones, sweet and sensual were these moments for Samuel, calm at heart, with the wind in his hair, as he headed for the highway. The sight of a captive bird, caught behind steel cables on a station platform in Madrid, had awakened in Daniel this continual suffering at being alive, when any painful sight pierces us, a field sparrow would die in atrocious pain before Daniel even arrived at his retreat, a monastery built into the hills of the town in the eleventh century, work in silence, be monk-like, otherwise you will be a bestselling author and no more, Adrien had told Daniel with brotherly solicitude and cool criticism of his work, I'm not talking here about real success but a sort of haphazard sparking, good fortune too, which your family's already given you, this monastery will calm your excitement for all the vanities you acquired after *Strange Years* came out, I was the first to acclaim the prophetic quality of your book despite a few youthful shortcomings, there you will get back in touch with yourself, you will be obsessed by the solitude of the mountains, but you will be more true to yourself, believe me, I'm saying this because I have a lot of respect for you, Daniel was irritated to realize the old writer's voice was still so strong in his ear, as he made his way up and down the corridor of the train, tormented, he knew he could neither save the bird nor free it, the sparrow struggled feverishly against its prison of steel cables and glass, die, go on, thought Daniel, do it now, but the bird battled on, its heart gasping with fear, when would exhaustion finally put an end to it? There were thousands of birds crammed among the pylons of freight stations like this, under walkways and train platforms, why did Daniel have to witness this one in its torture, a field sparrow imprisoned in the torment of industrial cities, just like thousands of men and women, Daniel was one of the lucky people, what was this exquisite tenderness he felt for each one of them, just childish sentiment, Adrien had said, follow your own path or you'll soon be complaining of writer's block like so many others, and Daniel lost sight of the imprisoned bird for good when the train shuddered forward, he saw some young Americans shoot him a mean look, why hadn't he saved the poor thing, they seemed to be saying, how heartless and cruel was he anyway? One who had not even noticed the bird incident asked him a more harmless question, are you off on a trip, sir? Probably, he too looked like a camper on his way through Spain, sir, why did they call him sir, him an anarchist writer, he was not about to tell them he'd been invited on a retreat with artists and writers of all kinds and nationalities, he'd likely just sound arrogant to these kids, as for labelling himself a writer, author of *Strange Years,* a book often lambasted by the critics, who was he to saddle this quintessence of youth with his problems, what did they know about a dictator named Hitler and the dog that fell victim to his madness, they were even younger than his own son Samuel, though they had not inherited the knowledge of pain in their genes, what they had inherited was the world, which amounted to the same thing, Arnie would be a terrific dance instructor for Samuel, Daniel thought, as he envisioned his son gliding high over the nest, like the wild white parakeet over an Australian pine, yet Samuel had needed to quit the island, he thought, and Arnie's latest New York choreography was going to astonish Samuel with its innovation and child-like daring; in this creation, the ironic *Survivor's Morning,* Arnie admitted to Daniel that he lived for the dance and nothing else, just to induce sharp, rapid awakenings, Arnie, like the vigorous bird slowly being exhausted by its web of cables and still set on staying alive, would he conquer or die? He held off the doctors and nurses he called stiff and measured, being in better health when he danced so very close to the edge, Arnie that splendid black feline of dance shows and theatres, frequently done up in a suede vest buttoned over a dazzling white shirt, a bone necklace at his throat, upright and stubborn, Arnie might well have been a preacher like his father, thought Daniel, this frenzied athlete of dance would know how to moderate Samuel's exuberance and unlimited self-confidence, Arnie would pass on to Samuel his passion for literature: Proust, Gertrude Stein, so little did Samuel read, and who could help but admire Arnie and his company with fifty choreographies to their credit, and the latest, *Survivor's Morning,* had won over Munich with its brutal inversion of *The Afternoon of a Faun,* in which Arnie lifted the veil on those sensual langours that little by little sap our vitality, victory or death, the millennium's only topic, Arnie said, knowing we're all condemned, we dare to confront death and put it on the stage, maybe he's crazy, Daniel thought, like the bird fighting against the cables, how would he come through this final struggle for freedom? Arnie defied all the conventions of classical dance, he frequently used deformed dancers, as long as they danced well, listen to the song of your body, Arnie told them, it's a hymn to beauty and danger, what could Samuel tell his father about all this, the shortness of life, death, these were not things he would have chosen, and what demons was Daniel sacrificing him to, was this just one more proof of the writer's selfishness, cutting himself off from his family to get something done, although he had recommended this surly isolation for Daniel, Adrien himself lived surrounded by people and every morning walked the hibiscus path to the tennis court, hand in hand with Suzanne; his son drove him to the golf course overlooking the ocean, not to be exasperated with the kind of solitude he imposed on Daniel, stiff and awkward in his striped flannel pants, he would gather around him students and researchers of a work whose mystery he alone could unlock, and with a full voice he would recite the edifying poem, Adrien's voice had not yet cracked like Jean-Mathieu's when it snagged on a reef of words, nor Caroline's with its sad and broken echoes, something she would take up with her surgeon, but that had nothing to do with Jean-Mathieu or Adrien,

whose anagrams bored her now that she had a more entertaining
companion than these grammarians who, steeped in erudition, rarely
conceded victory, and why these hermetic linguistic obstacle races,
instead of travelling and spending a small fortune, which at the end
of your life, she told Jean-Mathieu, is just not as much fun, hasn't the
time come for living without scruples or shame, vaguely troubling,
Jean-Mathieu thought, listening to his friend's pronouncements, that
she would forever do only as she pleased, I'm upset by this sudden
distance between us, he said softly, and who is this young woman who
now shares your life, at our age one should live modestly and be wary
of new acquaintances, but Caroline never paid attention to anything
but the tumult of her own impulses, thought Jean-Mathieu, she had
a constant need to combust and to flower, even though it was a bit late
in life, she was also a woman who mended quickly, who was ennobled
by action, definitely foolhardy, they all found themselves less and less
alone: Adrien, Suzanne, Jean-Mathieu, and Caroline, while Daniel
would soon be face to face with himself in a monastery cell, just like
Charles, who had left the world behind, first in a special centre in
Jerusalem, now in an Indian ashram at the foot of the Aravali Mountains, his soul transmigrating somewhere, the only one, thought Daniel,
to find the purpose of his mission on earth, with him it was an art, an
exercise in clarity and transparency, but why would Daniel emulate a
poet who could never be imitated, why a mystic when he himself was
carnal, a writer in a wholly different line, a living cohort to the illustrious dead, and in his one and only book, *Strange Years,* Adrien had
criticized his style as too slow and verbose, excessive in its often sinister
layering of atmospheres one over another, mightn't Daniel lighten up
a little in future, was there really so much to say about what his father
had lived through in the war, yet never writing a single line? It was
this voice of Adrien's hissing in ill-meaning undertones that Daniel
was to hear over and over again in his cell, where in the eleventh

21

century monks had hardened through fasting, there would also be street noises, the summer wind in the fruit trees, conversations with young people in coffee houses, the loudness of street crowds at evening would bring him alive with their gaiety, Daniel reflected that he had never written without at least one child on his lap, sending his e-mail, helping Marie-Sylvie get meals ready since Mélanie had started to be away so often, a leader among women she was, committed to fighting for the rights of women and children, when Daniel for his part wrote all day, expressing, as Joseph his father put it, the combativeness of an ecological samurai in his letters to the editor and his TV commentaries in favour of rehabilitating the Coral Coast, after all, thought Daniel, didn't writing a book allow him to point the finger at those the government had neither sanctioned nor punished, whether they were active destroyers of the coast or perpetrators of the most gruesome events in history, on this chaotic morning in a station in Madrid, and Daniel, unshaven and unwashed for two days, what had to be condemned was that monstrous stroke of bad luck that had held the bird captive, caged behind the cables of a train platform and deprived of the happiness of being what it was, a singing creature, and Polly would never make it back to Bahama Street as Carlos had told her to do with a few kicks, all the noise and yelling around him that noon, the gunshot, the droning of planes overhead, Polly was going to head for the sea, Polly and Carlos, once inseparable, both listening to the voice that called out to them, the voice of Mama, the sonority of Pastor Jeremy that Polly disliked, both together, listening, obeying, Carlos and Lazaro, inseparable, Carlos and Polly together had heard the thunder of the little piece of lead, then the ambulance siren in the noon air, alone Polly veered away from Carlos and the acrid smell of his rubber sandals, his smell, and when would all these fights be over, Mama said, battles and bruises, on Bahama Street no one slept or prayed anymore since Lazaro the Egyptian arrived, Polly listened to the sounds of water and its periodic rush to the shore pushing feathers ahead of it, bands of feathers on the heads of egrets, colonies of gulls pulling up on these shores before migrating to the coast of Sinaloa or Sonora, in the quick rustling of feathers and wings, Polly galloped toward the stormy sea, growling as she went at a boy swimming in the waves with a pair of greyhounds, we're first, we're first, he shouted happily, the sea that day was as warm as the sand and air, stepping out of it brought a shiver of delight, fetch the ball, we're first, shouted the boy, what was Polly doing here in the ocean without Carlos, this little dog that used to ride in the basket on his bicycle, Polly barked her come-on like all the other dogs, she was just as careful a swimmer, just as good at fetching the ball as those greyhounds now galloping along with the boy on their backs, but where was Carlos, why wasn't he diving furiously into the ocean fully dressed, stirring up the colours with his dark clothes, he was a no-good, his mother said, only no-goods jump into the sea with their clothes on, messing them all up, Mama decided they would always be part of one another, Carlos, Polly, and Bahama Street, slamming the door, she asked Pastor Jeremy if they had slept, if they had said their prayers first, and if they would go to jail. Carlos would have knitted his thick brows, swimming free of Polly, she could take care of herself, all of this sea and waves were theirs, he would have knitted his black brows and said, they're just White folks' dogs, Polly, you don't have to bark louder than them or bite them, you belong to me, Polly, he would have scowled, dripping with water and angry, as she shook herself after a plunge and a bath in the waves, Polly recognized the rancid smell of his wet clothes, the odour weaving together their lives, would they be immutable these fates, would they have time to sleep and pray, asked Mama, and the swelling water rocked Polly, living was forgetting about Carlos and his voice and his commands, she wasn't going to be intimidated by him, this water, this air felt so good; the doves, the mourning doves and the white-headed eagle are spreading their wings

23

over the sea, the ruby-throated hummingbirds are sipping at my rose bushes, I can see them all from the terrace, wrote Jean-Mathieu to Charles, oh, friend of mine living ascetically and so far away, do you know how much I have given up to earn this little domaine I've got, this lofty window just a little too close to heaven and to God, rather than His intervening in my life, I'd take sandpipers, the brown-edged feathers of His ducks on our ponds and lakes, fulfilled I am, though a little sad that Caroline has stopped paying attention to me, preferring the mundane chitchat of that lady companion, you know me, I hold friendships forever, in a few days, I'll be going to Venice by myself, the heat overwhelms me a bit, I wonder how many days and nights my herons have flown, Oregon to southern Idaho, then south to the West Indies, I get up at five to the sound of the waves and keep a log of their migrations, and when our ducks fly off to their mud inlets, swamps, and humid grain fields, let's hope the hunters aren't sharp enough to take them from us, couldn't you find it in you, dear friend, to repudiate that poem of yours in which we are all obliterated, humans and things alike, into what pit of burning, gnawing salt would you tip us with all our loves and hatreds, please don't submit us to this ordeal, are the words you chose equal to Virgil, I am eighty years old, and please reflect how with time we are touched by an incurable sympathy for all that lives, we welcome any and all paradoxes, the small boy I once was still shivers before me in the cold, my mother and I in the port of Halifax, his mother tells him to be brave, don't erase his memory with your salty, fiery rain, how charming is the child's face, even covered with tears, and I still carry him in me, please rewrite your poem and think of the confident child you once were, in poetry one cannot be overly realistic or naturalistic, why not rejoice in some sort of youthful collusion or rebirth, the way Caroline does, even though I long to have breakfast with her every day, the way I used to, I can understand how all of a sudden she finds me too old, after all, I too would enjoy the

light-heartedness of a young person, if I weren't so preoccupied with
my biography of Stendhal, I'm only up to the point of his stay in Italy
during the revolutionary wars, when he becomes an officer and has
not yet written *The Red and the Black,* let him be spared, he's still only
a child, I live beside him, with him, in this very room, I don't really
care about my posthumous work, soon I shall be in Italy, first I'll follow
Stendhal's footsteps to Milan, but what wouldn't I give, Charles, to
erase those lines of yours where you say that everything's corroded
already, everything that gives me pleasure, the splendours of life we
see shining around us so brightly, the sea as it appears at this moment,
the highlights of evening on my paper where my steel pen has traced
its calligraphed letters, corroded by this virulent salt, as you call it,
will even the white of snow be tarnished, these are the wanderings of
an unhappy soul, Charles, because what I see from my window cannot
wholly disappear while my eyes still see it, everything is inscribed in
memory, etched like calligraphy, the Mèrest bird's claw leaves its print
in the sand, in India, there in your ashram, are you not just a little too
alone, Charles, and Jean-Mathieu thought how much the immobility
of writing brought with it a weariness, so attentive was he to writing
generously, warmly, yet distinctively for his friends, was it already that
time of luminosity, that time when he wanted more than ever to dress
for a walk outside, time to work with Suzanne and Adrien on prepar-
ing the seminar on writing about winter in the North, what a spread
of bows, puffy ties, and smart-coloured shorts he had in his wardrobe,
oh, let the light of this beautiful day purge the pessimism he was feeling from Charles, or would it have been wise of Jean-Mathieu to be
honest with him, pitilessly showing him what a sad state his friend
was in, telling him about Frédéric's fall into the pool, the numbing
fight of that fleshless body against illness and failing breath, no, Jean-
Mathieu would say nothing, that was not how Frédéric had lived, he
thought, and who knows if this same Frédéric, once a celebrated child

25

prodigy on the piano, as Paganini had been on the violin, who knows if he had not just cut short a dissolution of worlds; invited by heads of state, perhaps they had shortened hostilities between countries with the sounds of their instruments, what a sweetness spread with them over these empires of men worn down by cruelty, listening to them play, dictators had smiled and fooled even themselves with false goodness only moments before unleashing their storms of evil, perhaps it was thanks to them the earth in its entirety was not yet on fire, Frédéric as a child and Paganini, thought Jean-Mathieu, in them God had polarized a momentary distraction that might save the world from that machine-like finger all too ready to press the switch, to the tune of a few sweet piano notes we would see dawn forestalling the most deadly of calamities, Jean-Mathieu would awaken in his stark white bed bathed in light, amid the chirping of birds of which Frédéric had always seemed to be one, even if for some time now, no one heard his music anymore, and during a brief train stop in the perfumed hills, Daniel felt himself come alive again as he strode the platform awash in the chatter of birds, an aviary appeared in front of him with a hundred golden canaries feeding on sunflower seeds from a passerby, singing and flapping as though in unison, and they could have flown away while feeding from his hand, but they all seemed held by the same cord of hunger to their cage, Daniel might have pushed the meddler aside and set the canaries flying off to branches in the mountains before they ended up stuffed into a box like those birdlings, scarlet tan-agers and red birds of paradise he had seen a man selling in Bolivia, but instead he just listened to them sing as he thought about soon being shut away in a retreat, a few hours later, as he jumped from the train, an ungainly artist shambled down the country platform toward him and cordially latched onto his arm, I'm Rodrigo the poet from Brazil, he said with a marked accent, I've read your book, and I believe like you that one's soul can come back, otherwise how do you explain all this confusion in the world, souls coming back, did I write that, Daniel asked him, sure you did, you remember, Rodrigo replied, you wrote that souls cast out because of the sins of the fathers and sacrificed too soon with innocent bodies come back to earth and lay waste to it with terror and crime, and furthermore, said Rodrigo, I'd say they're impenitent like their parents, I don't believe in innocence the way you do, they're fifteen- and sixteen-year-old replicas of Joseph Goebbels and his Nazi propaganda, hundreds of them, you can see them in the streets of Buenos Aires, it's the New Order, the Order of Blood, so this is what I should have written, thought Daniel, these shipwrecked souls are all around us in the slimy fog of ancestral wrongs, you'll see, Rodrigo shot back dismally, if he were not so unkempt, he might look a lot like Adrien, Daniel noticed, and proudly Rodrigo combed fingers with ink-stained nails through his hair, you know, we've long taken refuge in the silence and safety of monasteries, in the seventeenth century we were already saying goodbye to our mothers and daughters, and nowadays we flee frivolous wants and absurd ambitions, with Rodrigo as his guide, Daniel's car sped on to woodland roads and closer to his writing sanctuary; the room in a cloister he had so much wanted, and as soon as he began to doze on his hard mattress, hands clasped behind his head, he felt encased like those saints in their bone-filled crypts, Samuel his son was right when he had pointed out the moroseness of convents and cloisters, real life was outside, and even here he was tormented by latent morbidity, like the time Vincent had almost died from an attack out at sea, believing the clear sky presaged nothing else, Daniel had forgotten the hourly dose of medicine in the house, the prospect of sailing with Vincent had removed all sense of danger, all threats that he should have borne in mind, when suddenly a thin cough inflated Vincent's chest, and at the same time the sky turned heavy with black clouds, and what miracle was it that allowed Daniel just a moment's grace to preserve his son, how was it he made it up the hospital steps in time, his son in his arms, it would have taken an innate gift to foresee all misfortunes for such a sum of human errors to be avoided, understanding and already feeling better, Vincent had forgotten the inconstancy of his father that prevented him from being the perfect parent he made himself out to be, and what about the occupational ravages of a writer who, although at home, was also off chasing characters with particular physical or psychological traits, sometimes he questioned his companions shamelessly, pursuing everyone wherever they were, even when trying to relax, Daniel probed and consulted, weighing the underside of Everyman, because under each virtuous exterior lay cowardice and indolence, these were the right-minded women and men that Daniel portrayed in his books, their most hidden and cunning acts, that engineer he met on the train, for example, knowing he would never meet Daniel again, told him how he had killed a wild dog in Alaska, well, after all, he had to defend himself, didn't he, and anyone who crossbred dogs with wolves should know better than to set them free, crossbreeding humans, on the other hand, was even worse, Daniel said, observing the killer's jaw, which had been broken by someone's fist, it was said, he had taken a revolver to a pup he had raised for six months, maybe you think I should have given him a second chance, said the engineer, these plains dogs snatch their food straight out of the traps, I killed him out of pity, and believe me, I don't regret it, who was this guy Daniel anyway, an upstart busybody mixing in other people's business, it was with revulsion for himself that he remembered the engineer, after a lacklustre conversation about copper and oil extraction in the Arctic Circle, Daniel not yet noticing his protruding ears or crooked jaw, a vile act unfolded with the account of the wild dog shot point-blank, from inside a mediocre, ordinary man emerged a walking disaster, Daniel thought, the carcasses of baby seals strewed across his path too, with what indifference he went after their fur, massacring without another thought

salmon in their lakes, crab, halibut, maybe he had even knocked off a
few Eskimos or Indians, look, we've had this land for only about a
hundred years, an ill-natured Daniel had told him, this smooth-pelted
baby seal gets riddled with bullets from a helicopter, salmon get shred-
ded in a dam, and a wolf-dog whimpers for another chance, didn't he
bite you by accident anyway, after wandering for days, persecuted by
hunters and living on borrowed time, these creatures were somehow
connected to Daniel along with everything else in the world, the engineer wanted to train him like the other dogs, when suddenly he had
run off and been tied to a spike in the ice, then, his eyes caked with
frost, the wolf-dog had received a death sentence under the blank
arctic sky for having the misfortune of mixing with humans, finally
he crumpled in the reddened snow, this was the story of the wolf-dog
and the explosion of flames through its skin that Daniel was able to
write, sitting at the antique writing table that had been set up for him
in the room, Daniel thought his way back to the origins of life and saw
the fossil engineer as a man who was vulgar and crass from birth, an
exterminator of species more fragile than he was, unforgiving of any
life that was not his own, he would always be the same, wouldn't he,
no change was needed for a sparrow to be imprisoned behind the
cables of a train station in Madrid, for fledglings to be captured in
Bolivia, for a wolf-dog to be cut down in remote Alaska, Daniel was
writing, his computer screen shining in the nighttime cell, when he
heard beneath his window the voices of young people come to beg for
their supper, the only one we take together and have wine with, said
Mark and Carmen from the garden, where they picked through stems
and rocks with their shovels and rakes, we're artists, and we've always
worked together, they call us Debris in New York, that's where we
show our sculptures and paintings and installations; leaning on the
windowsill at sunset, outlined against mauve hills, Daniel watched
them mischievously looking for remnants in the earth, bits of glass,

rags, they even skinned the carcasses of dead animals, they were picking up the earth's leftovers, they said, signing themselves Debris, leavings buried among riches, they even made their own clothes from what others had cast off, they dyed them, recut them, sometimes carefully, sometimes not, this time Mark was wearing a rough homespun vest over his shorts, revealing his short, white legs and hiking boots, Carmen swept up refuse in a ball gown with tints of ochre, half open to reveal a garter belt holding up over her pink knee a stocking that was too long, these affable pixies roaming a dusty planet, thought Daniel, had chosen a symptomatic art, which might be one of the last vital signs of a world they might all be deprived of tomorrow, so urgent was it to gather up the last traces, confiscate the remnants, cement and solder them, sell them in galleries at exorbitant prices, for these symptoms, signals from a life form soon to be extinct, were as durable as they were precious, and time anchored itself to their chalky skeletons, petrified in a radioactive era, haloed with fear, twinned for pleasure, the young couple skipped off to their painting and sculpture studios, surrounded by geese and ducks, Heidi the dog following them, it was the farm belonging to Carmello and Grazie, the monastery's Italian cooks, Rodrigo said as he walked along beside Daniel, his hair lashing his neck like a mane, an elegant bohemian he was, nails black with ink, Daniel mused with Rodrigo's hand on his shoulder, quick, let's go to the refectory, Rodrigo said, the women love to eat, especially those devils Mark and Carmen, then after dinner, they'll just jump the monastery fence, scamper down to the village and dance all night, which boarding artists aren't supposed to do, and they have an exhibition in a few days, you'll have to come with me to their studios, there you'll see this holier-than-thou bunch, writers spoiled by success, the Best-sellers Circle, Rodrigo was on a tear by this time, a coterie to stay away from, and oh, how smoothly they settle down to a discussion of anything and everything, while Carmello and Grazie's little girls serve

them up cocktails and hors d'oeuvres, standing on ceremony under
the shade of the cypress trees, once a year they get together here and
talk about the financial impact of bad literature, why don't they just
call themselves the No-Can-Remember Club, because they're so filthy
rich from selling sappy novels that they've forgotten a whole century,
probably the most savage since humanity began, aren't you being just
a little too harsh, Daniel replied, name me one author who hasn't
hungered for fame. Balzac and Dickens were overjoyed at their huge
success, aha! exclaimed Rodrigo, sure, when you've described the
exploitation of working-class kids the way they did, or the hideous
social conditions of the time, why bother feeling queasy with all that
glory? How was Dickens supposed to forget that his parents were
locked up in debtor's prison, or that he grew up in a factory? And
Balzac, all those costly and tangled relations with women, you'll see,
my friend, none of this lot will come over and say hello, come on, walk
faster, absurd, aren't they, these sophisticated intellectuals being photographed by the paparazzi with their lapdogs, Lhasa Apso, Shih Tzu,
you'll see tonight, Boris and Ivan, there, over there, see their mangy
shadows, they'll empty the glasses and finish the butts left lying around
by the richer guests, but don't go dreaming that you can join this club,
your kind of honesty, amigo, doesn't churn out millions of copies of
the pap-of-the-day, be a bit old-fashioned, out-of-date, and go on
writing slowly and carefully, Daniel pointed out to Rodrigo that he
had several children at home, and that was what slowed him down,
Rodrigo grinned, then, you shouldn't have got married, look at me,
I'm a bachelor, he explained that the walk was long because the monastery had been expanded to house a library and a refectory in separate
buildings, so that the artists and writers would not be tempted to step
outside during the daytime, a bit spartan, isn't it, this rule about going
out only at night, Daniel asked, yes, but it has its rewards, amigo,
Rodrigo replied, I just love it when Rosina brings a bowl to my room

at noon, I say to her, oh, my Rosina, what have you got in that tin dish of yours, lettuce leaves again, a few noodles, maybe brown beans? Do you really think an ogre like me can write from morning to night with so little to live on? Look, don't tell your parents, but bring me some eggs and bread from the farm, then the kid scampers off to the sunflower fields, *Buon giorno,* Rodrigo, *Buon giorno,* in this medieval castle I slave in, Rosina brings me the air of heaven, I've breathed the scent of the fields, all I have to do is sit down at my table and play around with this poem, "In the Days of Pompei before Vesuvius Erupted," now wouldn't "Vesuvius Erupting in the Days of Pompei" sound more harmonious, amigo, what do you think? Distant, Daniel was afraid he had looked feeble talking about his children to a bachelor, he pictured Samuel's victorious face, and the physiology of love and marriage as Balzac showed it in his books, all that had been changed by emergency plans, the trepidation of a tumultuous time on the edge of volcanoes, and while Daniel had come to love late in life, Samuel seemed born for it, and what was the point in his grandmother's scolding him for his budding virility, the fervour of love was just one more blessing on these children of the times, who seemed to want for nothing, a time of innocence and wonderment, Mère said, thinking of Vincent and Mai's bodies, still small but about to be stirred by wild sexuality, she complained, bombarded everywhere by TV and cinema, Mère would take Mai and Vincent by bus on safaris to parks where thousands of hectares of an artificial Eden had been cleared and sculpted for them by masterful landscapers and architects, like God, the Tree of Life, the forest and jungle with its surviving animals, giant baobabs of the savannahs with rivers to slake the thirst of uprooted fauna, and on these lush hectares the rarest of plants, and whether the animals were real or sculpted like the Tree of Life, Augustino would realize, his grandmother said, that once in a legendary past, the world had been beautiful, then no animal was labelled extinct, the greenery had been transplanted here for this African safari and reconstituted flawlessly, so had the millions of plants saved from dying lands, yes, it was exactly the same, just for them, Augustino, Vincent, and Mai in their child seats saw a hippo emerge from a lake, a lion among the gazelles, an elephant, zebra, giraffe, like all of this recovering nature, dying and reanimated, the elephant showed its majestic head, wounded by ivory poachers, to Augustino, oh, let them do it as soon as possible, thought Daniel, let Augustino, Vincent, and Mai admire this procession through forest and savannah and crystalline waters, the Eden of leopards, roaring lions, gorillas, crocodiles, and rhinoceros, some of them wheedled away from the sadism of zoos, some of them dead before they were freed to these parks, oh, let them be quick, Augustino, Vincent, and Mai, and be dazzled by this rescued native paradise, these acres of brand-new luxuriance spread out before them, a very convincing kingdom of wild beauty, true or not or simply dreamed. And Jessica, sitting next to the flight instructor and her father, repeated what she had already said to her mother and younger sister before leaving that morning, there's nothing to worry about because I'll always be a pilot, flying till I die and till all the records are broken, like John Kevin's, he was eleven when he flew straight across the country in five days, and you'll all see, Mama and Papa, at seven I'll beat his record, I'll do three thousand miles in two days, and my name will go next to his in the *Guinness Book of Records*, oh, yes, I'll do it; she needed three cushions on top of her red seat to see the control panel, and the extensions under her seat allowed her to reach the pedals of the Cessna Cardinal, red like the bird it was named for, the black letters on her cap declared Women Fly, the grey peak casting a shadow over Jessica's clear blue eyes, her hair bleached by the sun and blown back over her cheeks and the raised collar of her black leather jacket, Mama, Papa, my mission's going to be to fly till I die, like a bird in the sky, a cardinal or a dove, they hardly ever stop to rest, this one time the instructor would be Jessica's student, she had logged only forty-eight hours of flying time, and he was afraid it was not enough but didn't say anything, the little girl had promised she would be faultless; almost 8:22, about one minute to takeoff, a very long minute for the instructor, Jessica admitted she had not slept a wink all night, the Cessna Cardinal was hers, he thought, almost a model, and although she had only forty-eight hours of experience at the controls, was it enough? Jessica, her father, and the instructor heard the sound of voices and applause on the tarmac around the plane, and she saw her mother with her little sister in her arms, come on back quickly, they all said, her black-gloved hand waved goodbye, I've been waiting so long to do this, yet all her mother heard her say on the cell phone was, Mama, can you hear me, it's raining, isn't it, is that what I can hear, it mustn't rain, Mama, can you hear it, Mama, they were still at the air base, Mama, can you hear the rain? That was before they had taken Route 30 to Cheyenne Airport, probably not later than 8:20 or 8:21, her mother remembered that Jessica had slept only two hours the night before, for her to accomplish this transcontinental feat the way John Kevin had, she would have to fly over California and not be afraid of long hours or rain, at 8:22 storms were already forecast for Wyoming, too much wind and rain, even an experienced pilot would hesitate under these conditions, but Jessica would not, we'll be taking off in a few seconds, a minute, she told her instructor, this wind and rain doesn't bother me, but he gently resisted, not wanting to disappoint her, California all the way to Falmouth, Massachusetts, will be exhausting if these storms build, he said, reminding her that she had slept only two hours the night before, he was suddenly speaking very fast as the fatal seconds ticked away, Jessica, we're late anyway, why not postpone this for a few days till these wicked storms dissipate, I'm not afraid of anything, she said, it was practically 8:23, too late to start discussing things, Jessica adjusted her seat, gripped the controls, and turned to her father, silent and motionless, Jessica cast him a winning smile, all teeth, thanks, Papa, for letting me do this since I was small, when we get back, Papa, we're going to see the president, by now everyone had heard her voice on radio and TV describing her flight plan to Falmouth as confidently as a grown-up, when she arrived to the applause of her admirers on Friday, after three thousand miles in two days, she would be celebrated, her father, her instructor, all three accomplished pilots, she had flown for the first time at six, a birthday gift from her father, and now at 8:23 the instructor was pointing out that visibility was poor, thunder, did you hear that, no, she said, just rain, that's all I hear is rain drumming harder and harder on the aluminum plane, the wind, listen to that wind, he said, and thunder, you can hear it, Jessica, but at 8:23 they were in the air over Cheyenne Airport, the three of them flying low, with difficulty in the wind and the storm, over Gardenia Boulevard and the Riding Club, they were headed northwest, where was it they were trying so desperately to drift, struggling against the drag of rough, sinister winds, green detonations, blinding thunder, the spectators gathered to watch them take off from Cheyenne cried out, they're in trouble, they're banking right, the left wing of the plane gave way in the wind, it's all over, listen to that rain, it's coming down hard, the mother heard it all, but the three in the plane were so quickly destroyed, even before their plane hit the ground, that they seemed to expire without even a sigh, slipping into night as they crash-landed, flames burning their eyes, thirst incinerating their throats, the words, *I'll fly forever till I die*, still echoed as the three of them disappeared into their seats, and where Jessica's Cessna Cardinal fell in skidding scraps of metal, rain fell through the calcinated Wyoming air onto the bodies carbonized in their red seats, and still the words echoed, *I'll fly forever till I die*, that was Jessica's gift, her sacrifice to the thunder, so let those who loved her dry their tears, at five she had known the ecstasy of horseback riding, of riding her bike to school in the snow and the cold,

maybe she had been born from Amelia Earhart's soul, her terrestrial
mother, a vegetarian who only wanted the best for her children, including rapture and delight, and these Jessica had felt on this second takeoff
before the rumble of fire and thunder on her eyelids, Women Fly, a
little higher up she had preserved the voyage of Amelia, and tomorrow
it would be someone else, for even without rest or relaxation, the dove,
the red cardinal, the Cessna Cardinal, all must fly like Icarus, Jessica,
so close to the sun and crashing into the sea, and her terrestrial mother
blessed the child who received at birth the seemingly real passion and
joy, the ecstasy her mother felt she must have had flying close to the
sun with her father and her instructor, all three never regaining consciousness, asleep in their folds of fire; a sombre ceremony took the
place of her triumphant return, and still there were presents for Jessica,
asleep beneath the ruins of the plane, and who can tell if her sleeping
ears heard the songs and tributes of solidarity from fellow pilots across
the country; little girls brought toys, their parents brought flowers,
there was a violet teddy bear to be her companion, and Jessica still
saying, don't cry, her only regret was that her mother, who did not
approve of toys in the house, refused to accept the bear at the farewell
ceremony, Jessica never used to play, she said, and that was Jessica's
one regret, the violet bear she couldn't take with her, her father would
have let her keep it; a last photograph taken a few seconds before the
flight of the Cessna Cardinal showed for all to see how closely father
and daughter were knit in pride at what they did and where they had
gone together, wed forever in air full speed, never to return, although
she had no toys, what Jessica did have was a pony and horses, and she
had overcome the intoxication of air at full speed, and rather than
being consumed by luminous flames of sunlight, the three of them
had died in the April cold, amid freezing rain, and the plane's dis-
membered carcass, rather than plunging into the sea, had somersaulted
onto a suburban highway, then a vacant lot, during her last meal at

Cheyenne Airport Jessica had implored Adam, the young waiter, to skip the oil in her fries since it wasn't pure vegetable oil, and he had told her he was working at the airport because he too wanted to fly, he could recite all the twin-engine transatlantic flights from the Air and Space Academy. He watched the DC8s take off while he served the customers, when he took a solitary cigarette break at the end of the patio, he could make out the buzzing of mosquitoes over the stagnant water as well as the approach of the tanker-plane that would wipe them out with blasts of a toxic brown cloud, or the impossible drone of larvae brought together in a sustained squeal of fright that elevated Adam's anxiety and his impulse to fly, now, as he remembered Jessica's clear blue stare, he found himself comparing her to one of those lizards he would like to see preserved, or those bluish dragonflies whose flight he had followed through the tropical gardens, amid these gnats and mosquitoes that never seemed to bother her, Jessica just went on eating her fries, and this older boy Adam, who found her so amusing, might one day turn into a botanist with all these gnats and dragonflies, a New Age vegetarian like her mother, soon he'd be taking flying lessons, he said, not long after this final little chat of theirs, of course he was never to see her again, and smoking alone that night on his parents' patio, he would listen to the rising murmur of the mosquitoes, the slap of waves against pilings, and think, the Cessna Cardinal's going to fly over the house tonight, and how could she just leave the earth in her high-collared, black leather jacket, she was still very near to him for sure, a little fly buzzing over the surface of the water after the storm, with his butterflies and dragonflies, flying forever till she dies, if Jessica had lived, Augustino wrote to his father, we'd be the same age, Daniel would have known nothing of Jessica's bravery, the tangible miracle of her life, as unexpected as an eclipse quickly slipping in and out before being noticed, he would never have known a thing about Jessica if Augustino hadn't informed him she was his heroine for the

37

millennium, they would have grown up together, Jessica always reaching to other galaxies, the landing strip where they saw a mass of metal from the plane was the one she often used, Augustino wrote, what dramas and pain have been etched here, she used to wonder, lots of questions, for instance, why did those who loved her allow her to die so young? He would write his father, I'm sending these words to you, dear Papa, and I swear that Jessica still lives inside us, it pleased Augustino that the words flew at once onto the screen, not with the heaviness of paper, but spilling out of the computer like treasure from a chest, carrier pigeons of thought, travelling far from Augustino and instantly arriving at the monastery in Spain where Daniel had withdrawn to write, and the name and picture of Jessica appeared on the screen, unforgettable and trembling with life for Augustino, who had stored data, films, documents, including this magazine cover of her face, drawn toward some cold and windy Elsewhere, under a grey-lined cap, all Augustino's heroines for a new millennium, those who would come next, young cosmonauts and astronauts with their cargoes of dogs and monkeys plunging in flames through lifeless space, in the movement of the stars, had they not been crushed too soon by the gods of air as well as the madness of a time that feasted insatiably on young lives? Daniel read his son's missives, hoping they would not come so often, suddenly these letters from Augustino appearing on the screen seemed crestfallen, like the sparrow caught behind iron bars in the Madrid station, or the wren flapping its broken wing that Daniel had found in the grassy field and nursed, then watched fly off unhurt into the sky, Augustino troubled his father's conscience, had his brain absorbed so much information, so many images, that already the past was reflected in the mirrors of his eyes? Daniel remembered as though it were yesterday what Mère had said to Mélanie on a trip to the Pyrenees when a communicant had been hit by a bus on the highway, the same way he should have said it to Augustino, don't look back, Mélanie, at that procession by the side of the road, don't look back, Augustino, at the light in Jessica's face. And how was it that Samuel had wandered into this part of Lower Manhattan, especially when he was already late for class, what would his professor say when he discovered his irascible side, suddenly it had shown itself, there where Samuel had stopped to check his car and saw a young hooligan with a hard face swipe the door, wash yer car? he asked, hiding a metal object in a polka-dot kerchief, with this hammer he was going to put nails through the tires of the convertible, calmly from his seat Samuel saw the truant sprint off, jumping nimbly between cars and onto the sidewalk, and the faded words on his worn-out black T-shirt were Honor, Work, Dignity, and when the boy got to the other side of the street, he stopped, leaned against a lamppost and crossed his arms, with the hammer in his belt and the dotted kerchief on his head, and yelled in defiance at Samuel, go on, defend yourself, rich boy, go call Mom and Dad on your cell phone, and next time you'll get... and he made an obscene gesture before disappearing among the shadows of the buildings, who knows, he might have been armed, thought Samuel, who promptly grabbed his cell phone, all the while thinking this was just the way the young thug saw him, insolent and proud at the wheel of his car, an expensive convertible his parents had given him, along with the portable phone, capitalist, the boy had yelled, Honor, Work, Dignity, but the street thug was just a thief, Samuel thought he had caught a whiff of hate on his neck, though he could not be sure in this racket of horns from behind or passing on the left: TransAms, Capris, Fords, nothing as nice as his, he thought, as he spotted a mechanic who could help him, who was he anyway, this no-good who dared to attack his car, one of the proletarian skinheads his father talked about in his book, like the ones who vandalized Jewish cemeteries in Buenos Aires, and in New York it wasn't just vandals, but sometimes indolent, unemployed Whites like this one, what his father easily imagined as an abandoned North American kid going shamefully hungry, crude parents incapable of feeding their overlarge family, no, he decided, this tire-nailer didn't deserve Daniel and Mélanie's socialistic sympathy, they would have explained it all: the economy's booming but the under-belly is hunger right here in North America, church food banks in all the large cities, trying to stem the tide of greed in society's leaders and feed their own, Catholic charities help out millions every year, lots of kids steal to eat, it's an abomination, Mélanie said, that one of the richest countries in the world still has 333,000 people going hungry, especially women and children, no, Samuel thought, this wan figure slipping away under its polka-dot kerchief, this boy wandering the streets, was just a walking case of aggressivity, already prone to larceny, Honor, Work, Dignity, what a joke, Samuel was thinking that about now, at home, Marie-Sylvie or his grandmother would be taking the dogs out for a walk along the seashore where he had often been with his brothers, a white parrot on his shoulder spreading its orange-tipped wings, while Samuel confided his longing to leave, leave soon, was it Samuel's voice, the parrot cooed with unbounded pleasure, nuzzling Samuel's neck with its steely beak, or his necklace of simulated pearls on fiesta nights, these were sensual moments at the end of days when light lay endlessly on the water, and when he was alone on the beach listening to the scratchy murmur in his headphones, or sweetly spent from being with women and the redness of sun on salty skin, a young man in a roomy car called over to Samuel, his hair was dyed pale blond and spiked on top, and he had an aura of being at ease with speed, uninhibited in his tight blue shorts, a quiet stare under the curve of his sparkling dark glasses, a mocking grin at Samuel showed off his pierced tongue, holding out the ring like some poisoned flower, Samuel thought, his strong hand around a girl who seemed poured from the same soulless, vigorous bronze, and Samuel began to suspect he might actually have something in common with them, he had that same hard charm of those who have never wanted for anything, what are you waiting for, get out of here, the boy shouted, and Samuel was surprised to find himself despising them, both of them, with their insolence, the rings and medallions in ears or on chests, with these trappings of freedom, the world would be even worse off than before, they were probably every bit as base as their parents, just as promiscuously rich and greedy, and Samuel listened to the boy's taunts, and felt he knew everything there was to know about him, the brand of underwear beneath his blue shorts with ribbed condoms in the pocket, sure he knew all about him, a clone but not a brother, a gross and phoney version of himself that he couldn't quite brush off, weren't they both heavy consumers, in-line skates, similar convertibles, nothing to limit their burgeoning desires, all needs he shared with this stranger, that must be why they were so suspicious of one another, yet still dumbly admiring of one another's virility; the hot asphalt of the street seemed boiling, and as the indifferent couple drove off in a meteoric roar, a wild girl with a delicate face haloed in blond curls appeared sitting on the sidewalk with a mountain of bags, had there ever been a bag lady this childlike, Samuel wondered, a schoolgirl, she recited uncomprehendingly a litany of horrific predictions from the Bible that lay open and upside down in her lap, for she was illiterate, but here she was, announcing that Samuel and all his kind, obsessed by their vile possessions, would be the millennium's victims, chosen for punishment, and what were he and the bronze couple going to do when the heavens opened above them, pouring fire on their heads, the wandering witch could only dole out misfortune to the passersby, although women were concerned about this misplaced tableau showing the Divinity of Modern Times, Our Lady of the Bags, a child of thirteen, who, like Joan of Arc in her village at Domremy, heard the voices of St. Michael, St. Catherine, and St. Margaret pleading with her to save France, these supernatural voices the little unlettered girl heard were denatured by a string of earthly violence, pestilence, and deluges that this brain, barely hatched and already damaged in a sudden accident, this child had been struck by a divine thunder, Samuel thought, and she'd die at the stake, not as a witch or a heretic condemned by some ecclesiastical tribunal, but because she could see the fiery torment that already embraced the earth, the bombs that one day could incinerate her while she was strolling along with her bags, or reading her Bible upside down, or just sitting on the sidewalk, dressed in her pleated skirt and clean as if she'd been washed by the rain, she was awaiting man's wrath as well as God's, hoping that His would take all of New York City with her, come on now, none of that is going to happen, said a well-meaning lady as she put a cool drink down beside the child, she drank it, eyes closed, and insisted incoherently that her voices had never led her astray, and what are you going to do on that day, said Our Lady of the Bags, will you be ready? A dream of happiness spread over her face as she lifted a frail hand to her lips, like a torch illuminating her dark life, this Coca-Cola she had been given held her to society as tenuously as the coin a poor boy has found in the King's garden, to a society that did not know what to do with its itinerants and still less with its wandering madmen, Samuel was afraid she was going to start up with her maledictions again, but instead she raised her delicate profile toward him and smiled steadily, it would be in the second week of May or June, she said mechanically, will you be ready, and went back to reading the Bible in her lap, I'm going to sleep out in the open tonight, meek as a dog begging its master for some bread, then the docile, disconnected voice caused Samuel to cry, it must be true, after all, as his father had said, that in these senseless times a doctor in a psychiatric institute would be on duty at night, hoping those who had no one to look after them would come back to him, those who turned out into the streets with sheets wadded up against them, standing like displaced scarecrows in front of cars, clutching bundles of belongings, old men,

42

children, addicts, arms crossed in the middle of an unhearing crowd, unstable minds that had been upset by those contemporary seers who had made the apocalypse into a trade, and the doctor, listening carefully to the story each one had to tell, thought there was no cure, no way out, these lunatics, obsessed by the paroxysm of the apocalypse that stirred, with the intensity of nothingness, lives barely begun, these went well beyond daily hygiene, turning taps on in all their buildings and apartments, water overflowing from all the sinks and basins in a spreading flood that would wash the earth clean and create life anew, others felt erupting through their skins all manner of cancers from a planet living on borrowed time, a woman and a man, still young, thought they saw, as they pulled a zipper, all their entrails and gangrenous organs spill out, and why were straitjackets needed to restrain people, who though crazed were as simple as this, pondered the white-coated clinician and researcher, when they were merely victims of the prophets of greed, and later, when he went home, scarcely seeing his wife and children, worn out and edgy from so many night shifts, the doctor was perhaps himself aware of contracting the virus of these afflictions he so carefully tried to cure, art lover that he was, he had taken his children to the Chirico exhibit, he had always thought that the great postmodernist painter had not been understood, because his paintings gave birth to a current of madness, persuasive and grandiloquent, that revealed the most powerful premonitions of modern man, Chirico's horses, for example, on a red, deserted plain before the gates of hell, with a farm with no animals and a trough with a thin trickle of water; obviously, he thought, these stallions, with flared nostrils sniffing the air of a reddened sky with still a few turquoise clouds, with flaming manes and tails, pawing the infertile and rocky earth, had been painted by a hand possessed of madness so as to make one live this torrent of fiery manes, in the fearful stiffening of posture, a landscape of destruction that was not just metaphysical, as long thought, but very real; the doctor would relay this insight to the people he worked with, usually at dawn as he waited for his patients to wander back, one still in the institute's sheets, another with a needle sticking into a vein and coming out the other side, when would they show up, sometimes he saw the horses, royal stallions weighed down among the ruins, under a reddish-tinged dawn burned into Chirico's canvas, ah, there they were at the door, as though waiting at the gates of hell; happy to hear the hum of his engine, Samuel told Our Lady of the Bags, as he called her, sitting on the sidewalk in her plaid skirt with the Bible on her knees, you're crazy, little girl, I don't believe a word of it, you know, because I've got sweet, sensual memories, like a day back on the water, sailing or sunbathing or loving, too bad Samuel had an appointment at four he was already late for, that's what his father was always criticizing, love, the wild girl quietly refrained, see love through the eyes of a child and hear the song of the angels in heaven, lies, what lies, Samuel said, while the strident waves of the soothsayer's voice dissolved in the air. On board flight 491, Renata thought how young and rowdy the kids on this plane were, and what a relief it was to make the first stopover in New York, they were on their way to Honduras, those girls running down the aisles are in my French class, said the girl next to her, our parents are waiting for us in Honduras, we won a study trip for having the best grades, all of us in the Foreign Language Club, maybe linguists one day, and their dizzying and excited whisperings had not prevented Renata from leaving her husband in first class to sit with them, the extra luxury seemed right for Claude, but for her it was a snub, and all at once here she was in the middle of them, uniformed schoolkids with teachers and chaperones filling up the tiny space with their turbulence, she thought at times she felt carelessly affectionate hands brush her hair from behind while she tried in annoyance to read and reread the paper for the death-penalty debate she and her fellow judges were to have tomorrow, still nothing could take away from what was written here, so fundamental was the dissidence, her ideas could only add to the unsure eloquence of a low-key voice, or a hoarse one, she felt overwhelming despair that executions would still go ahead tonight, what punitive doggedneas was it that drew out the wait until nighttime or at least a time when people sat down to relax after work at the supper table or looked forward to retiring with a loved one, the perverse dimensions of this harshness were unbearable, she thought, the vigils of countless opponents sent out prayers to the California prisons, vigils that had begun before Easter and before days full of torment, before the secret, ignominious crimes of evening executions, forging links in a chain of sheer habit; on Sunday, the roads had been blocked by carloads of family members visiting the reprieved on the other side of the death-wall, just a word of compassion from a Cabinet secretary or a retired senator could change the fate of these men, but it would never come, and these families under the shadow of steadily shrinking hope would bring in food and cigarettes every Sunday, definitely better to be terminally ill than to undergo this torment of waiting, torture ceaselessly reworked since the Inquisition, this is what Renata was reading while the lively and spontaneous band of schoolkids, with a world before them, played all around her, ceaselessly chattering, barely sitting in their places, she felt so much impatience for these adorable beings who treated her with such undeserved familiarity, she thought, another group of sweet and tender little girls beside her, dressed in pink taffeta, just as talkative, were edging Renata toward the window of the plane, we're still far from the Caribbean Sea, they said, the Gulf of Honduras, vast mountains, forests, banana and coffee plantations, Renata noticed their pointed shoes and white socks with animal patterns, the proud hands of a mother had shined their shoes and done up their hair like that of little dancers, showing off their ribboned gift boxes, dolls, and bracelets from uncles and godmothers, I'll get there

45

ahead of you, Renata said, and I won't hear the whole long story of your trip, but we'll meet back home, said the eldest girl, and what will you do later on? Renata asked, we're going to have lots of babies like our mommies, said the eldest, aware of the plane's sudden movement, we're going down, said Renata, see those big clouds, she reassured them; sweetly, confidently, the girls huddled against her shoulder, but she could not help being annoyed and feeling aggressive when she thought about tomorrow's meeting, later in the terminal she felt angry with herself for being so distant, so lacking in kindness or tact, when the vibrant liveliness of these youngsters had brought her out of her relentlessly bad mood, and she had not even felt ashamed about it; what monumental injustice, what drama would it take for her to stand side by side with people different from herself, but still close to her, whether she liked it or not, Claude had announced the news at midnight in their New York hotel room, they had not even had time to think about tomorrow's meeting after the long plane ride to Honduras, nor was there time for those condemned to die at midnight, right after their last meal, these children had not had time to get past the Honduran mountains the little girl had pointed to in her coloured picture book, see, she said, that's where we're going, me and my sister, it would take only a few more kilometres and they would be with their parents, and how had they all blundered like this, innocent passengers every one, into this mud-filled jungle so close to their destination? Surely someone could be held to account for ruining their lives, for saving mediocre magistrates, many of them symbols of the corroding world, held up by a conference in New York, in the midst of a ballet of children ready to dance through their lives, Renata thought, as her husband tried to calm her, no one could be blamed except luck, not a poorly performing captain, no flight mechanic who hadn't seen it coming, had they seen the guide marks on the runway on this foggy night, could it have been foreseen, was the weather radar functioning, a fault in the fuselage, no, no one and nothing was to blame, Claude said, you had to admire the rescue team who had cleared the ground with bull-dozers amid the murky crocodile-infested waters, or could you blame someone for losing touch and making a morgue out of this water and dung, a pilot, luck, God? Did it make any sense, thought Renata, in such a fatal wreck, that apart from an Indian reservation in the mountains, only a handful of judges had survived, what is there to understand, her husband said, the disaster that indiscriminately wiped out all the sparrows in the skies over China did not make sense either, nor the deer herds in hunting season, nor, on a foggy night, all the passengers on flight 491 to Honduras, including the French class Renata had been drawn to, pell-mell, without warning or pity, the disaster had scattered all these little girls in taffeta dresses, rosebuds, white hothouse carnations raised for beauty and delicateness, and Renata would still be alive long after they had lost even a semblance of life, sparrows, deer, guileless and betrayed, and the monk Asoka wrote to Ari, I am forty today, and I do not know how long I have left to inhabit this body, twenty years, maybe longer, but I thank you for the happiness you have given me, and you, more than any other benefactor, Ari, you on your island, editing our newspaper *The Evolution of Conscious-ness*, the philosophy of which follows me everywhere, you know I have been a monk for twenty-seven years now, and a pilgrim for seventeen, do you think the world is less warlike just because we want to redeem it whatever the cost? My parents had been trying to reach me for several days, even phoning a friend of mine, and at the airport when I got back from Russia I learned that my two younger sisters had died in June, I've been travelling a long time, as you know, often putting up with very uncomfortable conditions, so I did not learn about it till much later; Matupali, my only surviving sister, is inconsolable, I wrote telling her not to be sad, for perhaps their time had come to leave us, nourished by our spiritual teachings they knew the body is a temporary shelter; a foundation in London has offered me a place to stay, this is where I am writing from, my dear Ari, for a few months I'll be able to go on teaching those who quest for a better world and who come from all over, from every nation, ethnic group, and profession, to hear a message of hope. Yet I still cannot shake this cloud over my head, this certitude that I shall never see my sisters again in this life, and for how long, ten years, twenty? What more can I do than wish them a gentle journey, but this obligation to perish and, worse yet, to see our loved ones perish is perhaps the most relentless demand that can be made on us, Ari, and now in my fortieth year, I feel as though I've lived several lives; the sadness of seeing those orphanages in Mongolia, and it had nothing to do with the generous welcome they gave me, the venerable monks of Tuv Aimag laid on a traditional reception complete with chants and prayers, and yet the faces of those kids, often with no father or mother, still the oldest ones danced for me in the costumes of Ulan Bator, then gathered together to be blessed, and what courage they have, how much grace, to smile, these first victims of the atrocities of war, how could one ever forget them, these children of my own I'll never have? One day, Ari, when you're a father, look after the little ones and love them always from the minute they are born; recently, my teaching took me to the Oya Valley, a point beyond which it is dangerous to travel; an evil wind blows out of the jungle and across the road from both sides, insinuating fear into the trees, for ten years now, heavily armed terrorists have poured into the valley, killing hundreds of civilians and spreading dread wherever they go; once at an identity check, a soldier advised me to wait before crossing the road because it was mined, I suppose you're about to say, Ari, that a monk shouldn't be in that jungle, but when I walked alone into the bunker for the first time and the soldiers all had their guns trained on me, I discovered the reality of love, the bunker had been built around a flowering tree, vanilla-scented orchids from my childhood village it seemed like, through my binoculars I could see the pitiful march of the soldiers across the fields, faces clouded in black paint under helmets covered with branches, they were about to go on the attack, tired as they were, in their fortified hideout I saw the piles of ammunition, sandbags, automatic weapons, and I knew how pernicious they were capable of being, but one stood out from the rest, a young man who had adopted a baby monkey only a few weeks old, the boy's generosity caught on so that even the other soldiers were bottle-feeding the newborn, what a sweet contrast, dear Ari, the same bunker, the same men around a baby monkey, just an hour after ruthlessly destroying everything around them; they asked what I was doing wandering around in a place like this, and I told them I had seventy-five students waiting for me in a school, kids who walked several kilometres every day to a rudimentary school with none of the basic comforts, they told me the road there was mined, and the children and their teacher were probably no longer even alive, but, dear Ari, I insisted on heading off anyway, not realizing, as I should have, that the north of my Sri Lanka was almost totally devastated. It was an evening in March that I got there, wanting to set up an education centre in Colombo, there were more urgent needs to be seen to first, when the venerable Dhammasiri and some other monks came to meet me, we were overtaken by a line of trucks carrying the dead bodies of men, women, and children, I couldn't believe I'd come home to my own country, my own village. My friend, said the venerable Dhammasiri, being anxious about you displeases me, but I was most troubled by your journey through the Oya Valley, the school you wish to visit no longer exists, burnt, and we are completely without news of the students and teacher, you would be better advised to return with me to Anuradhapura and rest at the temple for a few days, it took us over five hours to reach Anuradhapura, and the heat in the temple was unbearable, and we were bitten by swarms of mosquitoes, but stopping before a pond where frogs were croaking, I thought of my sisters and seemed to hear them laughing, as though in a dream, although I had not seen much of them, having been separated from my family at sixteen when I began studying as a novice monk, yet all at once, sweet memories of my sisters invaded my spirit, there before the pond. After taking a shower with well water, I installed the mosquito netting around my bed, but I was perspiring and unable to sleep for thinking about all the bodies unloaded that day from trucks in the northeast of the country, what torment their families would feel receiving them; about four-thirty, I heard the sounds of morning birds and cocks, then as I sipped some tea, I saw again the burnt school and its ghostly brick walls. Where is all this violence leading, dear Ari, are these men barbarians? I remind you, one must practise Ajjhatta Santi, ideal harmony does not conflict with a reality that is so often hurtful, you must meditate in tranquility, Ari, release the tensions knotted inside you, my friend, you say you believe in the satisfaction of all pleasures, but doesn't this just lead you away from your morning meditation? I told you in Moscow they gave me a coat, I never wear coats, but still this one touched me, and it was very warm too, so you see, Ari, people are capable of goodness. Ari gathered up the night mail that the computer had brought him on waves of light, and as he read Asoka's words on the other side of the world, he thought about the weight of his own selfish desires that would bar him from meditating like his friend for a long time to come, at eighteen, the novice monk would be up at dawn, vase in hand beneath the folds of his sober orange clothing, questing for humility by begging food from the villagers, these same dawnings would always be chaste for Asoka, but exuberant and sensual for Ari on a sailboat with his girls and set for adventure with a load of hashish and red cannabis below deck, and how could he talk about this youthful excess of hunger for every kind of pleasure to Asoka, who as a boy had never known the enjoyment and love of women, the path of

self-denial had seemed an outrage to the flighty Ari, yet Asoka understood him well, and in recommending once again the peaceful silence
of mind that would surely come from meditation, he was conveying
a tender blessing, just as he had blessed the villagers during his appren-
tice-begging, and Ari realized Asoka afforded him divine protection,
holding him back from the abyss he took such delight in, women,
Indian hemp, which sometimes served as inspiration for his art, just
low-toxin drugs that would soon be decriminalized anyway, Ari told
him, there is nothing so peaceful as an artless, positive thought, Asoka
wrote back when Ari found himself shaken by instability, isn't that
always the way artists are, toxic to themselves through their art, their
suicidal stress, the way their work eats away at hope, and smoking red
cannabis had not caused psychic problems for Ari, just a more complete
visual sense of form in sculpture, whether black marble, painted aluminum, neon, engraving, sculpture, after all, he too could influence the
world and challenge it with his embodied thoughts, like his artworks
in public parks, he said, the *Surrealist Manifesto* had shaken up the
established order, hadn't it, and there were more and more such things,
including sculptors like Ari with their calcite stones and steel lettering,
Justice, Peace, and others were fighting a worldwide apartheid in other
ways, artists had enormous powers, even if they were shunted aside,
eyes aflame and hands stained with the black granite he was cutting
with a torch, rage boiling in his heart, Ari could have used the calm
hand of Asoka on his head full of uncontrollable desires, but although
Ari still edited Asoka's paper, the two hardly ever saw each other
anymore, of course he and the perpetual pilgrim wrote each other
constantly, could it be true, he thought, feeling as though he were on
the earth for a long time, that life is actually so fleeting, ten, maybe
twenty more years, as Asoka said, and how could the monk resign
himself with such cool diffidence to the deaths of his two younger
sisters, and Ari had never even known he had a family, did achieving

51

perfection mean neglecting a friend to the point of not confiding in him, but Asoka the exemplar had one fault, thought Ari, he doesn't think about himself enough, already ascetic, he had travelled to Russia without so much as a coat, was that really the way to perfection? Whatever experiences life may bring your way, Asoka had written, every single one is a treasure, don't forget, each instant must be ardently lived, for once he had accepted the coat from one of his Russian disciples, but how many hours had he walked in bare sandals through the snow without ever begging a pair of boots from him, the military bunker he had visited was nothing if not the Vietnam Ari had known revisited, the school, the students, and the teacher all disappeared in smoke, this bunker had been built around a flowering tree, was that really all the monk had gained from such a dark calamity? My body is my main source of strength, Ari thought, and those who had despised their bodily reality laid out their funereal shadows along the hills of Rancho Santa Fe next to the ocean, had been members of a sect called the Law of the Chosen Ones, and on a tepid March afternoon had, one by one in order of rank, leaders last, divested themselves of everything not properly destined to them, including their vehicles, or envelopes, as their bodies were called, for their masters had taught them this, eldest first, sexual abstinence, then castration, for these bodies, vehicles, envelopes were to be fervently thrown off before they departed on the Voyage, when they would all be one mass of bodies with heads inside black plastic bags, and Comet Hale-Bopp would pass close to the earth followed by a spaceship that the Chosen Ones would climb aboard, their vehicle-envelopes, meaningless objects in which festered a fatal mixture of barbiturates, phenobarbital, and alcohol, would be transcended during the Voyage to a solar Elsewhere where the gates of heaven opened, transcended, metamorphosed, these bodies they had escaped from; later, due to the heat, those who had lain lifeless in the seven pretty rooms facing the ocean would be taken away in

refrigerated trucks, the neighbouring millionaires never having sus-
pected that such a sheltered spot would suddenly turn out to be the
tomb of an apocalyptic cult, while all around them people continued
to bathe in their pools or play tennis, because no one had ever heard
a word against them, the owner being aware, of course, of their austere
lack of furniture, the large number of computers, and the giant TV
screen in the centre of a game room, they were studious and mysteri-
ous, and had left behind a computer drawing of the extraterrestrial
god they venerated and who awaited them like a distant star in the
astral realm; these followers of a fatal cult were no more gullible than
anyone else, Ari thought, but their bodies, mutilated by abstinence
and castration, had failed them, and in the silence, in the aphasia of
submission to their chief, they had yielded to the destruction of their
bodies and the suffocation of their spirits, not one among them, not
even the most brilliant, had sufficient health or critical sense to look
deep into the eyes of the fanatic who would crush them so satanically,
physical anesthesia was the goal of all these sects, thought Ari, seeing
the line of young and deceased of the Law of the Chosen Ones step
wide-eyed into eternity, how sad, all those bodies estranged by the
vague Utopia of a madman, each from its unhappy eternity would
look into the sunny room by the Pacific, would remember its death
agony, mouth and throat choking in the bag, stomach bitterly digesting
the alcohol and phenobarbital, this pathetic body lost forever, Ari
could not imagine so much horror as he contemplated the solidity of
his hand and arm scored by the work he did, his body was forever, he
thought, energetic, strong, and this hand would never stop sculpting,
and life could not go on without the strength of this impetuous body
of his. This is life's bounty, thought Jean-Mathieu as he walked, cane
in hand, toward Caroline's house, almost fully hidden by a crown of
palm trees, the light that heaven pours on us daily, and how thankless
we are, we take it all for granted, and now the threshold to Caroline's,

more and more forbidding in recent times, and her mailbox firmly upright and resisting the rose-laurels, what fine taste she has, always an air of elegance about her, as she herself pointed out, and in an instant Jean-Mathieu began to worry about the steep right slant of the calligraphy, perhaps she would exclaim as always, oh, how well he writes, like Chinese ideograms laid out in a pattern, but she might also notice the hand tremor and the suddenly concave lettering, then what might she laughingly say to her lady companion, that the trembling was a sign of age, or perhaps she would just remain silent, embarrassed at this unwelcome ugliness, and how might she react to Jean-Mathieu's invitation, dear friend, in a few hours I shall be leaving for Venice and summer, and I should very much like to dine with you tonight, I anxiously await your reply, he felt awkward exaggerating, come on, she would reply mockingly, we have a whole life to see one another, he was not going to ring the bell, just put the letter in the box and leave, you remember the beautiful Venetian countryside, how wonderful we found it, don't you, dear friend, did we go there together, when was that, she might ask, I bet we were very young then, nowadays I go to Italy only for a cure, see how firm my facial muscles are, one has to stave off old age any way one can, Jean-Mathieu would reply, I like the terraces where you can talk and celebrate all night better than those vast vineyards, and my modest hotel by the canal better than the architecture of the gardens, I wrote a lot of my books on those terraces, and Caroline would continue, you have to try to keep your skin from sagging, is this how their conversation was going to go, wondered Jean-Mathieu as he slipped the letter into the box, what are our final days going to be like, oh, how sly were these forebodings that undermined our happiness, un-lighting our way to darkest despair, betrayals, and forgetfulness, Jean-Mathieu said to himself, so near to the sea's song that he heard its smallest notes in the unfurling waves a few streets away, this long-accustomed music comforted him, pulsing

night and day in his temples, life could not be, without the incantation
of the waves at his door and beneath his windows, or without the
unceasing air of travelling the sea brought into his life, the exaltation
he had once known as a ship prepared to weigh anchor, he would go
to see Frédéric and hope against hope to get him out of bed, and Charles
self-centredly cloistered and writing so far away in India, one would
have to fear the worst for Frédéric if he did not have Eduardo and Juan,
it is true Caroline has always preferred those luxury places with swimming pools, was this how they were going to grow old, concerned only
with their rheumatism and arthritis and not with Jane Austen and
Raphaello's contemporaries, Caroline asked Charly if there was any
mail this morning, because she thought she heard the mailman's footsteps and the little bell on the gate, no, there's nothing, Charly said, I
can't understand why Jean-Mathieu hasn't phoned or written, Caroline
said from the satin canape where she was sorting photos into an album,
I can drive you over there tonight, if you like, said Charly, but he'll be
gone tonight, came the answer, I wonder if he's getting indifferent, she
thought, a little piqued, men do that, when the mailman came, she
was usually in the laboratory far from the rest of the house, where she
could hear nothing, what really surprises me, she said, is that he no
longer phones me, I'm taking you over there tonight, Charly said, an
odd smile on her fleshy lips, what a sweet child, Caroline thought, a
little Black in her, but her skin's a golden brown, no, if she didn't insist
on telling everyone, we'd never believe her, politely Caroline ordered
Charly to put the photos back in the album, what did I do, do you
know, Charly, with that picture of Charles and Frédéric in Greece, the
nightingales and poppies, they all lived in harmony there, writing and
painting all day long, I'm sure you've forgotten where you put it, said
Charly, I may not have memory loss, but I don't know any better than
you, don't be cheeky, Caroline said sharply, I'll find it, accusing me of
losing my memory, she thought, that's going too far for a domestic, if

Charlotte could be called that, she was a funny and entertaining hired companion, insolent like all these young people, it's true, like the private chauffeur, it had already hurt when she gave up driving the Mercedes herself, Charly drove very well but too fast, she would have to be reminded that it was not her car, the girl really wasn't too well trained, Caroline might eventually be able to whip her into shape, now, in her parents' house the servants had known how to behave, and what was this story of hers anyway, brought up in Jamaica by an American father who had retired to the West Indies after a career in the military, true or not, the important thing was that she was pleasant to get along with, a bit fearsome maybe, but Caroline liked that, it relieved her of the monotony of her thoughts and stimulated her memory, for Charly wasn't fooled by Caroline's lapses, why bother remembering when it was only from one day to the next anyway, thought Caroline, and where had she put that photo, and it was unforgivable of Jean-Mathieu not to phone or write, without being a complainer it was fair to say that life could be a bit of a nightmare when a friend let you down, or maybe there was just some sort of problem, this Jean-Mathieu business was really no worse than getting your glasses changed, the book definitely needed that photo of Charles and Frédéric in Greece, since I'm not allowed to smoke in the house, I'm going out for a few minutes, Charly said with her usual sulky humour, and she was already out in the garden, how empty the house is without her, and she's always outside, especially at night, thought Caroline, I don't sleep much as it is, and on top of that, she makes me count the time till she's back, me, who has never been in the habit of waiting for anyone, not Jean-Mathieu before nor Charly now, I never realized how horrible it was, and what does she do out all night until dawn anyway, those smelly cigarillos of hers, good thing she's gone right across the garden with them, now Caroline would at least get some peace, that's the way Charly went out, wearing practically

nothing, her dress was too short, you could see her swimsuit underneath, and she spent all day in the water, then left all her things spread
around the pool, magazines, books, cigarettes, Caroline wouldn't have
enjoyed being someone's mother, and although she'd had a full and
adventurous love life, she was definitely glad she hadn't had children,
still the house was full of life now Charly was here, yet what could you
make of this blasé, indolent generation, unlike Caroline, who had
become a pilot and a war heroine out of patriotic idealism, Charly was
a hybrid creature, neither boy nor girl, proud of her body and the
sexual fascination it exerted, back in the New York apartment this fall,
things would be different, they would be cut off from the casual pleasures of the sea, Charly would be less hare-brained and more malleable,
is that why they were so icy on contact, because their souls are metallic,
or is it just me who doesn't know how to approach young people,
thought Caroline, absorbed above all by Jean-Mathieu's silence after
they'd always been so close, and out on the wharf Charly crumpled
his letter with her fingers, the red-hot glow of her cigarillo would
reduce it to flames in an instant, Charly saw only Caroline for her
immediate, personal usefulness, so what business did Caroline and
Jean-Mathieu have loving each other at their age, how indecent, no,
gradually, everything would be erased, phone messages, Adrien and
Suzanne wouldn't be phoning anymore, too bad about Jean-Mathieu,
but the aging poet was far too attached to Caroline, he would have
demanded too much time and attention, and all that flowery letter-
writing, Caroline didn't deserve such passionate devotion, she was not
even ashamed to say her family had house slaves, well, not slaves exactly,
but domestic servants, Black ones that they were really nice to, exquis-
itely nice, Caroline said, and Charly asked if there were any Jamaicans,
what business was it of hers to ask questions like that, Caroline didn't
owe explanations to anyone, it's like Jean-Mathieu forever talking
about his poor childhood in Halifax, Caroline couldn't help that, that

was there, long ago and far over the Atlantic, almost a century away, Jean-Mathieu's burning letter of hieroglyphs was rocking on the waves, seagulls and pigeons flying erratically over the dense heat, Caroline wasn't worthy of the love of such a gallant, likeable man as Jean-Mathieu, she who pretended not to know about the slave trade, was it a long time ago or just another one of those memory lapses, Charly wondered, a people stooped in the sugar plantations, I love this majestic island where it's always sunny, they'd be sold, all my ancestors, to South America, North America, the West Indies, chained without any future, she thought, and it was this blood of slaves that flowed in her veins, though she herself had been born to freedom, not chained or auctioned off, but her father, a veteran with many Black mistresses, including Charlotte's mother, so young and easy for him to manipulate, what bitterness to think about the control he had over them all, mother and sisters, then suddenly there was Caroline on a magnificent island taking pictures of them all for her exhibition, stealing their souls, and that was how Caroline had approached her, while Charly was drunk on rum, dancing alone on the beach, come closer, step onto my liquid-crystal screen, there was the image of a girl bewitched by the dance that enchanted Caroline, it will be a beautiful exhibit, full of the charm of the West Indian soul, where are your sisters, I'd like to photograph them too, you're all so beautiful, call me at my hotel tonight, I'd like you to have supper with me, your mother too, although I thought she was your sister, when she agreed to be photographed for the collection, Charlotte remembered seeing Caroline's cold eye in the viewfinder, little by little she got around to asking Charlotte to come with her, since her mother said Charly liked cars like a boy and dreamed of leaving, travelling, she could be her chauffeur, wedded to the multiple, encompassing images of her camera, Caroline had told Charlotte, you'll like it where I live, all you need to do is drive my car, I already have a secretary and a maid, and oh, blessed was this island where they met, she said, too bad, for once Jean-Mathieu was not travelling with her, but he was giving a conference at some university in London, here it was so restful, and the trip to Jamaica would have been cheaper for two, but Jean-Mathieu had told Caroline he should not make this kind of trip anymore, she could have helped him through his money troubles, but it always occurred to her that he would have been humiliated by the offer of help, Caroline needed a chauffeur who would also keep her company, and whether Charly came back with her later or not, she should not give in, for one day she would begin to grow old rapidly, she thought, and the Italian cures were no use anymore, she needed a chauffeur because her eyes had to be protected for her photography; fractious, rebellious, and treating Caroline as she would her father, White phoneys, both of them, Charly had agreed, and despite the humiliation of ancestors flowing through her, there by the sea, as she burned Jean-Mathieu's letter to Caroline with her cigarillo, she felt the birth of an immense pride that could never be vanquished, now it was time for the debt to be paid, it was Caroline's turn to be subjugated and to atone for past wrongs. And this spring, Asoka wrote to Ari, has been devoted to seven weeks of teaching at Omega, visiting hospitals and orphanages in Sri Lanka, returning to Siberia and the Tuva Republic, and in the hospitals, the surgeons, doctors, and nurses confided to me they hadn't been paid anything for months, how can you treat the sick like that, Ari? On the way to Mongolia, when we stopped at Irkutsk in eastern Siberia, I was thunderstruck by the magical beauty of Lake Baikal at sunset, after that, I took part in a huge millennial conference in Prague, listening to thousands of contemporary thinkers and political and religious leaders exchange equally uncertain predictions for the future, is there any other alternative, Ari, than death and destruction? That is what a lot of them asked, including Nobel winners. I was deeply affected by a visit to a refugee camp in Sri Lanka, the one I told you about in the village of

Kebithigollewa, a place that reminds me, you remember, of the worst slums I ever saw in Africa or India, nearly two hundred families piled into suffocating rooms in huts with coconut-matted roofs, it's hard to imagine all these people living in such humiliation when they used to be farmers, all of them respected in the village, before the Tamil tourists poured in. Some of them told me how bad their lives were: no hygiene, using the woods as a latrine works for us men, but not for the women and teenagers who have to live in this degradation. Government representatives come and promise to help, then leave. Ari, as I quit the refugee camp, I realized how urgently something had to be done, an architect friend went with me on that trip, and she was as affected by all this misery as I was, so I asked for her advice, after that she volunteered to work at the camp, and we put in twenty temporary toilets, then we built more and more as the months passed, and paid for them by taking up a collection. When I was a novice monk in Colombo, I often walked by the massive prison-fortress of Welikada in the crowded outskirts near the markets and stone palaces belonging to senior politicians, that is where they keep the most dangerous criminals, but I didn't know they were women. You know, they also lock away innocent women and their young children, babies even. There is a committee to improve prison conditions, and they have a project to start a prison nursery where women can visit their children away from the hardened criminals. There is a huge iron door leading into the prison, then several sets of bars and gateways, everywhere women in civilian clothes or in prison uniform, the ones in white are imprisoned for life, the rest are there for no reason, their babies too, all in the same degrading conditions, and when only a small minority have committed even the slightest infraction, and often out of ignorance, some arrested for selling in the marketplace without a permit, some simply unable to get a lawyer. The prison cells they are piled into with their children are nothing like those in the West, these women sleep heaped together on the cement floors, with no way to wash, and the showers are monopolized by the violent ones. They were hesitant to talk about life there, but one finished by sobbing that she was there because her husband was wanted by the police for fraud and had not given himself up, so she and her child had been taken instead. The women's prison is going to have its nursery, still when I got back to the temple, there was no way I could meditate in peace for thinking of these young women, their cries and their children's stayed with me, and I do still feel sad when I think that things like this can happen, I embrace you, dear Ari, in friendship and serenity. Ah, why didn't he rest surrounded by the beauty and sunsets of Lake Baikal a little longer, thought Ari as he read this, there was always some charity Asoka was devoting himself to in Sri Lanka or Mongolia, would Ari ever be able to do this, give himself up, body and soul, to hopeless causes? While the monk was out building latrines, or defending the dignity of women in refugee camps, or visiting young mothers unfairly jailed in Welikada, what did a woman mean to Ari but the cult of his sensuality and art, serving his capricious instincts, an accomplice in his volcanic love of life? He knew how to paint a vivid portrait of the fleeting, ecstatic smile or the embattled concentration of a lover, to whom he refused the most desolate regions of his heart, and everything his senses were greedily capable of seizing from day to day, but this was not the prayer that Asoka expected of him, no, rather the courage of thoughtful acts that might redeem humanity, this is the imperfection of being an artist, he thought, his action is cloudy, his art full of the impurities of life, its vices too, or does art compress into momentary flashes the sense of irremediable loss that afflicts us all from birth? During the stay in Irkutsk on the way to Mongolia, Asoka had, after all, taken time to be dazzled by the beauty of Lake Baikal at sunset, so he was indeed a man like other men, meditating on nature and torn by a divine beauty and presence, this admission touched Ari's soul as though Asoka had whispered to him, I too understand love at times, yours, everybody's, your carnal love for all that breathes, in the dazzling beauty of Lake Baikal, Asoka had forgotten his deliberate detachment from earthly things, the deep waters of the lake reminded him that he too was sensitive and sensual, this detachment separates us from what we love most, beauty, sensuality, thought Ari, it is not of this world, this stolid commitment to a life of action, though, isn't it harmful too, a sign of the futility of Ari's greed for all forms of life and passion in his painting and sculpture? Who else could understand so well the fury of Goya in his sketches of war and catastrophe, his obsession with the ugliness and corruption of the eighteenth century, the artist as sorcerer, demon, analyst, and fiery troublemaker, he said, look, here is the scandal of pain, *que viene el coco,* watch out for the bogeyman, called a mother with a pair of children in her arms, but the bogeyman, whether Pestilence or Famine, marched onward in this drawing, indifferent to all, his monstrous face hooded, *que viene el coco,* watch out for the bogeyman, the millennium bogeyman, thought Ari, all these assaults on nature in a universe where droughts, floods, cyclones, and storms could not be controlled either, as though our evil powers had unleashed them on ourselves, this was also what Ari was trying to portray when a tropical cyclone tore down on the Caribbean, Ari refused to go when everyone else was evacuated, and from his window he could see the frantic whirlwinds that battered his house, day flipped over into night while he watched, it was as though the centre of the whirlwind were at his door, the sky was seized by the same churning that uprooted palms and lime trees from the garden, that forced pelicans and egrets headfirst into the water, that dashed the eaglet from electric wires to jarring sidewalk, *que viene el coco,* watch out for the cyclone, the tempest, winds tearing into beaches from the transparent blue air of day to the murk of night, still wedded firmly to the physical earth, Ari sketched and painted the beauty of ruins left by the storm, the cyclone would calm by dawn, and under the wind and rain, every radiant bit of wreckage would spring back to life. Hey, come on, squirt, grow up, get into it, Arnie Graal said to Samuel, I'm not putting up with slackers or latecomers in this troupe; see this space all around you, none of my dancers make a move you can't see, tonight you work solo, dancing's a shock for the body, a tornado, learn to move your body, it's your language, your breath, and your rhythm, you've got to let the African percussion go right down inside you, then listen to it from far away, what have you been doing till now, just dreaming, weren't in any riots at twelve, were you, seen your friends killed right in front of you, Harlem or anywhere else, and Samuel listened in fear to his teacher, all the while thinking about Our Lady of the Bags, and what if that lunatic's predictions were dead-on, then the city of New York was going down in floods, buildings and skyscrapers crumbling, and Samuel would be left with nothing, he who in the street only hours before had yelled, lies, all lies, and then taken off, free, at the wheel of his car, young, vibrant, and owed respect because of it, but what would he do if the prophecies were true? Of course he was intimidated by his dance teacher, laying the authority and discipline on thick with his students; Arnie had told Daniel he was an artist first and Black second, he'd spent a long time doing hospital laundry in the daytime and dancing at night, hardly sleeping, from Amsterdam to Berlin to San Francisco, he'd always danced, and Samuel felt that Arnie was guiding him through the darkness, the preacher-like voice had immediately stripped him of all confidence, as he stormed, think of the power, the majesty of nature in an animal's walk, I used to be healthy just like you, a rock, still am, and no one's going to break me, I created *Survivor's Morning* for the ones who leave without curing the Abscess, there have been a lot of shows for them, around the beds where they lay dying, I took my twenty dancers to them, falling like leaves they were, grains of dust, with a rabbi reading from the Book of Genesis, a woman chanting in Yiddish, we switched languages and sacred texts, depending on who it was, but we always sang in several languages, and we watched these flowers fall petal by petal, grain by grain, go on singing, they said, sing, and they were tired, so tired, others died other ways, from bullets, in a matter of seconds, while we were dancing in the theatre, yesterday an African immigrant, just an unarmed street vendor and garbage-picker, was killed by four White officers, and what had he stolen? Nothing, they say he was a believer and a hard worker, nineteen times they shot him, and because he was waving his hands, they didn't realize he was just trying to talk to them, the poor guy stuttered, and he died right there in a hallway in the Bronx, and the citizens' watch wasn't there at night, all Doumadi got was four killers, White police officers, protests, inquiries, no point in all that, Black men dying the way they do every day in our cities doesn't mean a thing, who cares about a garbage-picker like Doumadi, a street-sweeper or shoeshine boy? That's the next show I'll choreograph, the story of the garbage-picker, and you, Samuel, are going to have to prove to me who you are, up to now, all you've known is traditional dance, *well*, I'm gonna break you, you're like a sweet country flute, but you've got to know in this world the only sound that gets heard is thunder. With twenty dancers and a chorus of women and children, we could tear the world open with cries, and you, fierce kid, are you ready to sing with your guts? Samuel was staggered by Arnie, after the ease and serenity of his island, where instinct had lulled him into a languid laziness in the garden crescent around an inlet of blue sea, where grew the rare plants, trees, and flowers his grandmother had shown him, name by fragrant name, she cultivated exotic South American amaryllis from poisonous bulbs, the rain lily, the climbing pandorea in its immaculate whiteness, the African tulip, Philippine orchids, scarlet passion flowers with petals like stigmata, gardenias, white jasmine stars of India, Madagascar crowns of thorns, stigmata, thorns, why this association of flowers and plants with torment, there must be something sick about that, thought Samuel, why should the memory of distant sacrificial suffering weigh so heavily on human destiny, and when would we finally be purified by the blood of crucifixion, and why had his father entrusted him to Arnie, this strange aesthete of dance, why had he been propelled toward this inspired, dynamic, but oh-so-hard choreographer, who, even when the delirium of the dance carried his body into a state of trance, let nothing crumble before being rebuilt the way the other dancers did, as he himself said, he was solid as a rock, and that is how Samuel had approached Arnie, in awe and respect, he was moved at the thought of this man who had danced before crowds, who had just performed his fortieth work in Munich, and whose voice was a baritone with the inflections of a preacher; the gold amulet shimmering and glinting on his black shirt as he urged on his dancers, telling them not to please or love or hate the audience, but perhaps attack or surprise them, like oil thrown on fire, Samuel, my little man, he said, you're here to learn, so don't waste time, dance! Acacia, thought Samuel, royal poinciana trees, coral plants from the Pacific islands, olive trees from Texas, when would he see his grandmother, Augustino, Vincent, and his sister Mai again, Mai had been given the name of a missing child, gone for years now, ever since that month of May when they had seen her for the last time, just one file among so many others, so many kids disappearing every year, and so when she had a girl, Mélanie had passed on to her the name Mai, in memory of the real Mai gone at four years old, with a ribbon in her hair, who would have taken her, which friend or treacherous relative, where was Mai's predator, born in Ontario and now no more than a spring name, Mai, bequeathed to Mélanie and Daniel's youngest child, still one and the same kind of childhood that Mélanie would ferociously defend from vile predators, and Mère asked Augustino as they paced the rows in the garden, now can you tell me the names of these flowers and trees, I had them

delivered when you were still small, that's Jacobinia carnea, it likes to
be shaded from the sun, Augustino said, looking confidently up at his
grandmother, and African tulip, it doesn't like the cold, and the jaca-
randa tree from Brazil, the royal poinciana tree you used to give us at
Christmas, Philippine orchids, amaryllis, Texas olive, then, as she took
his hand in hers, he heard the frightened voice of his grandmother
saying, what's happening to me, Augustino, I can't remember their
names anymore, not even the ornamental plants I removed from the
house because Vincent couldn't breathe the pollen, now the roses,
acacia, and yellow mimosa, those I do remember, we had lots of those
before Jenny went away to have such a miserable time in North Korea,
whatever possessed her to go and be a doctor there, so far away, white
jasmine star from India, Augustino went on, China rose hibiscus from
Hawaii, you can eat their petals, you know, what a strange thing forgetfulness, Mère continued, now tell me, can you, Augustino, you who
know so many things, but he had already run off to the other end of
the garden, you know one must never forget anything, she said, thinking he was still beside her, not the names of flowers and plants, not
their perfumes, what happens to grown-ups who aren't like you, never
going to sleep when they should, is that they slowly doze off when they
shouldn't, and that's why they forget the names of flowers and plants,
but those yellow mimosas, we had lots of those when Jenny was here,
we sent some around to every room, she and I, that was when Samuel
and your mother and your father were all here together, we were a real
family then, from the patio, Mère could see where Augustino had
ended up in a chair with his feet dangling in the warm air, suddenly
bent over a pocket computer his parents had given him a few days
before, a new one, and he already had two, probably to make up for
their being away from home so often, Mère loved chatting with him,
but he wasn't listening, intently writing to his father, tapping away on
the keyboard at the letter that would get there and be read by Daniel

in his Spanish monastery almost instantaneously, and so this is how they all live, thought Mère, writing all these letters to one another, didn't their words lose focus and consistency written fast like that, each one piling up on somebody else's, elbowed by e-mail, and that was why a grandson had no time for his grandmother, and what exactly did they say to each other anyway in this patchwork language, where were they headed in such a hurry, where? Samuel remembered there were also poison flowers on his island, this fragment of memory and revelation, like a tumour, had come to him from his father's book *Strange Years*, his parents had hidden his father's cocaine addiction, why, drugs were a crime, weren't they, but Mélanie insisted their outlaw years went back to before he was born, and after that, in the wake of their excesses, this fragile and sudden new life had become even more of a feat of magic and miracle. It seemed to Samuel that, in this book, Daniel was digging up admissions of phantasms that had lain buried, and a paranoia that wasn't really all that creative, Hitler's dog, for example, professing an animal's blamelessness, and not embedded in history with his master's murders, and into what secret, unconscious terrors had his father stumbled on drugs, the twenty-first century's Jean-Jacques Rousseau, as Adrien ironically wrote about him, had he really given himself up to daydreams and decadence, Samuel could have done without knowing about his father's dissolution, he reflected, but how do you go about judging your parents or God, your creators? Besides, the boy who had lived it up like that had calmed into a more sensible man with his wife and children, and tolerant of others' aberrations at the same time, just as the writer in him saw the poetic side, so he knew Arnie as a prince of dance to whom nothing should be taboo, these two shared not only friendship but the same exhibitionistic sincerity, Arnie uninhibited, bragged how everyone wanted him at the baths or in the sauna, for the colour of his skin, for the strength of his muscles, sex was a feat, after all, he said, a performance, a rite celebrated in the steam baths to the glory of the flesh, he valued the courtly game of these rituals, and as the youngest of twelve children had never liked to be alone, so what was the revolution about, he would say, but impudently pushing back the frontiers of sex and race, unashamedly getting rid of them altogether, and at the same time pushing back the frontiers of death with them, isn't that what *Survivor's Morning* was all about, his multimedia masterpiece not only held audiences spellbound for three hours, but Arnie, whose art dealt with nothing but dying, nevertheless seemed to be perfectly fine, the Abscess that unfolded itself from inside men otherwise beaming with health was like the worm in the apple, it grew slowly as the dancers focused only on posture, then suddenly, Arnie said, when one of us left, we were afraid the rest of us would be worn away by it too, that's when it occurred to me that dancing around our friends as they died would give us a longer hold on them, and they said, sing, dance, but don't leave me, I'm so tired, and that was how they eventually slipped away from us while we were still at their bedside, silently like falling leaves, grains of dust, and they were already on the other side of sleep, shoeless, while we were still singing and dancing, and it's dance that keeps me alive, like the African custom of dancing to help friends cross over in the midst of their torment, you know, in the papers they accuse me of worsening and mishandling the feelings of people revolted by death, all we have done is carry people over, lull them to sleep with the rhythm of feet and the richness of movement, why shouldn't death be an exploit like any other, a performance, a baptism, or a marriage with the beyond, or just what it is, a dance score, a choreography? But Arnie's spirit shrank at the memory of his last performance, false bravado in his smile, Tchaikovsky did the same with his last breath, adventured into a symphony, the *Pathetique*, putting to music the vision of a certain October 25, when a glass of water from the tap would make him sick, and the second would kill him, long after the stomach spasms and

fever from a hot bath he should not have taken, whether he died in the
bath, like his mother, from cholera, or suddenly while composing the
symphony, he was aware of everything on that Thursday, October 25,
I believe this is my death now, farewell, he said to his brother in a
moment of heightened awareness, pioneer that he was, he knew about
the Abscess, he lived it, and a century later he would not be surprised
to find out that an unknown young, Black choreographer was doing
a very different *Swan Lake* or *Sleeping Beauty*, the music just as revolutionary as ever, the large white birds in my version would be black
ones, the ultra-supple necks of my African dancers curving under
threat of the knife, all whiteness suspect like the robes of death, my
swans would be by the roadside near a pond, lynched by teenagers of
the Aryan Brotherhood, one swan, just one, pinned to their shirts as
a badge of honour, in my version of *Sleeping Beauty*, she never wakes
up, the Goddess of Indifference in her tomb, when did she ever wake
up? Arnie had set off scandals he compared to those of Marcel
Duchamp, what garnered him the most criticism at nonconformist
rallies was how cynical he could be, I don't want to forget those plantations with their Black bodies swinging from branches for so long, and
in dance you can express anything you want, life or death, and I've
set up survival workshops in twelve cities, and I listen to what every
dying person has to tell me; I am an artist, not a healer, tell me, how
do you each see your death? I want to know, that's all, maybe I want
to get you to realize that those last moments at the end of a life are
yours and yours alone, still our deaths are a collective dance, what do
we see, what do we feel for the very last time? Am I cynical to want to
create a single dance for those disparate beings united by a single fear?
I want to see triumphant, determined souls rise up and form a circle
or an arch, there is more than just that euphoric image of sex and death
locked together, death has its vital force too, it's a new beginning for
everyone, we can all transform our mortality into a *Survivor's Morning*,

a little different for each one of us; I wrote a trio for young cancer patients, on the video you can hear them say, as they drown from the fluids in their lungs, some of us in this hospital are gone, but we're still here, what divine mystery do we owe that to? One girl said through her coughing, maybe God loves me, but where am I going? To this soundtrack I added a saxophone and an alto voice in the background, with a pas de deux for my dancers, then suddenly the music gets vehement, as though the dancers were attacking one another passionately, the ardour of these battle-steps comforts some people during the devastation of chemotherapy, a hand on that skin furrowed by malignance, a hand initiating a new caress of life and hope on this funereal skin, if only for a few days or even hours, strange, these survival workshops are suddenly becoming as routine as death itself, how could I ever again find the dividing line between art and life? I know art is the only power I have; these dance critics wonder all kinds of things about me; is he another Nijinsky steeped in African culture, judging by those flying leaps, the answer is yes, the experts say, but you have to watch out, he's also an impure aficionado of New York's baths and saunas, the Abscess will transmute his force and sap his art, being one of the most charismatic figures in Black Dance, he's been spoiled by his early successes. Has he already begun to slip? Some even say I can't dance, that I get literature, theatre, music, and pantomime all mixed up, who knows, maybe they think I'm some sort of Bible-thumper? I have all of that in me, the product of all the transformations of the century, the Me cult, a narcissism that appeals to a lot of artists these days, and as for this openness to African and Asian cultures, I simply let them speak and move and dance for themselves, but they never stop asking, who is Arnie Graal, a dancer-choreographer, mirage or truth, heir to Balanchine or the Snow Queen of sauna-land, still I could never live without protesting, or being rubbed the wrong way and being controversial, time's beginning to crowd in on me, but in his unfinished autobiography Arnie had written that he would never grow old, let others get unsightly liver spots, he would always be virile and never have wrinkles like his parents, his teeth would always sparkle, take me to death's door, he had said, dancing *Survivor's Morning,* on an autumn day, I'll write a discreet note for my brother and sister and mother, I'll hear the sound of the wind in the leaves, I'll listen to the *Pathetique* and close my eyes, I think I always knew I'd listen to that music and never wake up. Samuel had been listening to Arnie and thinking how similar Arnie and his father were, like brothers, both artists from an era of survival that Samuel no more wanted to know about than he wanted to listen to the wild predictions of Our Lady of the Bags out there on the sidewalk, his teacher and his father were an out-of-date generation, he thought, they would soon be left behind by the younger ones, come on, shrimp, learn to move that body of yours, Arnie's baritone boomed through the theatre, what's with the bitchy pouting, go on, dance, get up there with the other dancers and do what they do, I'll tell you what you're doing wrong, Arnie and his father, Daniel, would be amazed, thought Samuel, if they knew how recklessly hungry he and the rest of his lazy, sensuous age-mates were for a world that was comfortable, just comfortable, simply paradise, one they could wonder at even as they were creating it, nothing to do with the values of the old world, but a new one without a past or a memory, Samuel's ideas got tangled up in melancholy, though, what if his father and Arnie were right, and these youthful, naive, and inexperienced hopes were just a mirage, how depressing, he thought, no, no way, they're all boring and out-of-date these parents and teachers, although he did not want to consider where he'd be without them, annoying as their ideas were. That was Samuel, young, full of life and free, long hair falling in waves over his chest as he danced, and this dance was life itself, erupting in joy and the sweet dream of holding Veronica in his arms tonight, it was also a quest to solve the deep mystery of nature by which he was part of all those who had gone before, whether living or dead. And, although it was not her own, Mélanie was absorbed in the fate of Rafa, awaiting execution in a Jordanian prison, she was haunted by Rafa, whose face seemed to come between them even there, next to the door of his red car, as she was kissing her son goodbye, always he would be free, and Rafa not at all, she was set for Washington to chair a television debate with other female activists, Mélanie was proccupied with an inhuman Arab custom, which had endangered, even killed, many young women, brothers could kill their sisters who had been raped or had committed adultery, and Rafa, like Suzanne before her, had taken refuge in a prison, knowing perfectly well none of her brothers would hesitate to cut her down with a rain of bullets to the neck, of course they promised not to harm her, like Suzanne, if she came back home, as she would be forced to do today or in a few days, but she and Suzanne both knew the price of honour was blood, their own, and I deserve to die, Rafa confessed heartbreakingly to women like Mélanie who had come to save her, yes, I'm guilty, for three days, I had a lover, a working man, and for that I must die, just as my brothers and father have said, Rafa's thirty-year-old brother, like Suzanne's, would be that diligent, effective murderer, and to the other brothers he would say, it's the most unpardonable sin of all, even a girl who has been raped must be punished by stoning, it may not be her fault, but she has covered her brothers in the crime of dishonour, from her prison cell Rafa could hear the voices of Jordanian female activists outside, for the macabre custom was no longer hidden in sectarian shadow, and the victims themselves were denouncing it, together with Mélanie, they refused to let Rafa's brother kill her, enough of these crimes, a doctor who diagnoses a girl's ruptured hymen will within days be filling out her death certificate, cut down by fratricide, Rafa whiled away her existence in jail like a trussed lamb, and heard the voices of women reporters and journalists like Mélanie from

America and Europe struggling for the rights of women brutalized by fathers and brothers, others she heard condemning the custom of brothers stoning sisters, and from her own country, still others saying, we'll set an example by trying to put a stop to these vile murders, and we're prepared to risk our lives, if we have to, we'll call a halt to them in our own families, but the bewildered Rafa just kept repeating to her jailers, I am guilty, by my thoughtless acts I brought this curse on myself and scandalized my younger brothers, the honour of the father and brothers depends on the virtue of their sister and mother, these words have sealed my fate, and she heard the laughing voice of Suzanne's brother, remorseless, diligent, and effective in murder, tomorrow a teenager will come to this same prison gate and confess to police, I know I was wrong, she would say, just like Suzanne and Rafa, for such is the law, and Mélanie's intercessions for her, petitions to Arab embassies, television appeals to women in their homes, would not protect Suzanne or Rafa from ritual execution, and at exactly 8:20 the next morning, the brother would slaughter and bleed the lamb, was it under a fig tree that Rafa and the worker had embraced, and how many other girls would this same young lover cause to be stoned to death, just as pitiless as the brothers, the law would continue unbending, for many years to come, in a forgotten Middle East town, where men were as hard as the climate and the rough, parched, bitter earth, Rafa knew she would never see the riverbanks again, the worker, wrapped in secrecy, with his hands pitted by the desert sands, had fled, no, she would never see the Jordan's banks again, not a tree, not even the fig tree under which they had slept, Rafa heard the song of gunshots clattering skyward and continued confessing her wrongs, but what do you other women know of our tribal customs, our families and religion, the fierce and warring spirit of our ancestors, be quiet, a woman is a lamb and must never complain, Mélanie in vain gathered signatures on her petitions, while in the twilight, Rafa waited to pay the price of honour, a black bow in her hair was the sublime coquetry for herself or her brother, this is how Mélanie, unable to hold back tears in the car or at the airport as she thought of her, would see Rafa hours before her murder, would she one day be able to awaken her son to so much injustice, unending slavery obsessed someone like Mélanie, who revelled in intoxicating freedom; what was Samuel telling her about on that cell phone attached to his belt, girls, sports, dance, his teacher, could she send him some money for skydiving lessons, skydiving, was there anything more exciting, first, he'd be attached to the instructor, soon he'd be out of the plane in free fall, it would be a minute, no more, then the parachute would open, he'd send Mélanie a video showing her all about it, you know, Mom, you can do several dives a day, there are no words to describe it, Mom, from up there you see everything, the sea, the mountains, and what about Augustino, he would soon be twelve and wanting the same sort of things, Mélanie thought, the latest version of a game or video, he had to have them, although his grandmother refused to have them in the house, they still filtered in through all the pores and cracks at school, in the nearby arcade where Augustino went, Mère Esther told Mélanie that his vast industry of video-war had already ruined so many, and sometimes these imaginary battles went far beyond the earth and into space, or some ideal plane by the same name, she went on, terrified at the thought that Augustino was witnessing two armies battling it out in the heavens, but which heaven, she asked, haven't they already done enough damage to the earth, she stormed indignantly, but what was the point, she so despised the hold of this new cretinism on young minds, like some kind of religion, and now believers and atheists faced off the same way Whites and Blacks used to, it's a twisting, treacherous landscape, she told Mélanie, what a miserable excuse for a crusade, Good versus Evil, the Good Guys against the Bad Guys, and they bludgeon kids into imbecility with all these legendary figures hauled out to fight against

the hordes of nonbelievers, it was awful this cultivated stupidity Mère
saw all around her, and how could the healthy tissue of an impres-
sionable mind like Augustino's withstand the onslaught of this
electronic culture? As admirably alert as she found him, even Augustino gobbled up cartoon videos showing discussions on faith between
a talking tomato and a cucumber, the whole series titled *Vegetable
Stories*, mean-spirited dialogue oozing propaganda on Christian values,
why couldn't they leave the cucumber, tomato, and other garden plants
alone instead of sacrificing them in some religious campaign, there's
nothing that won't turn up, she said to her daughter, we've manoeuvred
ourselves into a materialistic shipwreck, hours after any disaster you
can see the debris everywhere, unplugged video games and albums
with no one to play them, giving off bizarre noises, but not an edible
vegetable in sight, scorched earth, no fruit, just these robot-objects
running around on autopilot, Barbies talking to themselves, no more
little girls, just chattering Buzz and Woody figures, the weirdest a
weird society can churn out after being hit by thunder, what most
affected Mère was a Van Gogh puzzle-doll with a detachable ear and
an expression of thunderstruck humiliation that in nightmare play
children could tear apart, it might also be the portrait of art murdered
by doltishness, yes, Mélanie thought, her sons wanted, wanted, wanted
increasingly expensive presents, which she usually gave them, unlike
her mother, since they had been growing up, there were fewer and
fewer family activities, more like social and political ones, she knew
her passion to defend the oppressed, especially women and children,
made her seem a little harder and weaker, less desirable to her husband,
so determinedly active that she almost dropped from fatigue right in
front of her children when she came back from a trip, but she did not
see how she could live without this intellectual stimulation, Esther
had always confessed to never loving children much, but she was, she
pointed out to Mélanie, a very responsible grandmother, giving

Marie-Sylvie, the Haitian nanny who had replaced Jenny, a part in the upbringing of the children, the upkeep of a substantial household, and the care of the dogs and birds, she was proud of Mélanie's commitment, but would have preferred she be a little less altruistic, bringing up grandchildren was a different way of looking after young people, she was still mortified by the memory of her sons, walking arm in arm with her mother in the damp morning dew of the garden, Mélanie talked about her concern for Rafa, waiting in a Jordanian prison to be punished by one of her brothers, she thought her mother, though silent, understood her dismay, just then Mai and Vincent came running up to them and asked Mélanie how long she would be home with them this time, Mélanie asked Marie-Sylvie if Vincent had had his hourly medication, was he being more careful about sports, they must be sure not to take him out on the sea, and he must stay in his room when he got out of breath, Marie-Sylvie was silent, and Mélanie thought, why did she look so vague and distracted, then Mélanie quickly picked up Mai and put her down by her mother, don't go, Mamma, said Mai, oh no, Mélanie said, with Mai's arm around her neck, no, I'm going to be with you all week, they would go out into the tall waves, and she would kiss Mai's and Augustino's wet foreheads and hair, while Vincent was being watched by Marie-Sylvie, and standing here in the garden next to them in tender moments like this, Mélanie reproached herself for giving in to her generous but nevertheless selfish impulse to defend oppressed women, she also felt swept to and fro in this gentle and sensual tide in which she and her children were drifting, swept and shaken, volatile herself, one day, a happy, fulfilled woman, the next, desperate for the women who would not survive the oppression of men. In the boat taking him to the modest hotel on the shore of the Adriatic, Jean-Mathieu thought, ah, Venice at last, home again, the way Stendhal was in Rome or Naples or Florence, Caroline neither wrote nor phoned before I left, and dear Frédéric puts on his robe and

gets his skeletal body out of bed only an hour a day, when Juan and
Eduardo wash him, he can barely drag himself under the acacia bower
so Eduardo can read the papers to him and light his cigarettes, he
rivets his eyes on us, nothing more, the sadness of his emaciated face
and grey beard, the mangy coat of an aging animal on the verge of
death, that's what my friend will soon be, just over there is the Doge's
Palace, and I can go and see the work of Veronese again, that has to
be where Stendhal's love affair with Italy began, so much art, and here's
the third canal bridge where I can see the setting sun and think of the
works of Titian, and look back on everything I've seen during the day
in the medieval palaces, remember, Stendhal's heroes despised the
dubious power of money, Jean-Mathieu wondered if he had brought
his notebooks, ah yes, the notes were all in order in the case on his
lap, Caroline would have been pleased he had remembered his blue
scarf and gloves for this trip on the water, where the air was often cool,
oh, how he missed those liners he had written about when he was
young, ever since his birth in Halifax, he'd lived near oceans and seas,
the romantic days of passenger liners were gone now, he had seen and
written so much about the nature of people in those cabins, here are
the stairs on the *Île de France* that Marlene Dietrich came down, nearly
two centuries ago a tiny boat left Liverpool with six passengers, and
who could have known that the equivalents of whole estates would
cross the seas, the *Île de France,* the multitiered *Lusitania,* the *Arctique*
breaking through the ice, the *Mauretania,* the *Kronprinzessin* with its
freight of gold and millionaires, floating palaces, salons overturned
by storms and cyclones, these same salons that had known the peace
of calm seas, musical evenings, no comfort spared for the high and
mighty, the others just there to serve, dining rooms and ballrooms,
imposing rooms with art nouveau everywhere on ceilings and walls,
smoking rooms where, for a long time, women were not allowed, the
cathedral-like *Aquitania,* distinguished couples dancing in blazers

and white trousers or hats in first class from Southampton, the main hall of the *Majestic,* with its palm court under a crystal dome, the *Leviathan* and its habitues from Newport dressed in smoking jackets, just as though they were still at home, the *Homeric,* comfy as an English home, with black leather chairs and painted floral and equestrian scenes, the *Bremen,* in courtly fashion spoken of as a woman, shining like a planet, early art deco in the main cabin of the *Queen Mary,* and then, all of a sudden, the last sailing, inexplicable silence on the ocean floor, enigmatic silhouettes, these liners and steamers gone like the poets whose lives Jean-Mathieu had written about, young John Keats and Thomas Chatterton, Keats writing sonnets from childhood and whose name would be written on the water as though he himself had composed the epitaph, what desolation that these odes and lyric meditations had such a short flowering, like Jean-Mathieu, Chatterton in his youth had signed on to a merchant ship for London to write and become famous, but the boat sank, what dreams, what odes to truth and beauty in these heads to be crowned by angels before they were by men, Jean-Mathieu's life as a writer had begun in London, and there Chatterton took arsenic in his seventeenth year, poverty and misery, how many condemned poets' names were written on the water, twisted by the cresting waves into a foam of gold and fire, Jean-Mathieu thought, he had loved Chatterton and Keats like sons while he wrote their biographies, and the favourite son, the one he only called Dylan, whose biography he had planned but did not know how to write, he had known and talked to Dylan and could never recover from his death, the pride of his village school, he too had seen the sea from his room, when had he written, time held me green and dying, green and dying, it must have been the verdant spring of 1930, April 1930 or 1934, between the ages of sixteen and twenty, like Chatterton, he had written 212 poems, later to be read in the magazine of the little village school, on bits of paper in pubs and taverns; his hair curly and lips fleshy, he was the adorable child-writer of his country, hair moistened by Scottish winds, round red cheeks, irresistible, his friends all worshipped him, and women wanted and loved him from the start, he wrote *The Map of Love* just before the Second World War, from a poet of so little realism, a geography of love in a world of genocide and hate; that view of the sea from the stone house on the cliff at Laugharne, and he had a second retreat at Laugharne called the boat house, where his children were born, and he loved his wife with such passion, Dylan smoking ceaselessly with his chair to the wall, worn down by the same material cares and the same despair as Chatterton, at the game of hide-and-seek one day, he broke a tooth, a sign of his inner distress and rooted dissatisfaction, and how could it not be sensed by those around him? His health and beauty have vanished, the painter Mervyn Levy draws a magnificent profile in black of the cherub of the village school, in this coal black drawing, the lips are clamped onto a cigarette, and the poet seems to be slipping over into night, he drinks and smokes to excess, but thinks of leaving for America, it is at a reading of his work in New York that Jean-Mathieu sees him for the first time, when that battered, inky figure has slipped over into the night, he writes and writes, and what exalts him still more are his anger and his indignation, and when his days are numbered, where are they but New York, America, and they will be the saving of him, Rage, rage against the dying of the light, he writes, who had not heard his hoarse voice in universities, theatres, or museums, where tirelessly he read, Rage, rage against the dying of the light, and Jean-Mathieu had offered to let him rest at home, but Dylan preferred the freedom of the Chelsea Hotel or a bar or tavern or pub, where he could write alone in the middle of a crowd, then on his third crossing to America, debt-ridden, troubled, and anxious, suffering from numerous ills, he still goes on reading his poetry wherever he goes, we will hear his voice forever, Rage, rage against the dying of the light, in New York, he dies, in his thirty-ninth year, having said to a friend, I'd like to go to the Garden of Eden, where I'd be so well off, body and soul, if I were unconscious forever, but he was already well into an alcoholic coma, was this the unspeakable desire of an unreasonable child, the coma that would last five days and nights in a hospital until, on the evening of November 9, he left us, night closing his heavy eyelids, not even having recognized his wife at his bedside, never seeing his little boy again, Jean-Mathieu was one of the four hundred at St. Luke's Episcopalian Church in New York for the funeral service, the young widow took the body back to the cemetery of St. Martin's in Laugharne, the one where, as a young man, he had buried himself up to the waist in leaves, green and young and living, there was a hymn in those days, "Nearer My God to Thee," then nothing, his voice was no more, at the bases of mountains and cliffs, in the November winds and rains of Laugharne, the name of the poet is engraved on a white cross, there he is, down in the valley, near the farms: of all the contemporary poets Caroline had photographed, it was this one Jean-Mathieu still kept, the poet in November, an autumn that would know no winter or spring, the poet chained to his torment, as though harnessed to a tree and the far-spreading roots of a nightmare carried a long time within and pulling him ever onward, Chatterton, Keats, Dylan, all their names written on the water, Jean-Mathieu saw the gondolier bend his head under the arch of a bridge, it must have been a panic-stricken swallow that brushed his temple while he was reviving sad memories, and here I am in Venice, he thought to himself, amid the murmur of water rippled by the gondolier's oar. Polly, all by herself, wandered off Carlos's usual path, sniffing the sea air through her ruffled fur, but where was he, what had he been doing, they were inseparable, as Mama said, wouldn't the park where the egrets gathered lead on to Bahama and Esmeralda streets, to Mama and the kitchen smells and the bowl in the backyard that was never empty and reclusive brown spiders with poisonous legs sleeping under

the rotten planks, this way didn't seem so familiar without Carlos, if
he had been there, she would have followed along down the street, of
course, and he would have said, run, and she would have been off like
a rocket, or maybe, follow me, and she would have walked at heel on
his left, stopping when he did, following orders when he wasn't scolding her, he had trained her, and a quick tug on the collar or with his
hand would stop her from rooting through garbage, he would have
fed and watered her, they'd have swum together in the sea, in the
garbage cans there were sharp chicken bones and eggshells, she
wouldn't be hungry or thirsty if Carlos were there, indivisible, inseparable, Carlos and Polly, Carlos and Lazaro, in light and thunder, the
piercing sound of an ambulance at noon, Carlos and Lazaro, and
Lazaro's Adidas watch, nasty pictures came to Polly's mind, the day
Carlos found her in the basket of a bicycle her first master had cavalierly
left for hours in front of a grocery store, then a tanning parlour, be
right back, he said, he was stuck-up and had a brushcut, and he'd put
a tight-fitting collar round her neck, and this smart young master kept
saying he loved her, with her reddish fur and quivering eyes, after his
tanning session, he'd be dark and glowing under his pale muscle shirt,
Polly was watching the motionless clouds hanging in the heat of the
sky, wrapped up in a beach towel, she could hear her own heartbeat,
was it her fate to end up like all pups abandoned in bike baskets, then
one day, Polly had not had to wait for her vain young master in front
of stores, boutiques, and tanning parlours, that was the day Carlos
had got on the bike and raced off with Polly still in the basket, not
barking, barely breathing, and from that day, they would be inseparable, indivisible, Mama used to say, like Carlos and Lazaro before they
became enemies, merciless rivals, Polly was panting with thirst, was
this route really going to get her to Bahama and Esmeralda streets,
maybe there was a bowl of water somewhere under the trees where
the egrets were pecking at the faded grass, in the shade of the palms,

clouds motionless in a hot sky, Polly had noticed them while she was splashing about in the waves with the greyhounds, and their master was happily shouting, get there first, fetch the ball, maybe with clouds like these, her fate wasn't inevitable, and she would soon find Carlos and Mama, the kitchen smells, the bowl in the backyard where the hiding spiders lay under the filthy planks, it was Carlos's fault they had got that way, Mama said, like the old cooler that had been negligently dumped outside and not repaired, Carlos's fault too, she said, he never listened to his parents, but was this really the way home, and how could she be all by herself so long, day and night by the sea and along the streets, without Carlos, when Mama never stopped saying the two of them were inseparable? No predators allowed here, Venus thought, but wasn't the estate master, Richard, Rick, as the Captain called him, though Venus didn't like their being together, wasn't he roaming somewhere near the house in the cedar wood, wasn't he always doing that, walking near the house all day long, naked to the waist, he drove the Captain's Lincoln Navigator like he owned it, Venus thought his cold blue eyes had a mean look when he said he had not given up the keys or left the place because he intended to look out for her, as the Captain had asked before he died, a young Black woman couldn't live by herself on hectares of jungle by the edge of the canal, I can, she said, but the unscrupulous manager did not leave, he said he wanted to be there for Venus's charity bazaar, when she sold her pictures and furniture, Venus was afraid that Rick was going to steal the Captain's paintings and furnishings, that he was a thief and a shifty fence, no, there aren't going to be any predators here, thought Venus, all she wanted with her were the dachshund and the iguana, maybe I could stand guard, Richard said when Venus told him not to come into the house, you're safe with me, Captain Williams always said so, why all this carrying on, Venus, I know about your past as an escort at the Club Mix, what's one man more or less in your bed, specially

since it's the Captain's fornicating bed, say, that marriage of yours
didn't last too long, your old man got it from one of his enemies out
at sea, lucky for you, Venus, you get to inherit his fortune, everything
he owns, come on, let me in, no, Venus said, holding out her arms to
push him back, he could tell she was afraid, there were drops of sweat
on her neck, he gave a nasty laugh and went off growling nonsense
into his cell phone, I'll get you one of these days, he said, this man was
a shameful stain, she thought, when he started gravitating toward her,
she felt the same humiliation as when a store clerk had called the police
because she had got a little menstrual blood on a black lace dress she
was trying on, look at my hundred-dollar dress, you miserable girl,
the saleslady had cursed, too cheap to put on underwear, she shouted
as Venus fled into the street, arrest her, and she would have been driven
away by the police if a woman had not come to her rescue, saying, let
her go, she hasn't done anything, Venus had wept at her degradation,
the blood had practically blackened on the dress, like a stain of shame,
why had she not torn it to rags, or clawed the sales clerk with her sharp
nails, Venus never cried, never bowed her head before White people,
but she had sunk to new depths, then all at once she had seen a girl
laughing and convulsing with intoxication ride by on a bicycle, she
was a poor girl from Bahama Street, and her head teetered under the
straw hat held onto her head with ribbons, hi, Venus, she murmured,
remember me, I was with you at the Club Mix, remember? Venus
noticed the pitted skin on her arms and legs, her face breaking out
too, pox maybe, syphilitic scars, a sickness the poor do not get rid of,
Venus had thought, why did I have to meet her on Bahama Street,
when they were escorts together at the Club Mix, Venus healthy and
beautiful, but the other one probably only had a few months to live,
no family either, but Venus had Pastor Jeremy and Mama, by what
miracle had she been spared, healthy and beautiful still, when the poor
girl from Bahama Street just faded in with six thousand other girls,

and who would think of these poor ones, Kenyan children, for instance, being wiped out by epidemic in Nairobi, this corner of the earth was filled with it, rats and huts and the bars of Majengo, hotel rooms by the hour, six thousand poverty-stricken women selling their bodies each day, some of them destitute mothers, so many recorded dead that a state of alert had been declared, and soon these six thousand would be joining them, working for the moment in brothels where men refused condoms, like candy without the sugar, they said, or eating it still in the wrapper, how often had Venus heard this in bars and hotels and shady rooms rented by the hour, and how were these poor Kenyan women supposed to educate the men who bought them so cheaply, didn't they say that condoms were a joke in the slums, if girls die by the hundreds followed by their kids soon afterward, it's because of the TB epidemic, or a spell by one of those fetish priests, or mosquito bites, beneath the very eyes of these men a time bomb was ticking slowly under Nairobi, yes, Richard with his taunts and sarcasm would have to go, thought Venus, he awakened all these shameful ghosts and the age-old struggle between races that had been forgotten with the Captain, who had won her so sweetly and gently, still, even with the house by the sea, the Lincoln Navigator, his wife, his child, as he referred to them, the ancient confrontation had still been there, in the background, masked by the pleasures of love, and the shadow of the predator, ever anxious to encircle you and subjugate you, remained, no, Rick was not going to trap her, and Venus remembered the revolver the Captain kept under his pillow, you never know, he said, about enemies from the archipelago, a boatload of tramps in the mangroves, a vice cop disguised as a fisherman, some plainclothes detective deciding to sweep the shoreline and marinas in a nighttime raid, you have to be careful of everyone, he said, pulling on his pipe, one hand fondling Venus's hair where it curled short over her forehead, Williams described Operations Clean-Up and Chimney-Sweep to her, lightning raids they

were, and did them a lot of damage, he would often talk this way when
the weather was uncertain just before he left for the Bahamas on his
seaplane, you've got to always have a gun in the house, he said, and
Venus admired the hardiness of her adventurer who never told her
exactly what he did when he was away, and even though she would
have liked him to stay with her always, still he was closer to her in this
room where she heard the roar of his laugh and the gasping in his
lungs, she stared at the painting he had done for her on their wedding
day, the bodies welded together, and Williams had switched their skin
colours, giving Venus the milky white and pink he had at sea, but not
weather-beaten like an old man such as himself, he said, a sunny
warmth emanated from Venus's pale skin, and for himself, the Captain
took Venus's dark skin and wild spirit, no longer able to tell who was
who, he would say, the fresh eroticism of this painting reminded Venus
just how much she had been loved and venerated by this good and
sensual man, and she reminded herself again, no predator's going to
get in here, though she was sure she heard Rick's footsteps beyond the
bay window, you don't have to worry about me, my little Venus, he
said, why've you locked the door, why not open up? I ain't no grey old
man, little Venus, come on, open up. The cutting short of all these
lives, Renata thought, high-school girls, members of the Foreign Language Club with their supervisors, an entire aircrew, the cataclysm of
flight 491, but Renata, her husband, and other judges safe and expected
at a conference in New York, just a brief stopover hours before crashing
into the mountains of Honduras, this rain of ashes and lives, lives as
harmless as animals led to the slaughter, flowers barely opening before
being cut off, was it nothing more than a continuous Slaughter of the
Innocents that we watch in hurt and helplessness, she recalled Franz
conducting Berlioz's *Mass for the Dead* near blackened ruins and amid
a rain of shells in Bosnia, then *The Childhood of Christ*, while the whole
thing was broadcast on television, majestic music, cathedrals, and

libraries in flames, as numbed children looked on, very nearly killed themselves, and their faces said as much, as if burned with the libraries, authors, and creations of the mind, yet still listening to the music of Berlioz as though its substance, its rich vocal and orchestral invention, were a victory of life and love over nothingness, was it Franz's sensitivity, the tenor of his orchestra or the sublime play of voices in this drama, it was as though Herod, even as he ordered the killing of Jewish children, was struck by the desolation of such bloodshed, as though as Mary rocked her son and called him sweet child, the voices and song made a multiple requiem that included the massacre and amputation of children in Zenica from mines, and the German doctors could never make enough artificial limbs from carbon fibre, and only a few of the Zenica amputees would get them, but even with expensive well-made ones, they would never replace those lost little legs, these were the ones walking through the night under blackened facades, children and mothers, these too were part of the funeral march toward life, and while Franz was conducting Berlioz's *Mass for the Dead* and *The Childhood of Christ* in Bosnia, Renata was thinking that pictures of war and the bugle call to massacre were an exquisite anguish for us all. The gradual sinking of the lagoon, thought Jean-Mathieu, the recurring floods, the polluted air, all of it threatened the works of art, Titian, Veronese, what a heritage would soon disappear beneath the waters, and on February 13, Wagner died in Venice just after his last opera, *Parcifal,* perhaps only a few steps from this family boarding house where I'm staying, the most mystical of Wagner's operas was put on in Bayreuth in the summer of 1882, had he sensed it would be his last, ominous that February 13 when he died in Venice, why is this nagging at me, is it because Caroline and I saw such a splendid production of it together in Zurich, or maybe Boston, it was a time when we both had the knack of travelling, and as he filled his travel diary with his dignified calligraphy, Jean-Mathieu reclaimed mastery over his life, the memory of Caroline was not entirely without pain, he appreciated the secrecy of his diary, he could wander through his own private labyrinths and still take comfort in the glow of sunset on the waters under his shuttered window, and everywhere was the clamour of life, voices of young people in the street, restaurants lighting up before a late supper, church bells tolling slowly, mournfully, this tapestry of sounds wove its own warmth and light around a writing man, he noticed, as he listened to the night that would soon wrap him in its sea dampness, for it was so heavy that the woollen scarf over his shoulders was already soaked, and the bedsheets were damp, he could hear the gentle slap of water, as though he were on board a boat again, tomorrow, rising early as usual, perhaps he would look at Paolo Veronese's *Allegory of Youth and Age* with the same wonder as he had done with Caroline, but henceforth, he had to agree, what had been allegorical, symbolic of immediate pleasures or remote expectations, was no more, now one entered into the picture and became Age cut off from lively Youth, yet standing there before Veronese's painting, Jean-Mathieu felt as though the vigorous Youth was painted as though it might leap out of its frame and rush headlong into life's pleasures, sad for Jean-Mathieu that he felt this impulse curbed in him while he contemplated Age, more than just an allegory now, and why would it be the last part of one's life, when Jean-Mathieu's intellectual powers were in no way declining, when he wrote more than ever, when he felt better than Caroline, who complained not of the physical effects of aging but of a slight weakening in memory, if she had travelled along with him, she and her more pagan sensibility would have liked to see *The Great Biblical Feasts* to whet her appetite, she would have wondered why he had brought her to see this *Allegory of Youth and Age,* it's so sad, what I like most about Veronese are the spaces behind his figures, filled with a whole mythology, a sort of architectural tableau, an entire theatre and its play of illusions mixed with real space, and everything bathed in that red light, but these conversations in Venice museums and palaces were a thing of the past, doubtless, because, with his cane and all his maladies, Jean-Mathieu, despite himself, had come to personify the *Allegory of Age,* and Caroline found herself still young and serene, like the *Allegory of Youth,* and now, amid the continuing din of life in the city, when it was time to dress for the concert, he thought it would be best to go back and lie down on his damp bed and wait for sleep to come, the pages of his travel diary were getting wet too, as the watery atmosphere liquefied his longhand on the paper and the sentence he had written early yesterday, *The Allegory of Youth and Age* by Veronese, and the sheets were damp, soaked by the evening air, an evening still red outside, as day was in Veronese's paintings, Jean-Mathieu was one of the lucky ones who would have a bed tonight in an Italian family boarding house: it seemed only yesterday that the young sailor's apprentice would have been happy to sleep on the bridge of a ship and look up at the stars, did youth really need to sleep? Our Lady of the Bags, as Samuel called her, the unlettered child with an open Bible on her lap, repeating to passersby who would not listen as they ran to the stores before closing time, yes, you will bear witness to the seven plagues of Egypt, right here, in the city of New York, for it is written in God's Book, a little after the new moon, the earth will tremble under your feet, my parents, who have gone to the Holy Land, have entrusted me with a mission to all you sinners, you who are ever greedier for the things of this world, and when you have all, you want still more, they have told me to sow the grain of the Word of God, my parents, who have gone penniless to Jerusalem, will see an Ark and eight angels rise out of the earth, and on that day of the equinox, when you turn on your taps, water will turn to blood, for all this devastation is foretold in the Book of God, why do you not believe me, my parents are in Galilee, where they will see before I do the Ark and its eight angels hovering in the air over the gaping earth, and you who do not pray will endure the seraphims's sword of fire, my parents are waiting for me there in the Plain of Jezreel, and for three thousand years we shall live joyous in paradise, which is promised to us all, yes, they wait for me there in the New Jerusalem, but before I see my dear parents, and I will, where am I to sleep? Momma, Poppa, soon I shall join you far from this demon earth, where no one offers me shelter for the night, for like you, Momma and Poppa, I have heard the voice of the Lord in the thunder saying, repent, for they will be afeared before these afflictions; the Bible tumbled to the sidewalk as the prophetess pulled her legs up under the pleats of her kilt, shall I sleep in store entrances or in parks with the flowers tonight, God alone is my rest, Jesus only is my truth, why won't they listen, or maybe they can't see me? In a few hours, Our Lady of the Bags would be no more than a vanishing silhouette in the night, of all the faces sliding by today, some sneering at her, she remembered the woman who in the heat had given her a Coca-Cola, bless her, she thought, and the arrogant young man with long hair yelling at her from the wheel of his car, lies, what lies, every bit of it, you ought to go back to school, she banished this face of Samuel's and spat in the dust, never would this boy find God, but for Our Lady of the Bags, very soon now all the stars would shine, and for her alone. How brutal the shattering of all those lives, Renata thought, and as they were collecting the calcinated remains from flight 491 in the Honduran mountains, yet so near the runway, a handful of judges and magistrates, like Renata and her husband, sole survivors of the catastrophe, were debating the death penalty in a conference hall at their New York hotel, Renata, Claude, and some others, fewer and fewer, were firmly opposed to it, others, in anger, even fury at times, maintained that the real question at issue was whether to lower the age of execution to sixteen or even fifteen, otherwise where was the deterrence in having such a severe punishment, how else could justice be rendered, there would be no end to child crime or offences on the campuses of universities and colleges, and no one would ever be safe in public in these cities and this country of theirs, the fever of crime was contagious, it was spreading through our local detention centres, whether in Arkansas or in Mississippi, these young killers were getting coddled too much, their mothers could visit them on Sundays and get letters from them, as if what they had done was not so bad, Ma, come see me, take me home. Ma, I'm only eleven, why'm I in here, and the mother is too stunned or too out of it to tell him why, because you're the youngest killer in the country, sweetheart, ten of your classmates are dead because of you, you riddled your teachers with bullets too, Mother might say, you've lost weight, you look pale dear, your lips are cracked and dry, I don't like milk, Ma, and the Kool-Aid here sucks, and all these mothers can see in their killer sons is fear and bewilderment, come take me home, Ma, children begging is all they hear, my son sang in the glee club, he doesn't understand what he's done, so young and heartwarming these criminals asking their parents if they can go home to the trailer and the striped cat with a stump of a tail, the guinea pig in a cage, such naive mothers, my kid cried, they say, that proves he's sorry for what he's done, doesn't it, please go easy on him, in that prison he asked them to give him a Bible along with his hamburger at lunchtime, but they refused, these sweet kids cry and moan, I want Mommy, Mommy, and the officer or sheriff gets all teary-eyed repeating this, he wants his mommy, he wants us to let him go home, but where were these fathers, mothers, and sheriffs when the shootings happened or the night before when these same kids were screaming vengeance: you kids at school, just wait and see tomorrow, and you, Candy, for making fun of me for loving you, just wait and see who lives and who dies, rivers and rivers of blood are gonna flow, and you, Candy, you get the first bullet for laughing at me, and she did, in the abdomen, and died instantly, are we planning on opening orphanages for these thugs who play with toy guns from the age of five so they can handle real weapons when they are eleven? Are we going to keep them comfy and cozy, maybe let them watch violent videos while they are in preventive detention? Did these fathers, mothers, officers, and sheriffs somehow manage to miss the fact that these boys were already Nazis in the making, with Blood emblems and such on their red jackets, or standing up in front of the class in fatigues, with knives in their belts and talking about handling a hunting rifle, practice-shooting in the backyard, did the parents and grandparents somehow miss all of this when it was replayed over and over again on the family videos, the young killer-to-be is so ready to take his schoolmates that his parents' house, as well as his grandparents', is already decorated in heads he has brought back from the deer hunt, his parents push him to take karate lessons, still he did play flute in the school orchestra, the mother would say, and he always had an A on his report card, he liked singing and phys. ed., and he had just joined the football team, normal students on the surface, having sexually abused their cousins or three-year-old sisters, and they had taken things from supermarkets, their ambush of girls in the drama class, killed with a .38 or a .357 Magnum was planned well in advance, and then later these suspects could say, Ma, come take me home, the milk and the Kool-Aid suck, milk and Kool-Aid, maybe the guard could bring them a pizza for supper, but innocent as they pretend to be, they never seem to ask about the victims, in less than ten minutes, Candy, Stephanie, Nathalie, and all the others would flow rivers of blood, Candy, you're gonna see who lives or dies, no, these delinquents are monsters, one killed his mother in Vancouver, another one, three of his friends in Kentucky, and only the threat of the death penalty can scare these destructive minds a bit, and what do we do, sheriffs, officers, and for today's conference, lawyers and judges, we escort these kids like grisly actors in a play, we lead them into detention centres covered in black, we spoil them like their mothers whose consciences are blind, these criminals who miss their mommies, who miss the fountain in the garden and the little sisters they raped, for blood has no colour or smell to the young actors in this make-believe, even the ones identified as Bloods, and we escort them, covered in black, and we watch over them so their distraught families can blindly go on, feeling nothing, and how many schoolchildren need to be buried before these criminals, now age eleven, twelve, or thirteen, turn fifteen or sixteen and are formally condemned to death? Renata's soul froze in terror as she heard these words from the judges, interrupted occasionally by vehement but sympathetic protests, including her own or Claude's or another judge's, but they would be heard, Claude said, we know the death penalty for adults is a crime against nature, and it would be a double crime to inflict it on minors for some thoughtless, unpremeditated act, minors too young even to buy alcohol or cigarettes, could such baseness even be imagined by those of us empowered to deliver justice; the eleven-year-olds now in reform schools and detention centres had mothers, fathers, and brothers, and have we thought about their distress, waiting like the eleven-year-olds held on death row, and Renata reflected that if her husband spoke of things impossible for him to imagine, it was because he did not realize, as she did being a woman, that the picture painted by the judges was about to become reality, countless executions of sixteen-year-olds or fifteen-year-olds, dangerous and armed delinquents to whom Justice regretted having shown too much tolerance, a horrifying vision of children put to death like the madman's Slaughter of the Innocents, what was inconceivable today for a Justice weary of its own indulgence, still momentarily lenient toward the very young, would soon be concocted by legal minds as some necessary and fair reform, it was all too true, she realized, these judges and magistrates, in order to appear more merciful, they too had sons and young grandsons, would, in an underhanded act of redemption, save the White schoolkids for later, the first execution

would be a Black boy of fifteen, and so it was that Nathanaël's life hung
in the balance, Renata believed, the life of my grandson, the grandfather
had told the court, is in the hands of the Lord and the lawyers, but we
are poor people, and maybe we can't save him, Renata could see
Nathanaël, handcuffed between two officers, one a hard-faced White
woman, perhaps just feeling overwhelmed, crossing her arms when
the decision came down, and another officer, a fat White man with a
pendulous jaw, these were the custodians of his life for now, and vigilant
they had to be, for Nathanaël was heavily built for eleven, and despite
his puppy-dog eyes begging for pity, they were on their guard against
him, his imploring eyes and pink lips, dressed for court like a man in
a suit and tie, look at those broad shoulders, he's well developed for
his age, I'm innocent, he said, it's not true, the guards shot back, we
won't be going easy on him, and in the four years till he's executed,
he'll be in an adult prison, I'm innocent, he said to the judge, my
mother's a night nurse at the hospital, and she said I could go out that
night, I was just aiming at trees and street lights with a .22 that was
stolen from a garage mechanic, I wasn't aiming at anyone, I was pointing it high in the dark, anywhere, I didn't even see the boy I hit in the
head, it was an accident, I swear it was, the prosecution had maintained
this was a fake confession, my son has difficulties at school, he needs
to be rehabilitated, I know him, he wouldn't hurt anybody, he was
aiming at trees and street lights, please let him go, Renata felt certain
that Nathanaël, the son of a nurse from Michigan, likely a single
mother, would be tried as an adult, and already she could see him at
age fifteen, standing between two guards as they took him to the electric
chair on that earth-shattering early morning, his destiny was the same
as Lorenzo's, an adult criminal and Cuban refugee once picked up
from a raft, he was accused of killing a police officer, and like Nathanaël,
he protested his innocence, it was some other guy, not him, how many
vigils and prayers for them both at the prison gates, but how many

vain prayers also from the opponents to the death penalty, and at dawn on his fifteenth birthday, the imperturbable guards and officers with arms crossed would explain to him, as they once had with Lorenzo the Cuban refugee, the routine of execution, a few days before, they would take him to a cell twelve feet by seven feet halfway to the death chamber so he could have his last meal, anything he liked, Lorenzo had asked for steak Delmonico, salad, brown beans, and rice, but Nathanaël was offered desserts, sundaes, raspberry pie, and chocolate, he would have enough time to enjoy all that, because he would not have his head and legs shaved like Lorenzo, they would leave him his hair, the hour of his death was planned for seven o'clock, the death chamber was white, freshly painted for him, and Nathanaël would be attached to the chair with three leather straps, a dozen or more witnesses would be standing on the other side of a glass wall, but Nathanaël would not see them, and the executioner, his identity a close secret, would be invisible to Nathanaël except for light falling on the eyeholes in his black hood, would these eyes be his hope, they trembled for a few seconds, such a slender hope, would they reach the governor by phone, would he in his generosity give Nathanaël a pardon? Executioners had to be rotated, of course, and the one chosen for the marriage in hell today sent shooting through the boy a voltage of such intensity that he felt successive waves of fire in his veins, an escalating series of deaths, and struck by lightning, the chains on his wrists like eagles' talons cutting deep into his hands, he would still be saying at the moment of his death, I'm innocent: thus they explained the routine of the death chamber to Nathanaël, who, his mother said, had difficulty learning, and when exactly would he understand what was happening to him? His mother had been working the night shift in a hospital specially so Nathanaël could get tutoring to help him with his school work, and now he was being tried as an adult, his guards reminded him, was his life in the hands of the Lord, as his grandfather said, or

94

his guards' hands, perhaps in the courtroom when accused of murder, he had already glimpsed his fate, Lorenzo the Cuban's fate too, and both would have wet sponges placed on their heads like a diadem to absorb the heat of so many electrodes to the temples, from the child's hair, like Lorenzo's shaved head, sparks would suddenly burst like a nest of flames, by what curse-driven mistake would that sponge be not from the ocean but made of stuff as inflammable as ether, and all of them behind the glass, witnesses, guards, officers, and spectators, would be sure the ball of fire would descend from Nathanaël's head right to their feet, would it be fire or thunder, brilliant orange flames gathering on Nathanaël's skull, there in the death chamber, and the blackened sponge, and the shaken Presbyterian minister, the same spiritual guide first afforded poor Lorenzo and now Nathanaël, would shout, my God, it's awful, we've all breathed in the smell of charred flesh, why, dear God, was it my duty to be with this convict, in the thunder and smoke and ashes, they electrocuted him not once but ten times, starting over and over again, what a damnable mistake, there should have been a wet sponge on top of his head to absorb the horrendous heat, but this one was cellulose instead and highly flammable after the heat dried it out in two seconds; relieved, the executioner collected his $150 in cash, tax-free, would he be glad someone else was doing the dirty work next time, would he remember poor old Lorenzo the Cuban refugee, buried in an unmarked grave somewhere near the prison, since he had no family in this country, no one would come to mourn, maybe a few death-penalty opponents would lay some roses, Nathanaël's mother, though, would be there to fetch his body on that windy morning, and for a long while, she would warm it beside her, the executioner might have a kind thought for the boy he had electrocuted at seven o'clock, his skull and hair catching fire with the sponge, maybe he noticed through the eye slits in his hood how young Nathanaël was, and if maybe for a second Nathanaël took him for the ghost of Superman, the prison's chief medical officer reported seeing no evidence that the condemned man had suffered, in my professional opinion, death was very rapid and humane, all the flames and incandescence of course provided a disagreeable sight, but I have examined the condemned and found only a few burns about the head and legs, we must remember this boy was a criminal, and we were right to put him to death, I ask you to consider that his death was a humane one; these judges, thought Renata, who would have imposed the death penalty on Lorenzo as an adult and on Nathanaël's fifteenth birthday, having already declared them guilty, would be forever tied to their victims, one, shortly after having signed Lorenzo's sentence, would suffer from leukemia, a proliferation of white corpuscles as great as the drops of blood from the smack of fire on Lorenzo's skull and the electro-burn coming from inside the living body, the second judge would be murdered with his wife in their house in Kansas, and what other psychological problems these judges and their wives had to endure, what mental injuries from those they had injured physically and tortured by fire to the very death, and this grieving was merely an extension of the judicial system, after all, what could the judges and their wives, already weak and senile, do about it, hadn't they hoped to live out their days in peace, hoping no drive-by killer would come up to them suddenly one day, the judge and his wife, lying side by side on the marriage bed, both ready to depart with clear consciences and leave behind the nightmares and silhouettes of Lorenzo and Nathanaël mingled in flames, for the judge was also a charitable man who had done good things, and why had he been forgotten, and if the sentence was unjust, if really Lorenzo and Nathanaël were innocent, as they claimed, it would make their judge the very worst of men, but how can we be sure, let him sleep, he is old and weary. Augustino e-mailed his marks in Latin and biology to his father, it was his grandmother who had chosen Latin, in his haste and delight, he mostly wanted to announce that he was part of a group of students aged eleven to sixteen, from fifty-four countries, who were invited to a summer brainstorming session on how technology could help improve the living conditions of children around the world, he had Mélanie's permission to attend the conference, although it was a long way away, for this first time, Augustino would express his ideas freely, for children could not always be told what to think, how to act, and they felt the need to express themselves, Augustino wrote, the Olympic Stadium would be their platform, and the grown-ups would come and listen to them in a worldwide press conference, Augustino already had his penpals' thoughts on his computer, Bhavani from India said, I want a world where children do not have to perform slave labour, Leon, twelve, from Northern Ireland wanted Protestant and Catholic schools to be connected by the Internet, Issy in New Zealand had designed an ecology web site, all had one thought, how to make life better tomorrow, how to save the animals and all living beings, Augustino very much wanted to travel by himself, but his grandmother wanted to go with him, I want to go see my friends alone, he wrote, but his grandmother disliked this self-reliance of his, going on about how he was just a child, even if he did know the names of all the plants and flowers in the garden by heart, and did Daniel know that the most precious of the butterflies in the island's botanical garden had survived Hurricane Damien, and the turtledoves alighted on the tree known as burning bush, and so did the Spanish needle butterflies on the hectares of green grass, the Flying Dragon on fluorescent wings with a pinkish tail, the Gumbo Limbo tree gathered in animals and birdsong of every description, the turtle pond was unrippled by blown leaves, and why wouldn't Augustino's grandmother let him play with a fun video game, it was the Good Earthquake, clean and nice, just enjoyment for the eye, why did she have to be so tough about it, he tried to explain to his father that the games his grandmother banished from the house made him master of the universe, in a very correct war — you had to beat Quake and Doom with lances of fire from the meteors and planets, worlds collided in tremendous explosions, and this bothered Daniel, because Augustino wanted to emulate the inventors of these video epics, those who had dreamed up Quake and Doom, with their invincible armour, were now millionaires driving Porsches and Ferraris, a goal Augustino wanted to achieve, and there were the Karmac games, where you could outdo the Spirit of Evil, a giant skeleton rising out of the cracks in the earth, Daniel realized Augustino was incapable of seeing this as the apparition of a third world war, a clean war, to be sure, or did Augustino realize it dimly already through his choice in games? The boy finished his e-mail to his father mentioning the prize in a drawing competition that would soon be given to an Hispanic student at the Catholic school for painting an African-American Jesus on the cross, backed by the red light from an ocean sunset, and a feather lying at his feet, as a spiritual sign from the Indians of New Mexico, some saw it as a dark, peasant figure, others as a girl or a child, it had been painted so as to be open to personal interpretation, other drawings in the contest showed a beach bum with his dog, Jesus as an astronaut (one of the youngest children did this), an athletic Jesus with huge biceps, this was the first time anyone at the school had painted a Black Jesus, some parents protested the choice of prizewinner and said no prize should be given, and they would not accept the symbolic feather either, and what did Daniel think of all this, although he was deep in his book, he was troubled by Augustino's messages, about Quake and Doom and Karmac and the morbid Spirit of Evil, but maybe they were also the yin and yang of his future personality, a personality in progress, after all, this phenomenal capacity for learning was the twinning of his organic gifts with the memory of a computer, he had the ambiguity, the inventive and disquieting alternation of yin and yang, on the heels of the Spirit of Evil, his letters spoke of the spectacular birth

of two white cubs to a tiger named Aehsha in the Oviedo Zoo, plus
the birth of a dolphin in a Florida research centre on Easter morning,
only the earth Augustino inhabited could be so illuminated with wild
tigers and dolphins, but what about the dark corner of his world, where
a game called Righteous Earthquake meant ruthlessly cleaning out
the Old World, in which Quake and Doom would obliterate the shadows, whatever the cost in calamity, and a mortality that was not to the
taste of his generation, born to deathlessness, in a perfectly functioning,
brand-new world, without cold or dark, yang would be as regular as
sunlight, and every living thing, plant or bird, all humanity in his
future world, would be happy when the Old World had been surgically
removed; reading these letters from his son, Daniel remembered a
visit he had made with Rodrigo to the musicians' workshop to hear
Garçon Fleur and his orchestra, there are angels among us in this
Spanish monastery, amigo, Rodrigo told him, and this one, although
his parents named him Garçon Fleur, came from Alabama, he looks
like a farmer's boy, but you should hear him play a Bach piano sonata
and lead a jazz band, he's simple and natural, like his parents, there is
also a young Korean violinist, twelve years old, a prodigy too, and she
dazzles you with her spontaneous revelations of Schubert, what could
be less alike, Garçon Fleur from Alabama and Bach or a little Korean
girl and Schubert? What heavenly gifts and miracles wasted on lovely
children in this monastery, when I, Rodrigo, keep on working away
at my rhymes, and the poet Pedro Lopez de Ayala was already doing
better around 1379 in his "Cantar a la Virgen Maria," Señora, he wrote,
*por quanto supe / tus acorros, en ti spero / e atu casa en Guadelupe /
prometo de ser romero /* just like me, amigo, this poet was a religious
man, he had many trades, translator, chronicler, follower of politics,
great traveller, too, I wouldn't be surprised, would that God had
bestowed on me, amigo, a spark, a lightning bolt from Pedro Lopez
de Ayala's soul, and the same lyric flights that moved his pen, nothing

bespeaks prodigy like the birth of Garçon Fleur surrounded by solid citizens who know nothing about music but everything about farming, Daniel and Rodrigo were fascinated by Garçon Fleur and followed him everywhere, but he was interested only in his drummer, guitarist, bassist, parents, and grandfather who brought out the greatest tenderness in him when he sat on the old man's knee and stroked his beard, a chubby little boy who played the piano and directed the orchestra barefoot and bare-chested, his wide-open, sleeveless jean jacket and fringed jean shorts had been embroidered for him by his mother, a turban over his waist-long flat hair, brushed and combed and sun-bleached, and which his mother was forever straightening before he went onstage, then he would step up to the piano or the podium, still barefoot, so relaxed he might have seemed insolent, whether he tackled the complexity of a sonata or a jazz improvisation inspired by musicians he had worked with in New Orleans, Garçon Fleur overflowed with a captivating and unpredictable musical imagination, notes cascaded from his agile fingers, Daniel had often listened from the window of the workshop, during his long and rigorous practices, and if Rodrigo was right about his theory of reincarnation, if Rodrigo himself, in that headstrong insistence of his, extended the rhymes of Pedro Lopez de Ayala, who died in 1407, if our lives were a series of staggering miracles, why wouldn't Garçon Fleur, born in Alabama, inherit the soulfulness of those same blues he refreshed with his lively, percussive cadence, and be this millennium's liberated son of one of Bach's children, perhaps one of those less beloved, Wilhelm Friedemann, whose inventive genius in shaping the sonata had gone unrecognized, this enigmatic and sombre son, the most inapt to happiness, so poor he died in misery, forced to sell his father's manuscripts, faithless son, the end of a dynasty, repudiated by success, yet still lavishly gifted, why might not this son of Bach have passed his immediate and eternal soul, as well as his melodic gifts, on to a Garçon Fleur so ready to take them up, and with an ease Wilhelm had never known? When the boy had finished his draconian piano exercises, he let off his exhilaration by teasing the goats on the farm, by running breathlessly through fields of sunflowers taller than his shoulders, or by going down to the village pub with his parents and satisfying his hunger for nachos, more, more nachos, he told the waiter, fingers sticky with hot cheese, while his father and grandfather happily drank down mugs of brown ale, and his mother discreetly brushed the boy's hair, suddenly, there, before the stark profile of the men, she would settle a look of sweetness on him, on his small hands, chubby like his face, Daniel noticed all this, then wrote it down, Garçon Fleur's mother seemed to him as admirable as Maria Barbara, Bach's first wife, about whom we know so little, except that she bore him his eldest son, Wilhelm Friedemann, the shining and wounded genius who was at home nowhere, and might it be that Maria Barbara was the one who gave him his virtuosity on the organ, or who helped him compose his first mass, one woman had born a disappointed Wilhelm Friedemann, another kept an eye on the health of Garçon Fleur, and loved him so that he could continue to remain balanced and robust, and develop more than just a reputation as a virtuoso, but also an inner life, while the men quietly sipped their beer, this Maria Barbara told her son that now they were going to study math, the two of them enjoyed the reasoning sciences, like the wooden puzzles whose secrets they undid with malicious pleasure, the boy never left a room without a wave of his pudgy hand to everyone and an artless smile, Daniel thought, she surely proved that his mother lived inside him, as Maria Barbara did Wilhelm, two mothers carefully guarding the immense and fragile spirits of their offspring. City, you are built on so many islets, thought Jean-Mathieu, an old man might feel tottery, never able to cross all your bridges or see all the art in your medieval palaces, his cane had brought him this far to the Doge's Palace and the Veronese he worshipped, the *Allegory of Youth and Age* now seemed less off-putting than when he had dwelt on his own decline, in fact, now the depiction of Age in the painting lent him as much strength as his intellectual efforts on the biography of Stendhal. Believing he knew better than anyone that, beyond the *Allegory of Youth,* so expressive and radiating inner light, not only did he find more youthfulness, but neither were there shores or bridges to these islets from which no return was possible, he felt a renewed serenity in having followed the path laid out for him, his train of thought went from Veronese's allegory to the paintings of Tintoretto and Titian, then came to mind Alvise Vivarini's *St. John the Baptist,* on whose face the artist had copied the features of a contemporary thinker, and forty years ago, Jean-Mathieu mused, he himself had been that hoary, bearded figure with bushy eyebrows, before he suddenly lost all his hair, of course, oddly enough, it was this bald, elegant poet with consciously fanciful clothing that Caroline had loved, whereas this Vivarini St. John, or this Jean-Mathieu from the past, had left her indifferent, he imagined the canvas so vividly it might have been here before him, the muscular physique, still holding a sensual attraction long after this voluptuous depiction, was he a learned dandy or a self-consciously and potently sexual thinker; his right shoulder, bared by the heavy green cape, his short clothing underneath showed thighs and a seductive leg, a runner's legs and aristocratic feet in delicate sandals, ready to race or else to dive into studious reading, in this attractive pose, he was reading a manuscript and pointing to it with his finger, that used to be me, Jean-Mathieu thought to himself, sensual and noble, still he felt himself to be the most ordinary of men whose life came down to being a fine ocean voyage under clear skies, how was it that he collapsed suddenly in front of the Veronese, his cane seemingly dissolved beneath him, his temples filled with a babel of murmurings; no, this couldn't be, Jean-Mathieu had never had a heart problem before, this was poor Frédéric's fate, who couldn't even leave the house, but Jean-Mathieu had always felt fine, only a second before he had been thinking about Justin's childhood in northern China with his father, the pastor, in those days, Justin wrote in his memoirs, I had a happy childhood, so happy I could not wait to get up in the morning, our thirst for life is as alive as that, then guilt puts an end to happiness, mine ended with Nagasaki and Hiroshima, I was ashamed, I cried, if Jean-Mathieu thought about his friend, it was the latter calling him back from out of his silent eternity. Jean-Mathieu felt like saying to this voice that disturbed his contemplation of the Veronese, I'm still in a hurry to get up in the morning, so don't call me to you too quickly, and at the very instant Justin's long-dead voice faded into the mist, Jean-Mathieu heard the clatter of the cane at his feet and that other noise, more obscure, like snow crunching underfoot, a subterranean sound, in his temples it seemed, or surrounding his heart, like that sad feeling of suffocation, a cottony fading-away, I've got to reach Eduardo, he's got to meet me at the airport, though Frédéric can't be alone, but Juan is there too, I mustn't get excited, it's probably nothing, oh, but this heavy breathing, what a nuisance, I've got to take a minute to phone Caroline from my room, I mean, after all, we just might not see each other again, dear Caroline, dear friend, why was he clumsy and pronouncing words so badly, and here came the suffocation again, cutting right through him, what pictures, what memories, and when was it he dreamed he was driving along a wave-swept wharf filled with a line of motionless, driverless black cars, in the dream, Jean-Mathieu was driving fast and dangerously toward the churning sea, when he saw coming to him the diaphanous silhouette of Justin, who said, where are you going on a stormy night like this, my friend, can't you see the other cars have stopped? What sounds, what a cracking from the rush of fluid in his veins and around his heart, he thought, and again he saw the Antonello da Messina painting he and Caroline had looked at in the Louvre, I'm an agnostic, you know, he had told her, but this Christ on the column upsets me, look at the baffled, begging face of this crucified man, his haggard, bloodshot eyes and mouth half open in a cry of rebellion and refusal to submit, there is our history, and Caroline had replied that Christian art repelled her with its submissiveness and suffering, Caroline and Jean-Mathieu and random bits of memory, yes, he would phone her from his room, he would tell Eduardo not to worry, it's just a malaise, but it might be a good idea to think about going back and seeing my doctor, but how was it, he wondered, that he fell faint right in front of this Veronese, tonight he would write to Charles in India, please come back, my friend, I can see myself at the end of a wharf in a turbulent sea opening as if upon a precipice, he would write that to Charles too, yes, tonight, I am thinking about these lines, Dylan, Dylan, I can't get over his loss, I seem to hear him recite these lines in the fury of the waves, Rage, rage against the dying of the light, he was so young, on the threshold of his life when he wrote that, Rage, rage against the dying of the light. When I heard the ambulance siren at noon, said Lazaro's mother by his hospital bed, somehow I knew it was for you, you were kicking inside me again, I knew you'd had a fight with your best friend Carlos again, he tried to kill me, he tried to kill me for an Adidas watch, Lazaro kept repeating, can you hear the sirens, Ma, it's noon, and he tried to kill me, they'll take good care of you here, it's nothing, the bullet just grazed your knee, you'll be able to walk in a few days, his mother said, but why didn't you just let him keep the watch, why all that blood on the sidewalk and in the street right in front of Trinity College, when's this hemorrhage going to stop, Lazaro asked as his mother bent over his bed, you have to pardon him, son, she said, Carlos really thought the gun wasn't loaded, and you've taunted him so many times, we didn't give everything up and come all the way to this country for you to be like your cousins and brothers with their bloody feuds, do you want to be like them, Lazaro, vandalizing the temples at Luxor, massacring tourists, that's the land of blood-revenge we've left behind,

I don't want to be one of those women burning incense sticks at the death of their sons, and what do you go and do out there on Bahama and Esmeralda, you get into a fight with Carlos, your friend, when we could at last live free from the threat of war, and you go and start one with him, we left behind the discrimination between men and women, and I had no intention of waiting and making tea or coffee while armed men, cousins of yours, hold meetings and preach discord and hate, we women were always left out, cowed behind our veils, even in universities, like untouchables, stoned for adultery, all our rights taken away, young women with no faces, forever masked and hidden and curtained from men, even when we studied, and our university teachers refused to see us, untouchable, banished, and massacred everywhere, in deserts or Afghan dirt, our relatives wander among rows of funeral ditches looking for their sons, how will they know mutilated teenagers from those khaki militiamen's rags now turned to uniforms for sand-sleepers, and you, son, you fight with Carlos, yesterday a twelve-year-old schoolboy threw some eggs at front doors for fun, and a woman came out of one of them and killed him with a revolver, he messed up my door, she said, what kind of country are we in, a peaceful place or the sands of Afghanistan, with all these buried schoolchildren? After everything we were running away from, you and me, acts of terrorism, countries rife with crime and plague and cholera and malaria and shortages of water and all sorts of things that eat away at us, and here you go and fight with your friend Carlos, all this barbarism and war we want no more of, the sickness, hunger, thirst, drought, and death they bring, instead of working our land, we kill each other over and over, and just like your bad brothers and cousins, you get into fights, Lazaro's hand went down to his knee and brushed the dressing, yes, he'd be up in a few days, he thought, soon he'd be able to walk, but he'd nearly died for a watch, his mother's presence, the elegiac tone in her voice, her face no longer veiled as it had been at home, with her hopes of peace and harmony in the education of her children, the new sense of freedom since they had come here, everything about her annoyed Lazaro, nor did he appreciate her success as a goldsmith, yet it afforded them a comfortable living, a mountain bike, a watch, gifts soon swapped with Carlos, too bad his mother, his unveiled mother, was wrong, Carlos deserved vengeance and more, his cousins and brothers were only following the purity of their religion, the manly code of blood, Carlos would have finished him off if he had not shouted, he's killed me, and the dirty, lying killer ran away, Lazaro thought, he picked up old syringes on the lawns along Bahama and Esmeralda, and he hung out with hookers who left behind used condoms and needles, you had to install locks on all the doors on Bahama because of the vandalism, a watch or a bike swapped with Carlos, that vandal, that druggie, I'll get him, Lazaro thought, so you don't remember, Caridad, his mother, went on, anything about where we came from with swarms of helicopters keeping us up at night, plastering us with napalm, fire and smoke swallowing up our beaches and forests, women and kids crying and clinging to the roofs of vans to get away, lined up all along the streets carrying mattresses on their backs, the forests burnt, the wildlife on the beaches destroyed, the sea with waves the colour of oil, monkeys in the mountains howling in desolation, wild boars screeching from the flames in the forests, dogs abandoned in the streets and so hungry they came out by the hundreds at night to chew the legs of our children, you don't remember all that, do you, son, the country we left behind, no water, no bread, just murdering commandos, I sold everything I had, all our family owned, and you, you fight Carlos, you want us to go back out into the streets with our packs on our backs, have you forgotten everything I've done for my children, Lazaro? But Lazaro thought of his mother as just a woman, and he was a man, so why weren't they separated by a white curtain, besides, every word she spoke inspired mistrust in him, and on top of

it, this Carlos, this lying thief, had humiliated him that noon in front
of Trinity College, even knowing the cops were never far away, Carlos
and his dog, two shadows in the sunlight, and seeing that her son had
his back up, Caridad touched his forehead, saying, don't let hate grow
in your heart, son, and Our Lady of the Bags, as Samuel called her,
had been walking a long time through the streets of Manhattan with
her bags and supplies in her arms, one could hear the noise of her tin
cans and crumpled cardboard echoing in the night, and now she
dreamed just of stretching out in a grassy park, because all the stores
had been closed for an hour now, and she would have loved to sleep
in a bed, wash her face and hair, slipping quietly to the back of a restaurant where she could deliver her body up to a haven of water and
rest, would this be the night she would see the Apostle again, the way
he was when he preached in the parks and on radio and television,
raising his arms to heaven in his white robe tied with a knotted cord
around his waist, this Apostle with clear eyes and a blond beard, who
one day had told Our Lady of the Bags, here is a Bible that you may
comprehend the mysteries of God, not realizing she could not read,
go and be simple, and with that there was such a burst of heat and
light from his robe, the crucifix around his neck, and his arms raised
heavenward, that the little girl would have liked to stay with him, even
if she were only a raindrop clinging to his robe, surely it was he she
had sought, he whom neither rain nor snow could sully in summer or
winter, he seemed not to know hunger or thirst, and all who met him
seemed refreshed, his name, which he refused to have pronounced,
the Apostle without name, even this title was spoken with utmost
deference, thought Our Lady of the Bags, whether in the mining valleys of Hazelton, where his prayers had fought the miners' depression,
or in New York, where he had defended street people, the Apostle had
informed Our Lady of the Bags that she was not a real itinerant,
because, being a little mentally confused, she should never have left

the institution where they had taken her after her parents died; Our Lady of the Bags said with sudden annoyance that her parents were waiting for her in Jerusalem, then, said the Apostle, take the vow of poverty with me, for your life, my child, will be comfortless like mine, I would wish to be a drop of rain on the garment of Jesus that nothing can sully, neither rain nor snow nor muddy streets, why won't you let me walk with you, Apostle, where I am going you cannot go, he had replied, can't you see I have neither mother nor brother, ah, who are they, mother and brother, I may not stay long in any place, I've travelled on foot through fifteen countries and forty-five states, and I may not stay in this city, sometimes at night I assemble crowds in the fields for prayers, they come from far and wide, sometimes three thousand people a night pray with me, and I tell them, pray for yourselves and go home without cares, and they listen to me, these devotees of God, and feel only joy, sometimes I sing, and they forget their troubles, this white robe was stitched by no slave of Industry, no one toiled to clothe me, for it is the tunic of the sun, and Our Lady of the Bags said, oh, do please let me travel far away with you, and the Apostle answered her, where I am going you cannot go, what would we do in the Shenandoah mines and the sharp, cold coal dust, men want me to awaken them to faith, and faith, my child, is the flower of the mines; Our Lady of the Bags had once again pleaded not to be left alone, where was she going to sleep tonight, down in the subway tunnels to be surrounded by gangs like the Vampires or the Lords of Chaos, all wearing grotesque masks, the Vampire Gargoyles carving a V on their victims' foreheads with a knife and beating them on the head and neck, true vampires of underground caverns and corridors, and despite the capture of their adolescent leader, they still roamed free in the subway entrails and stairways, filling the little girl's soul with dread, and the Apostle, placing his hand on her head, said, child, go back to the institution you ran away from, and I will pray for you, for remember, I have neither

brother nor sister, Our Lady of the Bags was never to see nor hear him
again, except from time to time on TV or radio, this Apostle that
neither snow nor mud could sully, and who fixed cars or shone his
light on the miners of Shenandoah, no, Our Lady of the Bags had never
seen him again. They have to learn the love of music in school, said
Julia Benedicto to Marie-Sylvie, who was holding Vincent and Mai by
the hand in the school music room, and Vincent will learn the violin,
Julia Benedicto was already recruiting students for next year, and she
was proud of the training she gave the Island Youth Orchestra, Marie-
Sylvie glowered openly at her, who was this Cuban anyway, both were
refugees, but one was already guest violinist with the symphony orchestra, and the other chafed under her guise of domestic servant, no
matter if Mélanie and Esther called her an excellent governess, one
who enlivened them as no one else could, and under her abasement,
her grudging subjugation in this rich folks' house, Brahms's Concerto
no. 2 will be on the orchestra's programme this year, Julia was saying,
some recent composers too, Kodaly, perhaps Ginastera, the children
must start attending concerts now, Brahms's Piano Concerto, Marie-
Sylvie thought, feeling as though the children's fingers in her moist
hands were somehow an intrusion, here they were, listening to Julia
Benedicto talk about music while they had lunch at noon on the palm-
shaded terrace by the sea, the maitre d', all dressed in white, was
discussing the menu with them, and they, as well as Vincent, Mai, and
Augustino, beautiful and intelligent, raised their whimsical little faces,
while her crazed brother went about town banging his head against
the walls and yelling, they had been saved by the Coast Guard, every
one of them, and sent back to Port-au-Prince, how desolate to be sent
home when you have no home, first one boat, the *Resolute,* then
another, the *Madrona,* would disembark them all, women, children,
Chinese immigrants, Dominicans, after their wooden boats, decks
collapsing under the weight of so many passengers, had in vain brought

them to Key Biscayne, and Marie-Sylvie thought of them sailing as always with no radio or lights, in a vessel no more than sixty feet long, and sitting there, Vincent, Mai, Augustino, and their nanny, Marie-Sylvie de la Toussaint, eating without appetite on a restaurant terrace, what would they do if, all of a sudden, these repatriated expatriates had jumped out of the boat and climbed ashore, gripping the terraces with dark hands or running among the tables with nowhere to go, nowhere to hide, He-Who-Never-Sleeps, Marie-Sylvie's crazy brother, cried, these displaced people had been surrounded in the Bahamas to prevent them from landing, yes, they had been seen running in between tables, then throwing them into the ocean, chairs and all, overboard, and where were they all going to hide, in the churches and temples, Mozart's Overture to *The Marriage of Figaro* would also be on the programme, Julia Benedicto said placidly to Marie-Sylvie, they have to learn music appreciation very young, it's their grandmother who wants them to study it, Marie-Sylvie said suddenly, weakly, although this submission to Esther's or Mélanie's wishes was only feigned, and Marie-Sylvie thought resentfully that Julia Benedicto had been luckier than she deserved, educated, whereas Marie-Sylvie was just a servant with no ambition, everyone knows my brother and I kept goats, she thought, on the hills covered in patchy grass, we'll be having concerts in the parks, on sailboats out on the water on calm mornings or evenings, Brahms, Manuel de Falla, Camille Saint-Saens, concerts for the entire family, Julia Benedicto went on, but Marie-Sylvie heard nothing but the voice of her brother, He-Who-Never-Sleeps, screaming at the male nurses as he was being interned, in hundreds they made it past the naval marina, jumping into the water, racing on foot through the lights that lit up the sky, leaving restaurant diners gaping in amazement and taxis honking, so much noise in the town that it was like a melon exploding, they had come from Monrovia and Ghana, all under arrest, all in captivity, handcuffed on the banks of the Miami River, women attached to one another by the hands, dirty water dripping from the clothes of men detained by the Coast Guard, some got away in a Jeep, others drowned, what was music, that song of instruments and voices, wondered Marie-Sylvie, what was it, as she sat listening to a concert in the park by the sea on a Sunday afternoon with cooing turtledoves, that drew detestable families all in straw hats, and all the while, the race of the handcuffed refugees was on, through the city and into wall after wall, it would be good, Marie-Sylvie thought, if they stormed the restaurants where people were eating crab and crayfish, kicking down the doors and snatching pieces of bread as they ran between the tables, nimble as eagles on prey, in this jumble of thoughts, she wished Jenny could still be with her in Daniel and Mélanie's house as she used to be, first Doctors Without Borders in North Korea, next in Colombia, working on whatever disaster presented itself, she had not much time for Marie-Sylvie, in fact, she had written that she should not let herself be overcome by the corrosive feelings of exile, from a North Korean village called Yong Yun, Jenny wrote that famine and malnutrition were taking lives all around her, yesterday forty children under two, tomorrow double that, an acute human crisis, we don't have enough food, one hears nothing but crying, children scratch at the painful swellings caused by hunger, and I put them to sleep in narrow orphanage beds that will also be their coffins when they can no longer cry, I lie down next to them to try to make their deaths a little gentler, I sing for them the way my mother did for me, I place my hand on their foreheads and feel the icy sweat, I wrap them in grey blankets, Marie-Sylvie read these letters from Jenny and thought back to her beginnings with her brother in the remote village of Jeremie, where they still burned witches for practising black magic, where a sick child died soon after one of them came to his bedside, Marie-Sylvie thought these witches leaning over the cribs were none other than Famine and War, the pestilence that had crippled her brother's brain,

the same black witches Jenny was fighting now that she had abandoned
Marie-Sylvie to gloomy solitude, what was the point in waiting for her
to come back, when she would be off again to Colombia in a few weeks
to take medication and shelter to those found under the rubble, when
sports stadiums would become morgues and buses would be makeshift
operating rooms, that would be Jenny's life, while Marie-Sylvie would
have nothing to do but cater to spoiled children, and she was ashamed
of thinking like this, remembering Mai asleep in her arms one day
after one of their Sunday lunches in a restaurant, not wanting to move
and disturb her innocent sleep, her jaded heart was filled with joy, and
she had thought, they don't know me, they know nothing about me,
and yet they love me, suddenly confident again, she felt the future hang
less heavily on her, if only the children could always stay this small,
they would never come to judge her, with a determined, less submis-
sive air, she collected them from Julia Benedicto's music room and
drove them home in Mélanie's car, promising Vincent they would go
out in Samuel's boat today, as long as the sky remained cloudless,
Mélanie would not have agreed very readily to this, but she was not
due back from Washington for another day yet, and what was there
to be worried about in such fine weather, after all, Marie-Sylvie could
sail just as well as Mélanie, so they would at least go by tomorrow, if
the weather stayed nice, she told Vincent in quiet annoyance that
Samuel's boat in the marina bore the proud inscription *Samuel, Southern Light.* Someone's ringing the doorbell, said Caroline, but I can't
get it, I'm in the darkroom, Charly, feeling languid, was not about to
answer it either, she was too busy putting on black nail polish to match
her lipstick, coming out of the darkroom, Caroline had pushed Charly
aside and told her to get dressed, you don't welcome visitors in bikini
briefs, but we never see anyone, said Charly, stretching as she blew on
the nails of her right hand, then all at once, she saw him, he was there,
it was him, Eduardo, the Mexican with tresses, Eduardo, Caroline was

talking in a low voice near the half-open door to the garden, what are
you saying, my friend, Caroline said, looking blank, you're leaving for
Italy tonight, no, it can't be true, Eduardo, she stammered, laying her
head on his shoulder, no, my friend, this can't be true, and Charly,
seeing them like this, wondered what they were up to, what they were
plotting, now they're hand in hand about something, but Caroline had
deliberately pushed Eduardo toward the garden verandah, she did not
want him to see her usually tidy house in this disorder, nor the dusty
tinge to her hair, for she had let her visits to the hairdresser slide, and
what a menagerie in the living room, three angora cats Charly had
just got and a Yorkshire terrier whose fur needed better care, God,
what a mess, Caroline sighed, as she noticed Charly sulking with
lipstick stains on her fingers and one foot in the pool, better get dressed,
said Caroline, I'm going out and I'll need the car, her voice was tone-
less, she was thinking with sadness about the publication of the book
of photographs she had prepared with Jean-Mathieu, those portraits
of poets from the past century, wasn't the whole project in doubt now,
she said to Charly, her heavy eyes looking away from her to the lime
trees and rose bushes that needed watering, and that rag doll stuck
through with needles on Charly's bed, that was a bad sign, wasn't it,
nobody's allowed in my room, Charly said, not you or the maid, I live
here, this is my home, Caroline replied, suddenly crestfallen in front
of this off-kilter girl, what made her think she could ever make a
chauffeur out of her, she was just a savage, and that male doll, pierced
with needles in the arm and chest, was hateful, she would have to get
rid of Charlotte, particularly now that Caroline was sure she was stealing money in small amounts, here and there, but maybe that doll was
some sort of sex toy for Charly, she went out at night with it in her
handbag when she got on her motorbike, just like a boy, now all of a
sudden she was passive and languid, Caroline had imagined life without
her, an uneventful life locked away in an old folks' home, then senility,

Eduardo had brought her disastrous news about Jean-Mathieu this afternoon, but the report had to be a false alarm, her good friend would get better, she would get this unbalanced girl and her fetish obsessions out of the house, she probably could not help lying and stealing because of her background, Charly was a half-breed, wasn't she, and Caroline would have the courage to say, get out, Charly, I no longer want to see you here, a thought suddenly stirred in her, maybe after Charly had gone, Jean-Mathieu would come and share her house, the dear man had always adored her, since they were both getting on in years, she was afraid they would make a pair of foolish old lovers, yes, that's it, Jean-Mathieu would be back, and they could go out and travel together, the awful news Eduardo had brought today was a lie, what's wrong, asked Charly, all sweetness again, is something wrong, Caroline walked alone into her room and said nothing, is it that absurd to think that people over seventy-five, like Jean-Mathieu and me, are condemned by society to forswear love and passion, why was it ever decided that we would be incapable of desire and sensuality, when, faced with the stupefaction of old age, this is all we are, beings begging for love, none of us has the courage to admit it, not Jean-Mathieu nor I, today's bewilderment had given Caroline a migraine, or were her senses simply thrown into confusion, which was it, she wondered, suddenly alarmed at the idea that Charly might leave, whenever they quarrelled, and it was almost every day lately, Charly had threatened to go and join her friends in Thailand, she would go to Bangkok and get a better job, or maybe the beaches at Surat Thani, or the island of Ko Phangan, and Caroline could already see her dancing till dawn on moonlit nights, a ring in her navel, perhaps wearing only a fisherman's green coverall, there the attractive, slim-waisted youth lived only to dance, Caroline thought, drugged stupor and ecstatic nighttime pleasures, a new civilization is being born in us, Charly would say, for she really believed in herself as the heir to the paradise of the islands, for three dollars a day you could rent a bungalow on the white sandy beaches, with its coral waters, this was the new Greece, and people came from all around the world on this idyllic quest, Charly said, from London and Japan, young tech refugees from Silicon Valley, children of the New Civilization with no morality, thought Caroline, tattooed with rings in their nipples or navels, how would it play out for Charly, death by overdose or sexual promiscuity, a careless drowning in the coral seas, Charly had not yet sensed that it was dangerous to live on a constant high from all these temptations in the real world, no, Caroline would not tell Charly to leave, even if she found the girl sneaky and dishonest, Charly's presence in the house might in fact be malevolent, but Caroline would no longer be able to live alone, this migraine, this insidious weariness, and why did Eduardo have to come in when she did not want to see anyone, he would have done better to stay and look after Frédéric, and what about Charles, why was there no news of him from India, especially since the critics had loved his last book, then this horrible news about Jean-Mathieu, no, not true, Eduardo said he was leaving for Italy tonight, and he would come back with Jean-Mathieu, Caroline would wait patiently, this anxiety and confusion would last only a few hours more, yes, she would be patient, Eduardo had said he might be back the next day with Jean-Mathieu. Carlos was thinking he would be safe behind this old building, at least until sunset, although the sun was still scorching in the sky, a hen with her chicks clucked amongst the garbage in the yard piled with car tires, odd bits of metal, empty soda bottles with stale leftovers in them, this was where they sold crack or traded marijuana for a loaded gun or a car hood, the walls were peeling white paint, and blue paper was taped over the openings where windows had disappeared or been broken and gaped black mouths, who would ever live here in this crumbling house, thought Carlos, sponging his forehead with his T-shirt, Lazaro and his Adidas watch, what blood-spattered ghosts rose in the hot mist

from the streets and sidewalks to the sickeningly warm sea, for the
fire of the sun would warm and crumble everything eventually, the
heavy red flowers like those of heady Cereum grapes, which open only
at night, the fleshy fruit of the avocado, lime, papaya, and mango trees
the birds so delighted in in summer, the gelatinous liquid from these
fruits would have trickled through Carlos's lips and calmed his raging
thirst, poinciana and orchids, sweet-smelling frangipani blossoms,
but all these fruits and flowers and plants were as luxuriant and efflor-
escent in the heat of day as under waves of night breeze, the gardens
would still be in flower while Carlos knew only fear and condemnation,
retreating into caves or trying to glide unnoticed at night along the
brushy banks of the canal, the Isle of Trees, and the harbour, where
the oyster fishermen's boats drifted early in the evening, their motors
almost noiselessly slipping them through the glow of blinking navigation lights, yachts weaving across the folds of water, masts and flags
raised, the men on them in a hurry to unload their offspring, as smelly
as the oysters in their buckets, sons with muddy legs who had camped
with them under the pines on the Isle of Trees, on the mangrove coast,
where Carlos could steal a boat anchored in the sand and sail to Venus's
house, just hoping that one of those mischievous characters camping
in the bush didn't see him, they'd harpoon him like one of their sharks
whose tapered carcasses lay bleeding in the sun, that's it, farther on
he'd be safe, Lazaro, the Adidas watch, the ghosts dissolving in the
heat of the mist rising from streets and sidewalks, and pigeons and
doves strolling confidently down these streets and sidewalks amid the
cars, and Carlos thought about what the officer had said, no bars on
our jails, but no rest in our cells, if they arrested Carlos, it would be
to send him out to clear the Brazilian pepper forests where the air was
unbreathable, he'd build highways, with his hands and feet in the
thorns and thistles and snake-filled swamps, ten hours a day, he'd
swing a pickaxe in the stabbing sun and the summer tornadoes, no

ball and chain necessary, this was prison reform, you'll go and cut brush and bushes till the forest is cleaned up and whole highways have been built by the sweat of your brow, the officer told him, and we'll have squads to watch over you, no bars, just hostile brush, crocodiles, poisonous snakes, the deadly residue of Brazilian pepper, and count yourself among the lucky ones on this earth, in Asia, now, they'd inject you with venom from a poisonous flower, and you'd be rocked by such violent hallucinations that little by little your mind would let go completely, and they'd have to shut you up in the funny farm with all the other nut-jobs, we don't know exactly how many of ours die on the job in this brush, no sir, the officer couldn't say, Carlos thought, the Blacks who built the highways under a torrid, leaden sky, only the unarmed sheriffs watching them were White, that's it, Carlos thought, they'd send him to Brazilian pepper forests to become intoxicated by their deadly pollen, like Asian prisoners by the lamphong flower, they had become deranged too, or else they died without a name or anything to identify them, not a trace, Lazaro, thought Carlos, it was Lazaro's fault he was going to jail, no way, he would escape, he'd put fear into all of them, his broad hand, so open to animals, now swept the hen and her shrill chicks under the shell of a car gradually crumbling in the filthy yard, sure, it would be simple to escape, he'd slip into one of those boats under cover of night and just slide on by the port installations, the naval shipyard, the docking basins, the regattas with their sailboats and skiffs ready for Sunday's race, the express catamarans, empty while their captains stayed out drunk until dawn in fishy, man-smelling taverns, he used to walk Polly there on her leash, the big cruise ships, the sleepless *Wolves, Grounded, Legendary,* and *Oasis* that went out for four days of non-stop fishing, flags wafting in the breeze, but first Carlos had to make it out of here, here no one and nothing should live, not even the chicks and their mother, fluttering and cackling and hanging on to life by the merest thread under the body of a car, fluttering and clucking after their mother, when Carlos thought he heard someone crying, and it seemed to be coming from inside the tumbledown house, he pushed aside the blue paper covering one of the windows, and through a shade-filled hole he saw the little Black boy, about five years old, in a checkered shirt and very short jeans, sitting on a bare mattress and swallowed up in the filth around him, obviously no one had taken care of him for days, Carlos thought, what he held on his knees seemed bigger than the boy himself, a semi-automatic, yeah, I know that gun, Carlos thought, it's a Davis .32 like the one I stole from the Cuban cook, just for self-defence and not supposed to be loaded, again he saw Lazaro tumble to the ground, the Adidas watch and so much blood in the heat-cloud rising from the sidewalks at noon, although he looked half starved, the five-year-old seemed bolstered by the gun in his lap, it made him into someone dangerous, how many firearms were there in the shack anyway, and cocaine and crack bags, someone was going to open that ramshackle door any moment now, maybe the kid's father or uncle, and he was gripping the gun close to him, I'm not waiting around here until night, Carlos thought, and he gathered his thick hair under his cap, it was enough to give him away, and there must be a photo of him in town from his first offences, small stuff, though, he thought, nothing to get him in real trouble, a few days in an institution had been enough to set him straight, his mother said, there was another picture from the boxing championship of him and Lazaro, both indestructible in the ring, the hen's cooing and the kid's crying came back to him as he stayed close to the walls covered with white blossoms, he thought jasmine would come out and spread its perfume only at night, when he had made it over the water to Venus's house, he'd have nothing to be afraid of, nothing unless one of those big sailing yachts held a sinister omen like maybe a flag with the skull-and-crossbones glinting in the night. At the Temple of the City of Coral, Pastor Jeremy was saying to the flock, heed Reverend Paul, for he speaks of the soul and it alone, as you will see and hear, he is here to deliver the sermon, here to speak of naught but the soul, stay still in your seats, dance and move no more, here is Reverend Paul, boomed Pastor Jeremy, please be seated all, the Reverend Bishop has come all the way from Texas to speak of your souls, and he stepped aside to leave room for Reverend Paul, thinking that these fresh young evangelists had some nerve thinking they could so easily enter into the secrets of the soul and of God, it was a bit pretentious, since we could really know nothing of either, these young ones had a different way of speaking with crowds and rallies all around them, so little time we have between the moment we are born and the moment we die, preached Bishop Paul, what is it, a breath in time, dear friends, just a breath, God has placed in each one of us an idea like the one He had when He made the world, a perfect idea, this is not one of your typical sermons, thought Pastor Jeremy, what's he going to say next, think, dear friends, went on the vibrant minister with his eyes shining and glasses slipping forward, yes, think, that between your first breath and your last, there is time for you too to know the greatest, most perfect joy of all, I'm not talking about success or the accumulation of wealth on this earth, but the idea of accomplishing a grand and joyous plan that God has invested in me for every day of my life, that's how it is for each one of you, my friends; I've written a biblical pageant with thirteen parts that will show you what I mean, my friends, and you can see it in any theatre on the island, yes, Pastor Jeremy thought, now these new evangelists have turned into movie actors, and gone is the poor life the Lord showed us, they've got the bank accounts and the cars, they're forever travelling all over to preach to people in the thousands. In the beginning, Reverend Paul had a church with only about twenty parishioners in Texas, now for four years he's had 25,000, he says, and this African-American preacher wants to have people of many nationalities and creeds, Whites, Hispanics, professionals and workers, yes, said Pastor Paul, I forget neither poor nor homeless, and in my seventeen books, seventeen biblical stories to date, I think of them all, for everyone has a soul, and each soul has its anguish. Seventeen books, thought Jeremy, and on his foreign crusades, he says he's met people of over fifteen nationalities, what youth, what ideas this young man has, when does he find time for prayer, obviously he has no family, what would he do if God had given him children, like Venus dishonouring them with her men, or Carlos, the thief, who had not been seen at home for days, or Le Toqué, Deandra, Tiffany and all the others? In his sermons and preachings, Pastor Paul touched on everything, didn't he, sensitive to the abused woman and spiritual guide to all who confided in him, staying in touch with prisoners in more than six hundred jails throughout North America, he had spent several hours on his latest visit to a Louisiana jail, where they called him the Shepherd of Shattered Souls, the Doctor in the Kingdom of the Forgotten and Dispossessed, was this not asking too much of himself, Jeremy wondered, could you make an industry out of religion, prayer, and preaching to so very many? I've heard the call of the Lord, replied the Shepherd of Souls to such questions, the Word must be heard far and wide, I listen, and what I cannot do, God will. Freedom is an instrument that takes many forms, some think a minister is only a man of prayer, God has told me, go, and never stop thinking of something new, be creative, for the Creation of God is in every one of you, be neither deaf nor blind to what I have given you, modern man is a consumer, and why would he not consume the language of God through us, men of modern needs, can spirituality alone light our way? No, for we also have bodies that like to consume, we live and we eat every day, we watch TV shows, not all of them are Christian, we are a part of the new era we are living in, we pastors, we don't want success, we want to heed the call of God through these thousands of souls that every day consume more than they can absorb.

Standing on the outside looking in, we think what happens to others can't happen to us, but it is in our very homes that our wives and daughters are molested, and we do nothing to protect them, our pastors won't talk about the cruelty so many women undergo in their own communities, I wrote about these goings-on, and I exposed conjugal and domestic violence, who among our pastors makes the effort to heal other than with the abstraction of words in their sermons? Souls are first and foremost wounded bodies. I was overcome with sadness when I saw my mother die of cancer, and I asked myself why, when she was dead, they said she was in heaven, all of them, they're all in heaven now, these deceased whose bodies have been wracked with ills, well, yes, they may be in heaven, but does it make us feel better about not having supper with them tonight? Or not seeing them at the table tomorrow? No, our sadness is the greater to know they won't be there for supper tonight. It was during Reverend Paul's sermon that Pastor Jeremy thought back to Carlos and Polly, where were they, and why hadn't they been home for two days, Mamma said a seventeen-year-old didn't always spend the night at home, but still, where was he, what had he gone and done now, he wondered, Le Toqué did not appear to know where his brother was either, he had been called Le Toqué, or Woodenleg, at school because of his limp, and this was an injustice that should be corrected, God had given the boy a birth defect that was not his own doing, what would Reverend Paul say to that, was it a sign of God's perfection, the illustrious bishop, the Shepherd of Shattered Souls, the spiritual healer of women and girls the world over, did he hear the hoarse crowing of the cock under his own window, did he see the two jerks in the front pew laughing and chattering all through that soaring sermon of his, one in a straw hat with muscular arms protruding from his clean T-shirt, well, more like a muscle shirt, actually, was that a way to dress when you came to the Temple of the City of Coral, this lout reminded him of Carlos again, they looked

similar, and the other a nice piece of work too, the pastor thought, on
his left arm trembled a tattoo that read Grandpa and Grandma, may
they rest in peace in their grave, Pastor Jeremy signalled the two to be
quiet, trying to whisper with his trumpeting voice, show some respect
for the Shepherd of Shattered Souls who's visiting us today, Pastor
Jeremy couldn't take his eyes off the one that looked so much like
Carlos, and wondered where on earth his son could have been these
past two days. Sitting next to her son's hospital bed, Caridad said to
Lazaro, don't turn and face the wall as though you aren't listening,
you used to kick and fidget inside me, when we lived in Egypt, your
father Mohammed used to beat me when I was pregnant with you, he
locked me up in the house because I wanted a divorce, women weren't
allowed to do that then, and I had asked for a divorce because he locked
me up and mistreated me, while he was whipping me, I used to say,
what's going to happen to my baby, I wanted to run away, but he held
me captive, it took me a long time to realize I wasn't alone, other
women would soon be getting divorces too, that was before you were
born, you are the son born of my rebellion and my pride, and now
what do you do, you can't even pardon your friend, did I rebel for
nothing, are you going to turn out just like him, your father, Mohammed? Oh, our husbands kept us prisoners, but they were allowed to
divorce and marry any number of women, according to religious
tradition they could have as many as four at once, and they often did
without even needing legal permission, but we divorced women
couldn't expect any financial help from the fathers of our children,
and how we had to fight for even the most elementary rights, and you,
Lazaro, you can't even forgive your friend, gritting his teeth, Lazaro
thought, oh, and who said so, some disgusting wiseguy in a university
dared to say men and women would soon be equal, what a lie, I'm
obedient to the law of blood, just like my brothers and cousins, I am
the son of Mohammed, and this woman corrupted by newfangled

ideas isn't my mother, no, men and women will never be equals, the sharp pain in his knee and the burning fever in his temples made him wish heartily that Carlos would be arrested, interrogated, and thrown in jail, and as soon as he could get up and walk, he wouldn't listen to his whining mother, he, Lazaro, would avenge himself, that day, he knew he was a man. Just a few more hours, thought Caroline, and Jean-Mathieu would be back, their book had to come out, a poem by Jean-Mathieu and a black-and-white photo by Caroline on facing pages, always only well-known poets, they could not be compared, she thought, Jean-Mathieu would be honoured in this, for Caroline's art of photography was one of resemblance and precision, life exhaled beneath these seemingly impassive faces, guilty of indifference, Caroline was not one of those courageous photographic artists who had documented the most dangerous, petrifying images of the previous century, no, she was not one of those men and women whose cameras had decried famine in the Sudan or in Ethiopia, her heart had not been corroded by the visions of those plains, for if like one of them, the moving Kevin Carter, she had photographed the little Sudanese girl, all skin and bones, attacked by a vulture just as hungry as she was as she tottered toward an aid station, staring, empty eye in bare head after the attack, or if she had taken a picture, whether yesterday or again tomorrow, of the disaster on the Sudanese plain, the bodies of babies with eyes wide open, still at their mothers' wrinkled breasts, perhaps she would have committed suicide like the photographer at thirty-three who wrote, I'm sorry, I'm leaving, the pain of living has killed all the joy of living for me, I'm leaving, I'm very sorry, and what a heavy burden this picture of a child attacked by a vulture will be on everyone's conscience, the photographer died of carbon monoxide poisoning, and was it Caroline's fault if millions of women and children were about to die yesterday in Sudan or today in Nairobi, humanitarian organizations would send tons of food, because the rich countries

123

and fairly comfortable women like Caroline were always shocked to see skeletal shapes on their television screens, and who was to blame for the food arriving so late, the sight of these little skeletons in their mothers' arms was unbearable, Caroline thought, whether sleeping or eating or using the computer or cell phone, you couldn't forget these women and children, they were dying, and who to blame, indifferent and guilty of it, Caroline could think only of Jean-Mathieu coming back, no, they would never be apart again, they'd have breakfast every day by the sea, what was it that pessimistic Eduardo had said, Caroline dear, it's possible you won't see Jean-Mathieu again, but no, it wasn't true, she would see him the next day, or at the latest, in a few days, they would walk arm in arm; it is to the great photographic journalists that we owe the world's collective memory, Caroline thought, these photographic creators of modern pietas took their subjects anywhere they found them, revealing them in the heat of the moment, in a war or social crisis, in the poisoned air of the fishing village of Minimata, Japan, the deformed modern pietas of a mother bathing her daughter Tomoko, paralyzed and convulsed by mercury vapour, or a Japanese mother smiling at her child with arms and legs crucified by mercury poisoning, a smile whose mute compassion no work of art could convey, only the momentary sensitivity of a photographic genius could do it, the photographer could reproduce, as though drawn by hand, the inky layer a tire factory laid over the inhabitants of a Romanian town ruined by dictatorship, cooked in coal and born degenerate; looking at such photography, could we still be on the earth, thought Caroline, could we still hear the song of turtledoves in the trees like today, or had the trees in that Romanian town all lost their leaves and birds amid the smoke, the air cooking and cooked like the air at Hiroshima seconds after the conflagration, Justin had described these women and men in his books, rising clothed in ashes no more than seven or eight minutes afterward, and that moment following the bomb signed in

blood and ashes the dawn of a time when we would never be the same
again, was this how Justin defined victory in the Atomic Age, a calamity and these people rising clothed in ashes, wool socks, and boots,
just men leaving home for work, what is this we have invented that is
worse than hell itself, was this how Justin put it, a deterioration of the
universal conscience, he said in his books, Caroline had not always
shared his pacifism, could there never be a just violence? Often cool
to the suffering of humanity, Caroline had preferred to look for beauty
and harmony in a world where the beautiful and harmonious had
been denatured and disfigured, what might her skillful handling of
physiognomy not accomplish, the adult profile of Mozart painted by
Lange, so swiftly with her camera she had illuminated the features of
this pure soul, the forehead too high, the graceless cheeks tinted red
like the lips, the eye contracted under its lowered brow deep in thought,
for the intensity of the music lay beneath these assembled features of
the soul, how she would have liked to paint those brows, that mane of
hair on Mozart's head, the shirt collar on his brown jacket, Caroline's
art knew how to pay tribute to all these figures inhabited by grandeur
and simplicity, how happy she could be doing that and nothing else,
in the tempest of creation Mozart's profile was also that of Yehudi
Menuhin, crystalline and yet secretive, had she known him as a child
prodigy, perhaps she would have kissed him as Albert Einstein had
done, exclaiming, oh, heaven, now I know that God exists, though not
everyone shared the spotless glory of this son of Russian immigrants,
not all realized he was a patient messenger of peace sent among us,
audiences in New York marvelled at him already while he was still
growing up, while Anne Frank was still growing up to be sacrificed
with them all, dying of typhus in Bergen-Belsen, a normal child who
no doubt would have preferred not to be special, not to fulfill such
great expectations, Caroline thought, nor be the standard-bearer of
trampled human dignity so young, that photograph of her seated and

smiling, legs and shoulders bare under braces and a summer skirt, was it taken by a relative or friend, her father Otto perhaps, in a flowering field of white clover, self-assured in the serenity of that moment, not an inkling on that summer day in 1935 Holland of who would be at their door; if only she could have stayed longer like this in her father's sight, in this white-flowered meadow, smiling into the future with the sun warming her slenderness, before becoming the monument raised over so many other names, if only she could have long continued to be the enthusiastic student writing at her desk, if only she had not had to grow up in that dark little room in Amsterdam, where she wrote prophetically, almost divinely, about the noiseless coming of the death machine, long after I'm no longer here, I want to go on living, she wrote a year before her death in Bergen-Belsen, thinking only of the joy she could give to others, how could she know the pain she would pass on to the entire world, as though an angel had told her that this diary of dispossession was written not just for herself, but for all those about to be born in the death camps and for all those who would not survive, it was for them that she wrote this story of her relentless struggle in which, all at once, she would accept with lucidity that this world was nothing but misery and death, will we all be struck by this thunder, this discharge that, for the moment, we can barely make out, and yet still one day, peace and serenity will return, am I right to listen only to my conscience? Noiseless though it was, she heard the death machine coming, even as she wrote in that dim back room in Amsterdam, never seeing the colour of the sky, never going to libraries or cinemas, never seeing young people her own age, oh, if only she could still be that smiling child her father had photographed against a field of white flowering clover, perhaps she would not have become that little girl who had seen and foreseen everything there was to see, including the final horror someone else had photographed, the road to Bergen-Belsen on Liberation Day, where an eight-year-old walks past thousands of bodies piled high by the wayside and under the trees, without looking at them, a boy walking swiftly through this mortuary of a landscape, straight ahead, not looking back, likely wandering for a long time without home or country, tomorrow to be turned back from the Palestinian border, walk, breathe, live, but above all, never look back, this thought seems to be written in the premature lines of his baffled forehead, if only Caroline did not need to see or know about the unacceptable pain of impotence and sorrow, if only she could photograph that which is gracious, some pleasant part of existence, like the aesthete-craftsman Eugene Boudin painting gracious silhouettes on the beach at Trouville, never would she be one of those photo-engravers, not merely skilled, but who expired with their epoch, still leaving their mark on its etched plates, as life itself knits together broken fragments, no, for Caroline exquisite charm was everything, Mozart's profile as Lange painted it with exactitude, the hands of Menuhin, all sorts of visions of music and dance, the euphoria on Jim Morrison's face set off by the leather suit and red stage-grotto, she would have liked to take his reverse profile too, hands wrapped around the microphone, body upright as he sang, shouldn't everything, everything about them be preserved, the dogged forehead of Glenn Gould cleft by a thick vein, the grace of Nijinsky or the seductive Rudolf Nureyev? However close or remote from us, these bodies existed free from our corruptibility, for no photographer could pervert or alter their enduring beauty, their frozen grace, fixed forever like the faces at a meal painted by Caravaggio, it was too late for Caroline to make up for her lack of courage and many other weaknesses, why admit these sad thoughts when she lived solely for life's comforts and contentments, least comfortable of all was this waiting for Jean-Mathieu, where was Charly, she would have to take the car and get medication for these migraines, this was no time to still be in the pool, the house was such a mess, she'd have to get the maid and then think about going to the hairdresser's, I have to be ready when Jean-Mathieu gets here, she was murmuring evasively, what's the weather like over there, he's got to have a good trip, I've got to see him, but I'm not ready yet, from the pool, Charly heard this broken voice and thought, she's an old woman, she's going to be more and more cranky and difficult, maybe I shouldn't have torched Jean-Mathieu's letter with my cigarillo, that artistic, flowery poet's idiotic writing, it could be the last love letter she'll ever get, but at least in scattering the burnt and blackened words in the sea, Charly had exorcised her angry demons, the meanness her mother had criticized her for back in Jamaica, but this kind, elegant man, Jean-Mathieu, would probably end up being abused by Caroline the same way the maid, the secretary, and Charly herself were already, besides, Caroline was far too taken up with him, the acid perfumes of water and the burning letter, no, she was not wrong to do it, she reflected, this master race Caroline belonged to could never be offended or shocked enough, Caroline greedily scooped up all the presents Charly brought her, the angora cats that Charly piled onto her lap while offering a nuzzling head and lying eyes, and that she never stopped complaining about, they were paid for with my own money, Charly, that's all you do is spend, I'm not rich, you know, what do you take me for anyway, I've got to summon up the courage to get rid of this girl, Caroline said to herself, perhaps her last love letter ever, and Daniel, walking along the road lined with poppies, was still dissatisfied with himself, he had written so little in that stark little room, and soon it would be time to rejoin his family, it's not healthy writing without a child, Mai or Vincent, on your lap, how confusing it all was, because when he wrote at home, he did not see much of them, he just liked having them nearby, maybe the poppies along the road sent these pungent memories, why didn't Samuel write from New York more often, were they paying enough attention to Vincent's delicate condi-tion, still his father was the one who nearly killed him when he went

walking by the ocean and forgot his medication, maybe it was just as
well Samuel didn't write his father too often, you'd never know he was
the son of a writer the way he scrambled letters and sounds, when was
he going to learn to conjugate verbs and handle grammar, in one of
his letters he had written, Dear poppa, dont you feel out of plase, out
of your deth and unwanted in your Spanish monastry with all those
writers and artists my age, Im sure you feel kind of lossed and adrift,
your old, you dont relax enough, Daniel felt like protesting, but I'm
not even forty yet, who on earth told him I was old? Descending to
the poppy-lined road under this gentle June sunlight had steeped him
in melancholy, he thought, Rodrigo, on the other hand, made a point
of avoiding it and napping or writing in the cool shade of his cell, how
slowly and sweetly this afternoon flowed by, and even the writing
slumbered as Daniel looked over his notes, standing in front of the
patch of sand used for bowling with the dog Heidi, who briskly left
his side to run off, legs flying, to the woods, would this vault of leaves,
dark even in full daylight, bring him the answers he needed for Augustino's pointed questions before nightfall, or would he just go on with
his morose meditation until he reached the sunflower field where you
could hear the laughter of Garçon Fleur, then the path covered in
heady, thorny, yellow rose bushes, all the saps and perfumes that spilled
out of the earth at this time of year, what self-indulgent laziness, he
thought, walking the poppy path, the woods, the underbrush hummed
and sang, under the balcony of the artists' workshop, Mark and Carmen
in their reclaimed and resuscitated clothes were sorting through the
creative rubbish they had collected, would Daniel even know what to
say to Mark tomorrow, when he displayed his paintings of nothing
but stuffed animals, or his fish and shellfish, lifeless trappings in jars,
like the painter Damien Hirst, who exhibited grey, fragmented calves'
heads in vices, so tangible was the torment that the viewer had to look
away, by putting these works on show, these embryos of death, Mark

and Carmen seemed to be saying, look and see what universe we're living in, they intended to go still further than their English mentor Hirst, and Daniel was naive to think these exhibits were not alive, the animal heads in formaldehyde and behind glass were still in decomposition, and evaluated at $500,000 apiece in New York and London, according to Mark, all of life hung on this organic decomposition, he seemed perfectly rational when he spoke, Daniel thought, and when he got up at dawn to record the birds singing, he probably knew everything else about them too, from incubation to maturity, life starts in the eye, the look a bird gives, he told Daniel, binoculars in hand, had Daniel ever heard the banded fly-catcher, rare in these parts, or the moustached tomtit that nests on the ponds of the South of France, or the red-rumped reddish swallow alighting in the Mediterranean basin, was it possible Daniel was one of those deaf and senseless men unable to tell European birds from North American, sure a lot of species are already extinct, the sparrow-hawk owl, last captured in Belgium in 1943, the black-throated thrush, last seen in 1936, and Daniel listened to Mark's litany of regrets, was it really the nightingale that had woken him during the night, Daniel asked him, it was, he replied, when the warblers had stopped, and their song is a concert of inventive melodies, Daniel reproached himself for being irritated that these brilliant crescendos had woken him up in the night, he knew he could never win with Mark, and Giotto, what do think about him, Mark, the twentieth century paid a lot of attention to Giotto, and do you know why, because his painting gave God a human face, at least that's what the experts say, bah, the fourteenth century's full of artists like him, Mark shot back, in every medieval church, he shrugged, all those Madonna-and-Child renderings were too much for a poor peasant like Giotto, so he fathered a new art, broke all the rules and revealed truth in the human face, this little speech of Daniel's was boring Mark to death, hiking boots firmly planted, he stared at Daniel, Giotto would have been

better to paint landscapes than foist off on us his belief in a god that
doesn't exist, he fumed, there is nothing that is not born and does not
die, it's life's accident, followed by decomposition, that's what awaits
us all, and that's what our teacher Damien Hirst is trying to say, all
our life long we cannot conceive of dying, so from here on in, art has
to be insane, Marc Quinn painted himself with his own blood, quarts
of chilled blood, can you understand that, Giotto, oh, farewell, Giotto,
the words rolled like stones from Mark's lips, just as Carmen called
out to him, Mark, come and see what I found with my shovel, a woman's
dress, maybe she was killed here, shoes, socks, bra, all practically
intact, once again, Daniel had failed to convince Mark that Giotto's
faces came to us perfectly revealed, Mark would say, of course, the
beautiful, oblique blue gaze of Giotto's model was nothing more than
a screen for his ulterior religious motives, for him, the mysteries of
faith and supernatural inspiration in the Renaissance painters were
neither true nor praiseworthy, still wasn't it miraculous, sublime, to
see three peacocks suddenly on the scarlet-petalled poppy path, this
morning he had come down it ill-tempered, and now here they were,
standing with their splendidly rounded plumage fully spread, right
here on the pink tiles of his and Rodrigo's kitchen roof. Amigo, look
who's come to see us, Rodrigo called, did they come from Carmello
and Grazie's farm or simply from heaven? Three divinities, Daniel
thought, who knows, maybe a visitation from Giotto, lightly perched
on the pink-tiled roof, in the same red-and-green-specked colours,
they offered themselves to the eyes of Daniel and Rodrigo like butterflies on the grass, a miracle, thought Daniel, you see, amigo, they're
well adapted to captivity in the monastery gardens, and now they're
gradually getting used to us too, just when you're thinking about leaving, my friend, it's a visitation or a miracle, three magnificent plumed
peacocks, the sudden poetry in this display assuaged some of Daniel's
fears of living far away from friends, though he still did not know what

to make of Jean-Mathieu's silence, it had been weeks now since he had written, Charles in India too, miracle or visitation from heaven, voices, the thoughts of each of his children, came to him from across the sea and the dark forests where boars took shelter from the hunt, soon, a few hours from now, he would be touched deeply by sunlight on the purple hills, now, hastily wrapped in his icy bedsheets under a wooden ceiling quickly abandoned by the heat of day, he would listen for the first evening notes, the endless modulation of joy of the nightingale. And what would Marie-Sylvie have done in North Korea or Colombia with Jenny and Doctors Without Borders, she who had always made it alone with her brother He-Who-Never-Sleeps, and under a warm summer sky, with a calm sea, how could they think she wasn't capable of sailing Samuel's boat by herself, it had been docked for so long with no one to use it, there, there it was on the horizon, she explained to Vincent, sitting next to her on the boat rocked by the waves, the starting point for the transatlantic race of the great white sailboats, all those crews at sunset on all those distant seas, and Vincent clapped happily, they were out in a boat at sea, how nice and sweet Marie-Sylvie was, letting him do all these things his grandmother would not, days off from school, a ride in the boat, and sometimes she even forgot to make him take his blah-tasting medicine, too bad his grandmother was making him do music lessons with Julia Benedicto, *Southern Light,* the name Samuel had chosen for the boat he got when he turned twelve, that was outrageous, she thought, and so was that Julia Benedicto girl, a refugee bringing piano and violin lessons to the island, free Sunday concerts out on the water, she ought to be showered with spray and mist and drizzle during her concerts, that outrageous girl, who was going to listen to her and her virtuosos play a string quartet by Schumann or Brahms, when they sent back all those who came from Cité du Soleil adrift on rafts and old tires, *Southern Light,* Samuel's boat could take them a long way out under the huge sky, thought Vincent, out there, the air wouldn't hurt his lungs and his breathing would be easier, his cough wouldn't rasp so much, he wouldn't be so short of breath, and then later on in bed at night, all the painful symptoms that left him wheezing from dyspnea would be gone, and he would be able to grow up like Samuel or Augustino, he was already more athletic than they were, Augustino hunched over his computers, though just as inaccessible as Samuel, barely speaking to their younger brother and sister, Vincent and Mai, yes, his brothers would respect Vincent, he was going to be a baseball and football player, he had a batter's helmet, a bat, and a glove that swallowed up his hand, he would be head referee or quarterback, anywhere, as long he was in the middle of the action, tight end maybe, but always on the offensive, Marie-Sylvie seemed to have a knack for the tiller, and Vincent dozed off, we're entitled to have some fun, the two of us, she said over the sound of the waves, no need to tell your mother about all this, Vincent, it can be our secret, besides, Mai would be too jealous, and she's way too small to come with us, I've got the right shoes to play, mumbled Vincent sleepily, I'll play tackle, this little trip will be our secret, and no one will ever know, said Marie-Sylvie, no, no one, said Vincent, surprised at how well he could breathe the warm, unoppressive air. The flight attendant in charge of seeing the passengers were comfortable asked Eduardo, accompanying the poor old gentleman, if he wanted to carry his case on board or have her take care of it for him, it was pretty thin, thought Eduardo, not like Jean-Mathieu's usual pile of heavy suitcases filled with art books, now all he had in this one light bag Eduardo carried were some shirts, a blue scarf, and an old-fashioned hat for the sun and the rain, he had told his friends he was travelling light this time, he also had a newspaper and some notes on the Italian masters carefully transcribed in his decorative hand, as though time were no object for Jean-Mathieu, who had just begun to think about Piero de la Francesca in the middle of a lagoon in Venice, in the *Legend of the True Cross,* Jean-Mathieu had noted that Piero de la Francesca had depicted one of the most unusual crucifixion scenes of the Renaissance, so damaged by time, then restored to its original splendour, this work was profoundly disturbing in its fresco of bloody battles, beheaded men asleep on orange plains with a crowing cock, then the back of a man seated on his bed or maybe a pallet, being seized by soldiers carrying a cross for him, and this young man seems to be saying, no, I won't, this cross is not for me, and what are you doing here as I rise on this bright, shining day, no, take this cross away from me, but I hear the cock crow, has the time really come for me to walk toward it? Perhaps the Tuscan painter thought these things, Jean-Mathieu wrote, no one should die so young and on a day like that, do not fix this child to a cross; the work was left incomplete in 1458 and only finished in 1466, so much did the painter recoil before the horror of the cross, no other notes followed these on Piero de la Francesca, perhaps Jean-Mathieu's soul had been wrung by this painting of a young man surprised in his bed by the armies of grief, and in his room at twilight by the water, he had written no more than the beginning of a hasty letter to Caroline, scribbling like a schoolboy, I'm writing this in a notebook just as I leave, but the ink was bound to run in the humid air of the room because he hadn't closed the shutters and windows that gulped in the rain-soaked wind and sea, Eduardo thought; come along, old friend, we're going back to the island and all our friends, he said as they left the house in Venice carrying a small valise with a few books and notebooks, a scarf, and an old-fashioned hat, he felt distraught bringing a mere phantom home with him. He's running off down the steps, no, he's just under the Captain's bedroom window, he's calling to me from the patio, and right there was where Rick stretched himself nonchalantly and laughed, his steel-blue eyes blinking in the sunlight, you can't deny, he went on addressing Venus, your husband was a great one for the drug trade, sure he was a pretty slick artist, but maybe he was really just a gangster like me, I mean, I was his closest associate, in fact he was the one who broke me in, now, wasn't he? And overnight, here we were, importing cocaine and marijuana together, what do you think of this story, Venus? I was young then, didn't have a record for anything except a few petty burglaries that got me a few weeks' time, hey, I was out of work, what would have happened to me if it weren't for your husband? Before Williams fell for you, this house used to be our headquarters, and you should've seen who hung out here, the same bigwigs who ran after you at the Club Mix where you used to sing and dance every night, remember them, Venus? The ones who used to pay you by the day or the night, the buyers, the investors, the lawyers, they were our customers too, but your husband never sucked up to them, because we were the kings, the hashish was unloaded every day in the mangroves, and the boss always had a car for me, great years those were, and we had contacts all over South America, of course your husband had a few enemies, although part of his charm was he didn't scare anybody, he was an artist, even in business, and he never stopped doing his erotic painting or loving music and women, oh, the women, you betcha, we couldn't help making people jealous, the biker gangs weren't all that crazy about us either, young as I was, I still went around with an attache case full of bills, Williams had his yacht, the one sitting empty in the marina, don't you worry, Venus, I never killed anyone, just managed the estate for your husband, his most faithful associate, never even carried a gun, the Captain sure knew how to sail, though, there were a few deals to close and scores to settle at sea that you don't know about, they did find a few dealers done in with a bullet to the back of the head and washed up onshore, it's a world where anyone can be gotten rid of quick, even the invincible Williams, Venus wasn't paying attention to his taunts from the patio by this time, she had the cell phone to her ear and was listening in terror to her sobbing mother, is it possible, she wailed, that Carlos's picture is on TV, it was the one taken at the boxing match with Lazaro at Trinity College, they had separated the two faces, Carlos was a fugitive sought in the attempted murder of his friend, and anyone seeing him was to turn him in, my son Carlos, she moaned, when did it happen, Venus asked her mother, a few moments ago, your father's at the Temple, and he still doesn't know about it, now the whole world will know it, Carlos, my son, accused of attempted murder, listen to me, Venus, your brother is not a killer, I know my son, you've got to defend him, Venus, he might try to take refuge at your place, in that place of sin, Venus, you know your husband was a no-good, and that manor of yours bought and paid for with vice and corruption, but if he comes there tonight or tomorrow, you've got to protect him, defend your bother, I'm his mother, and I'm telling you he's not a killer, save him, Venus, listen only to God's voice, let it be your guide, as she listened to her mother crying, Venus thought of Perdue Baltimore, who had once sung at the Club Mix, then had swiftly put an end to her clandestine activities and gone on to study and graduate in criminal justice, working at the Bureau of Corrections and Probation to pay her way and gain some experience working with juvenile delinquents on the island, Perdue Baltimore would defend Carlos, she thought, she had graduated, she was determined, and according to the island paper, she was about to go on studying science and technology, of course, how could Venus forget her, the pride of her race, black gown and diploma, when she quit the Club Mix she had said to Venus, why don't you come with me, there's nothing for you here, spending the night in holes like that singing for men, you're worth more than that, Perdue had been born in the Bahamas, the daughter of George and Rita Baltimore, and been a success, she called Venus her sister and friend, yes, Venus would consult her, and Carlos would be saved this humiliation and shame; everything Venus loved and protected was safe from the predator's fury, the Captain's

dachshund at the foot of the bed, the iguana whose yellow-scaled back
she rubbed with her fingers, and you had to pray to Jesus in your
misfortune, Mama told her, your father's still at the Temple and don't
say anything to him, we'll get help, Perdue Baltimore's going to help
us, Mama, what was it Pastor Jeremy said in his sermons, didn't he
always say we're never alone, whether in good or ill, in joy or sorrow,
never alone, Venus repeated, drawing closer to the window, where she
saw Richard lighting long bamboo sticks soaked in mosquito repellent
for the evening, he was relaxed and laughing, the belt in his jeans
hanging loosely on his hips, the night fishermen would be drinking
in the waterfront taverns by now, thought Venus, they wouldn't take
out to sea until later, their unlit craft waiting for them in port, and
Rick the predator was still in the garden, roaming around the house,
apparently watching the sea as it lay all about them in a din of birdsong,
and the pelicans flying low without pausing for rest, and the blooming
jasmine would soon embalm the night in its perfume, no, the predators would not get Carlos away from her, just hope it wasn't too late
before she told Perdue Baltimore, he's my brother, Carlos my brother's
in danger. And Renata found herself wondering who among all these
judges, magistrates, and criminal lawyers brought together for four
days in the same New York hotel for a conference on the death penalty,
who among them would inflict this outrage on fifteen-or sixteen-year-
old Nathanaël, would it be the judge who admitted transferring
Jonathan from a juvenile detention centre to an adult prison at thirteen,
regretting only that the accused was too young to be executed, still in
prison for life, Jonathan would have all the time in the world to think
about the atrocity of his acts, deeds of unspeakable cruelty that these
judges and magistrates had to be reminded of; Jonathan was accused
of first-degree murder for beating and stabbing a little girl, just a child,
a neighbour he had often played with in the street, the murder with a
knife and a baseball bat was deliberate and premeditated, and where

was Melissa, eight years old and gone for three days in the woods near Jonathan's house, and Jonathan was seen taking part in the search like hundreds of other volunteers, but where was she? Inside the rippling mattress of the waterbed she and the murderer had shared, Melissa's body was found covered with the same deodorizer and incense as the rest of the room, and does a child really act like that, asked the judge, or are we talking about a monster? A remorseless monster who merits a remorseless penalty, if he were two years older I'd have liked to give him the death penalty, only by making examples can we stem the tide of sordid crime in our country, perhaps teenagers used to be innocent, probably they were until they found out the world was a depraved, perverse place, then they lost all sense of morality and all respect for human life, but when did that happen? When they wrote a final letter to their parents saying they were going to bomb the school and kill their classmates? Or was it when they were popular as athletes but were secretly stealing from their mothers and torturing animals? They live near golf courses, lakes, and ponds with the brightest kids in North America, and live in nice houses, prosperous, fenced, and flowered, with names like Enclave or Oasis, and it's payday, marijuana day, and today the young criminals are loose and looking for fun, in school it's Adolf Hitler's birthday, the young criminal writes in his diary, it's a day to rock-and-roll, it's 420 day, because he's figured out the marijuana code, it's got 420 chemical ingredients, and today Adolf Hitler is reborn in Prairie School, we fully embrace Nazi mythology, this day in April will leave behind a souvenir of blood for all, and I mean all, those who sing in the choir and those taking Bible class, everyone is going to remember how this year is marked in the school yearbook, and they said we were the generation that would never know sacrifice or pain. Whoever said things like that about us is going to get a wake-up call! The judge said, innocent, these kids loved cartoons, especially *Pinky and the Brain* and *Animaniacs,* they were scared in their houses built on solid rock, hearing the coyotes outside howling at night, a lot of them advertised the massacres way ahead of time with graffiti on the school walls, we're gonna kill you all, you've got to die, they had written on that day in April, then finally, they slipped on their summer shorts, skin bared to the uncertain April sunlight for Hitler's birthday, you get tea biscuits at eleven-thirty in the morning, and you don't expect to get killed while you're waiting in line to eat, who was first to spot the pair of dark silhouettes in raincoats on the school roof? Who saw those balloons full of shaving cream explode? Initiation, maybe that's all it was, or an end-of-year prank? When exactly would the school's walls collapse, the day they had free cookies in the cafeteria, the day of the fake bomb or the balloons? Yes, it was cookie day when the floors split wide open and the janitor said, get under the tables and desks, something's very wrong, what's happening, the day the metal lockers blew out, there was running in the stairs, and the library filled with smoke, the day of the jungle, the plot, the cafeteria and library transformed into sepulchres, no one daring to turn and face the columns of fire, to the barricades, the smooth and easy generation that was never going to know sacrifice and hurt, to the barricades, today's Hitler's birthday; cell phones weren't going to save them now, as they called parents or local police from classrooms and toilets, wherever they were hiding, calling out to God, it was written that they would not be spared, what a great night to die, students to the barricades, it's time to pray on this April day, kids, why don't you ask God to wrap you in steel armour, because you're all going down, one by one, why not? Tell us why you should live. Stop crying, you injured ones, it'll soon be over, you'll all soon be dead. Then they took a young student by the neck and shot him, bye-bye, Peekaboo, hey, here's one nigger all by himself in this class, we got to do him, and so died Isaie, who wanted to be first in his class precisely because he was Black, a pipe bomb is easy to make, they e-mailed each other, and you can wipe out a whole group in seconds, the recipe's easy, a screwdriver and nails, and Hitler's 110th birthday attack is on, and we young criminals will go up in flames, like sitting on a keg of gunpowder, days later, bunches of flowers on the snow, and propane gas in a sinister package in a bag, assorted nails, and they had grown up in Deer Prairie and Oasis of Flowers; young as they are, should not these criminals be tried as adults and given the ultimate punishment? Would this judge, so meticulous in his account, be the one to impose justice on Nathanaël, accused of murder at eleven, haggard and handcuffed between two White guards in a Michigan jail? Yes, Renata alone could conceive of it, soon, in scarcely a few years, the decision would be taken just like that, they would reduce the age for executions to sixteen, then fifteen for Nathanaël. Caroline told the hairdresser she wanted something a little younger looking for her date tomorrow, this puffy hairdo made her look older, she said, and she did not like braids or buns, too severe, and certainly not perms, what I want, she said, is a fringe, well, you could say what you liked to a hairdresser, couldn't you, not like Charly, holed up in mulish silence with that snigger and sneer of hers, Caroline's hairdresser was a patient man, who sometimes told her she was beautiful, a little more sporty and not quite so prim, he said, there now, that suits you better, tomorrow I'm getting back together with someone I love very much, Caroline said to this patient man whose fingers brushed her neck in harmless sensuality, it was normal to confide things, she thought, my fears of the past few days have begun to fade, along with those nightmares that seem to stick to the skin, how awful those dream images can be sometimes, she could recall one of a tropical fish with bloody fins swimming toward her, when she suddenly awoke, thinking this was a recurring premonition that had come to her just before a president or senator was assassinated, or some other ominous event, then she would sink into complete devastation, and a crime or a murder would seem wholly

unredeemable, and she would grieve, even surrounded by thousands
of people, her hairdresser understood this, too, when she said, isn't it
awful, my friend, all that we've lost, the two of us, in less than a century? And shrugging, he would say, ma'am, it is sad, I agree, for we've
lost the brightest and best in society, then he noticed her expression
harden, annoyed that someone in his modest situation could speak of
an elite she herself belonged to, for they were her family, she was thinking, touched by a charisma of distinction, what a shock and what an
injustice that, at the height of their powers and in full glory, yet more
insidiously mortal than the rest, they were killed in their limos, struck
down during a speech, that their offspring, in celebrity twos and threes,
disintegrated in the sea in private planes on their way to a wedding,
or a party, or a happy reunion, their suitcases straining under the
pressure of evening gowns and formal wear from the greatest New
York fashion designers, and now drifting with the tide, these beautiful,
clear-eyed young people, bereft of their pearly smiles and thinly veiled,
persuasive arrogance, whose aristocratic bearing was denied nothing,
is it fair, Caroline wondered, that this princely, statesmanly line be
disrupted and laid low by disaster in a matter of hours or days, the
abrasive ebb and flow of the black ocean stilling the silvery voices of
women so young, Caroline was so repulsed by unhappiness, especially
this kind, that uprooted princes and kings and in an instant obliterated all trace of their kingdoms and rank, every bit as anonymous, she
told the all-enduring hairdresser, as those poor people wandering the
seas in rafts, this is what was shocking about it, it forced everyone to
be the same. The hairdresser's attention had drifted, scissors in air,
and it took a moment to respond, how artfully you do this, Caroline
exclaimed, I don't know what I'd do without you, and as she was saying
this, she heard her voice break, and through the crack in it she felt a
stab of pained dissatisfaction, wasn't she really saying to the hairdresser,
you don't like me, you don't approve of me, do you, she thought, and

one day no one was going to hear this voice anymore, just like the silvery voices of the noble young women killed in the fog on the seas and oceans, that is what she was saying, love me, save me from myself, but no one heard. In the hotel room, Claude said to Renata that she ought to hold onto her judge's humanistic objectivity, you could not go feeling sorry for Nathanaël or Jonathan, noble and tender sentiments, of course, but these were simply criminals and had to be judged as such, you could not just moderate the conviction or the punishment that was in store for them, and she listened to him and resented his detachment when she needed him to be flexible and more sensitive to the plight of the mothers of these young criminals, both working mothers, but he was already changing to play tennis before dinner, why not come and have some fun with him, he said, the conference would not reconvene until noon tomorrow, so relax a little before having dinner with friends tonight, as he quietly left the room, Claude noticed how she concentrated, head in hand, on her files, it is not good for her to be so wrapped up in these kids, he thought, as he went down in the elevator, he could still hear her say that there was no way he could help her get over what was going to happen to them, he could not wait to breathe the air of the streets and let sport lift the weight of so many worries from his shoulders; it was the mothers as well, Renata had said, often perfectly innocent women, and wasn't innocence the ultimate depth of every living thing? Even convicted women still keep this feeling of innocence; too bad Renata was not with him here in the cool evening air, Claude thought, we've got to find a way to keep other people's problems from overwhelming us, this innocence Renata talked about, wasn't it also a matter of spontaneously letting go in the joy of the moment and not always worrying about tomorrow? Was it possible to take joy in life, Renata wondered, when one often judged the actions of others, as she did, and knew a woman called the Black Widow had just yesterday gone to the electric chair after fourteen years, all of them

waiting on death row for their turn to be executed, all of them holding
onto a treasure of innocence that had been squandered and brutalized
by a chain of awful events and by an escalation of wrongs that could
not be set right, all they had left was their secret shame and perdition,
when at six o'clock in the morning a harsh light swept their cells, the
ritual began: the meal wagon rolled along the bare cement floor,
through the narrow opening in the cell door, each prisoner reached
for her tray, on Mondays and Wednesdays they spent ten minutes
washing together, one hour a week they would go out in the yard, two
at a time, they had a game of softball, one of them said she had committed the perfect murder against her dentist husband, another, the
Black Widow, said nothing and for a long time professed innocence,
a husband and a companion killed, a son crippled, she had been accused
of all sorts of things and denied them to the end, four thousand days
she had waited in her cell, until suddenly one morning, just after the
wagon had rolled along the bare cement, they said they were coming
to fetch her because it was a long way to the tip of the Florida Peninsula,
she would have to give up the security of the women's maximum-
security prison and her familiar routine, infrequently punctuated by
visits from her lawyer and her family, but for a long time now, the
Black Widow had had no family left, there were just five of them on
death row, and they knew everything about each other, yes, we like
chatting, they said, and watching TV, just a black-and-white one bolted
to the wall, we have to get up on the toilet seat to push the buttons;
we're still women, even if they lock us up and humiliate us and search
us every day, look at these brick walls around us, there's a woman's
touch all over, the rose pink or orange sherbet walls, if they eavesdrop
on us, we plug up the holes in the walls with sanitary napkins, but
what do we do with these uniforms? There isn't much choice, we get
potato-sack dresses or blue shirts with shapeless pants, they want us
to be ugly right to the end. Some buy lipstick and eyeshadow from the

prison canteen, some dream about bubble baths as though they were
a pardon, all hoped there wouldn't be any execution, but the Black
Widow's would happen, and it would be the first in 150 years, she killed
her family with arsenic, she was a quiet one but demonic, she would
take her last plane ride on a Thursday night, polite, she would even
thank the pilot and the officer who spared her the eight hours in a
truck, for the execution, she would dress the same as the men, a stiff
shirt buttoned in front, dark pants, no shoes or socks, her head would
be shaved in the early morning, and execution day would be a day like
any other, that's just the way life is, the prison administration finally
got around to deciding that she could wear eyeshadow, she had not
said much or admitted much, but she so wanted to be remembered as
a good mother, which she claimed she was, and that was it, the death
of the Black Widow, guilty of every crime, and her death was an inexor-
able fact, nothing could stop it, Renata thought, but beneath all these
murders and her apparently just death there lay still another crime, a
woman who had not always been known as the Black Widow, under
this and her other lost names lay a buried treasure of innocence that
no one knew, and along with the executed widow went the names of
other condemned women, condemned for drowning their children in
a river near the house, Susan and Theresa, cold-blooded murderers,
they said, diabolical women whose deeper innocence, although still
present, was no longer visible, so contaminated were they by the shameful gestures born of long-buried shame; and in these same cells along
death row, Susan and Theresa were going to wait a long time, though
even tomorrow made too long a delay, because every bit of extra time
was suspect, yet what did anyone know about them? At eleven, both
of them had attempted suicide, far off that time and long before they
were putting their children to bed at night, while the idea of death had
continued to grow inside them before their children were conceived,
then, when they were born, it returned, fragile, why don't we all cover

144

up in bed together, they had thought, and may the Guardian Angel of Suicides watch over us forever, and may he come with us and sink into the mud of lakes and rivers where no one will ever see us, our shame and pain and secrets gone too. The Black Widow, Susan, and Theresa had all dreamed of dying with their children, although all three had been saved by the instinctive will to live that gripped them at the last moment, and there perhaps lay the buried innocence of these women, Renata thought, the salving eleven-year-old suicide after undergoing acts of shame, the shame of secrets so often accumulated then denied, the wreckage of their lives could be purified only by sacrificing their own children, that was what Theresa, Susan, and the Black Widow believed in this innocence of theirs, and by their deaths, these little ones had shown them the way to a redemption fully paid for in blood; Claude, wearing only white shorts, shirt, and tennis shoes, and feeling an imperious vitality, sent the ball over the net to a player he was not familiar with but wished he could get rid of the thoughts that were still bothering him, this Juan Tevez, an Hispanic refugee in the country for only two years, had managed to stoop so low as to drive a boy of twelve to his wooded campsite at gunpoint and rape him, and had made things worse by killing the child, in a moment of panic, when he saw the police cars around the boy's house, perhaps he had realized there was no point in running away, perhaps he had honestly planned on dropping the boy off at his home after the rape, then had been unable to resist the temptation to murder. Whatever the whole sordid story, Tevez had raised his right hand and sworn before the court that he had raped and killed Timmy, yes, I am Juan Tevez, the young man with brown hair and a well-trimmed beard had said inaudibly, I took him with my gun to the grove of avocado trees on my campground, and I raped him, then when I saw the police in front of his parents' house, I went back and killed him, then I cut him up and buried him under the trees, tonelessly he had recited the capture and the crime, and the parents, the pastor, and all those who had loved the gentle boy cried through the funeral, saying, we'll never have him home again, no never, savagely abused twice over by the Cuban, schoolbooks and exercise books scattered over the wooded campground were the last remaining traces of Timmy in the avocado grove, a sweet boy loved by everyone; Claude wondered if the murderer had been one of those refugees out in the life-saving boats whose fingers the others wanted to cut off to identify him as a convict, then dump him in the ocean. Was he one of those scattered to the wind by a dictatorship, along with the others in the makeshift boats? If men and women who were still sane during the crossing wanted to toss a man like Tevez in the ocean after taking a knife to his fingers, what would a rape in the new country matter to him, when he was already an outcast at home? He was bound to be executed, and the case would bother Claude for a long time, what if his wife was right about this lost innocence, he thought, of course she tended to be misguided and soft, even plain wrong, for Tevez was a free man until he saw the police in front of Timmy's house, so why did he get himself in deeper and go from abuse to killing, maybe these murders would be incomprehensible as long as judges were incapable of clarifying them right back to their darkest origins; what are we all doing here on this large, twin-hulled catamaran Isaac has rented for us, where are we sailing to, Caroline thought to herself, annoyed that the wind was blowing under her cloth hat and getting at her new hairdo, Charly had driven her to the jetty and promised to be back to pick her up in the evening, Charly, all of a sudden meek as a lamb with Caroline, probably just an act, sure, they had both stroked the dog's ears and curly flanks, and Caroline had said, sweet Charly, what would I do without you, and as Charly took off along the shore in the car, Caroline found herself mobbed by all these faces and bodies, some old and wrinkled under their hats, and others young, Adrien had taken her arm as though she could not get up the gangplank by herself, and what were they all saying, my dear Caroline, what a terrible experience, we've been thinking of you, now doesn't your hair look nice, dear friend, said Suzanne, she always notices when her friends are elegant, thought Caroline, heading straight for a seat on the boat, why are they buzzing around me like bees, she stared at them from behind dark glasses, what's going on, there seems to be something special in the air, would the worn planks on this boat hold out through the trip, that's Isaac for you, magnanimously inviting us to his island and calling it The-Island-Nobody-Owns, knowing perfectly well it's his, I hope he has his horse- or golf-carts there to meet us, nothing else there but the sense of isolation, dirt tracks, and no electricity, what a hermit the man is, then when he starts to get tired of his friends, off he goes, his isn't a modest fortune like mine, but I'd still rather stay at home with Charly to read to me by the pool, thought Caroline, it was annoying these insistent looks she was getting, we know how much this affects you, my dear, said Adrien, Suzanne's affable and winning husband, an old friend, he had on a red sweater and white pants, really, it's so hard to believe, I prepared a short speech, which of his poems do you think I should read, my dear? I can hear the boat's motor, are we all here, he asked in his stage voice, and they all turned to face him, tall and majestic, the venerable writer next to whom Caroline suddenly felt slight and frivolous, I did tell him not to go off by himself, but he wouldn't listen, he suddenly said in a low voice, bending his tall silhouette toward her, there, the boat's moving, too bad the weather's a bit rocky, I'd better tell all those young people on the bridge to come and sit down, The-Island-Nobody-Owns, is it far yet, Augustino asked his mother, almost everyone's here together, Mélanie said, your father, your grandmother, and you, Augustino, at last you're all here together with me on this boat, her head was on Daniel's shoulder, he's got a few grey hairs in front, Caroline noticed, apparently Samuel's held up in New York by some dance recital, Mélanie and Daniel have begun to change too, still they're an exquisite couple, when Isaac's gone, I'd love to be their age and above all have their fortune, well, Rodrigo said leaving Daniel at the station, I know, amigo, you'll be back, maybe even before next summer, you still haven't finished writing *Strange Years,* but don't forget us monastery poets or Grazie and Carmello's little girl who brought us lunch at noon in a bowl, or the hospitality of the countess who put us up here and her hundred-year-old servants, ancient like herself, there to iron skirts and dresses and make tea at four o'clock, tasting a carafe of red wine with the mistress at mealtime, this giant castle behind us, with its museum and dusty old artwork, a chapel for the pious woman, down the stone steps each morning came the gardeners who took meticulous care in decorating the castle with bouquets of pink and white roses spread out across patios, lawns, and sunflower fields, day and night, three cats, two rabbits, and a tame hare shared the greenery of this wonderful estate and went to sleep at night on the soft carpet at the feet of the mistress, this is the bucolic atmosphere you've been writing and thinking in, amigo, and now look how sad you are at losing a friend, but you must go, amigo, the train's pulling in, oh, and don't forget those three peacocks on the pink-tiled roof, forget nothing, and feeling happy in the closeness of his wife, Daniel could still hear Rodrigo's voice suddenly through the song of the waves, pitiful the way Rodrigo had to give him the telegram announcing the death of a poet, a world collapsing, happy the man, like Daniel, who had a wife and children he loved and all those books to write, of course both the books and the children could be the source of problems and grey hair over the forehead, what's wrong, where did it come from? Mélanie asked, holding him in her arms, he had lost weight, happy the man who lived through the pain and joy of life without complaining too much, Daniel thought, distraught as he was at the thought that he would never see Jean-Mathieu again, yesterday it was Justin, writer and philosopher, and today Jean-Mathieu, mentor, friend, and father, and tomorrow, what, perhaps Frédéric, who never went out anymore, or Charles, in self-imposed exile in India, the terraces and patios by the seaside were slowly being emptied of the sensitive and subtle thinkers and artists who worked under ticking fans in summer, and if Daniel had picked up a few troublesome grey streaks that would make his son Samuel exclaim, poor Poppa, you'll soon be forty, thirty-eight, Daniel corrected him, not that many years older than you, even if Daniel knew it was not true, there really were quite a few years between them, more than he felt comfortable with, but how did Samuel manage to grow up so fast when his brothers and sister were still children, well, yes, if Daniel had got grey, it was because of his book, this forced retreat in the Spanish monastery and the culture shock that had worn and confused him, he thought; they all had a part in his collapsing morale, the Debris and their macabre rummagings, Garçon Fleur and his skill at the piano, the young Korean and her mastery of Schubert, all those he had met for a brief hour at the summit of their art, out on the grounds or in the workshops at the monastery, where each exalted in his or her performance, Rodrigo too, with his jet-black hair and beret, telling Daniel every morning as he got up, come on, write, amigo, and what of those caricaturists, Boris and Ivan, who had made off with his cigarettes, his phone card, and his pocket computer, what can you do, amigo, Rodrigo said to him, they were brave enough to flee their dictatorships and stand up to them with remarkable satirical skill, often savage, I admit, but look at their background, will you, Boris and Ivan both came from alcoholic parents, and one day both were abandoned in front of the Division of Radiation and Chemical Weapons so they'd become soldiers, it didn't take long before they became young Turks in the Children's Brigade and learned at once to handle a Kalashnikov on the combat training fields at Kantemirovskaya, they lived for training and barracks life, and how proudly they looked forward to their shiny combat boots and fur caps with the red star, then one day they revolted against all that, but never forget, amigo, they're still hungry young wolves, maybe I ought to wait till they sneak off with my writing table, pen, and notebook too, said Daniel, who seemed to be the only victim of these thefts, keep calm, amigo, Rodrigo replied, didn't we have full stomachs while they had to beg for a blanket or a piece of bread? So Rodrigo was right, the same as Mark and Carmen when they snubbed Giotto; they all think art is a scandal, Daniel thought, no longer feeling thunderstruck by Mark and Carmen's latest audacities, with them we enter into a post-volcano, post-crater period of reflection, Rodrigo said, and wondering with his finger to his lips and moustache, Daniel thought it was flabbergasting the way they had already managed to get galleries to buy their inglorious remains, debris, and rubbish. These are installations in anger, Mark said, but the most indecent of their exhibitionist art was the one on corporal art; somewhere Mark must have had a streak of nostalgic respect for a more conservative art form, for he had painted a torso in one line of black gouache on white that harked back to the self-portraits of Georges Rouault, though without the ascetic sobriety and religious torment, yet in a different way, Mark had the same qualities as this candid but unmalicious painter, that's me just as I am, under my hat, said Mark. He and Carmen had painted and tattooed one another from head to foot, here we are, they said, bodies decorated in every possible colour, like in African ceremonies, you know, the great tribal chiefs making razor marks on their skin to celebrate victory over an enemy, Carmen's face seemed to be marked with sunflower seeds then covered in yellow spots of paint, her arms with a blue puzzle, and her breasts bringing forth reddish thorns and a plumed bird, and on her stomach it said, write on me, this bespattered, contrived, falsified, misleading, and decadent corporal art exhibit that Mark and Carmen had made themselves into seemed to be a nightmare that Daniel was awakening from only now on the boat, finally calmed by Mélanie at his side, he had rejoined her, kissed her, and loved her the night before, and now they were all here together, Augustino just a few steps away, intrigued by the omnipresent camera Caroline had already succeeded in explaining to him, why didn't his mother give him one like this, then Mélanie briskly stood up and shook her hair in the wind, Daniel was worried she would not sit down beside him again, he would have to tell Augustino that, no, parents could not always buy children everything they wanted, he thought to himself as well how unpredictable Mélanie had always been in love, always an active woman, a fighter, she had protected her inner space from everyone, including her husband, her delicate profile resembled her mother's, who at that moment was coming toward her on the bridge, as the boat bounded over the waves, Poppa, how many more hours' sailing before we get to The-Island-Nobody-Owns, asked Augustino, it isn't even in sight yet, Daniel explained, but these little islands with sandy beaches, where they've planted Australian pines, are called Man's Island and Woman's Island, but The-Island-Nobody-Owns, which actually belongs to your uncle Isaac, is still a long way off, Mélanie was saying to Esther, I know my children will always remember Gandhi's name, because he was talked about so much in the old century, his generosity and compassion were revolutionary, and he'll always be remembered preaching before the ocean, he loved using symbols like water, salt, and fire in his sermons, and his style was hypnotic, he knew how to hold a crowd that revered him and called him Mahatma, Great Soul, utterly tolerant, peaceful and nonviolent, cut down by violence, yet transcending matter, but would Rosa Parks and her calm defiance of White racists, when she refused to change places in a bus in Montgomery, Alabama, would she be remembered, Albert Einstein would be, of course, Mama, he didn't just create the theory of relativity, he knew how to be popular, but it took him too long to get around to fighting for peace, much too long, yet they called him the pioneer, the cowboy, the bright intellectual superstar, because he did indulge his narcissism, he loved having his picture painted, clowning in front of a crowd, playing the violin well, or just being a mathematician with his head in the clouds, still, little by little, we found out about his doubts and fears and hidden shames, was it simply that he realized, through an atomic war, that science was fallible and could be responsible for the devastation of millions of lives? Naturally, we will remember Nelson Mandela and the liberation of South Africa, but about a woman suffragette called Emmeline Pankhurst, a mother of four like me, who founded a women's movement in 1903 and crusaded long and hard for the vote for women, ridiculed by all, most of all Winston Churchill, who called these women harpies and cats whose whining should be ignored, but still in 1918, said Esther, thanks to this courageous woman, women got the vote in England, you see, Mélanie, perhaps nothing is in vain, no act of bravery, Mère had listened to her daughter and thought, what passion, what vehemence, she's more faithful to herself and her ideas than I was all those years, Jean-Mathieu's unexpected end could also be mine at any moment, but Mélanie has years ahead of her, strange she couldn't resist having one more child, Mai's barely started to grow, and Mélanie's embarking on a new life with her, and is this what she really wants, this extension of herself into a more comforting world when it's already so hard to bring up boys, having had little to do with her own sons since the divorce, it was easier dealing with her grandsons, and her sons had always sided with their father the surgeon, pretending to know nothing about their mother's intellectual success, her museums and noble causes, but what was most on Esther's mind for the moment as she stood next to her daughter on the bridge, was to keep the straw hat tied under her chin with a ribbon from flying off any way, or worrying about whether it made her look silly, she threw Mélanie off balance when she said, Mélanie, do we really have to remember every single one of the petrified century's irreparable failings and faults? I think our children will have ideals of their own and not just the ones we leave for them, then, as her daughter looked at her in alarm, she fell silent, but Mama, Mélanie said, my children must remember absolutely everything, we can't live a decent life without knowing what has gone on before us, isn't that what you always used to tell us, Mama? Did I really say that, mumbled Esther vaguely as she clamped down on her hat, I must have been very young then, Mélanie, but you'll see, with time you'll find you don't want to think about all the madness in the world, these past few years, all I care about is horticulture, the trees in our garden, Russian liturgical music, why Russian music, Mama, exclaimed Mélanie, you've always liked Italian opera, oh, I like everything, I always have, Mère said, but I've learned to lower my ambitions and desires, she knew Mélanie was unpleasantly surprised by this, maybe it was this ribboned hat too, her daughter was not sure she liked it, and Mélanie's attractive mouth enlarged with a bitter wrinkle, is it true, Mama, that now you think about nothing but your trees and flowers? They're deserving of it, said Esther, all these trees deserve my attention and all my efforts to keep them alive in a world where every day nature is ravaged, have you ever really looked at the gold tree, or the Caribbean tebebuia, there are two hundred varieties, they grow in the streets, sometimes they're called silver trumpets, and in summer they grow yellow or pink blossoms, the Bombay tree in our garden is also very nice, and the weeping banyan around the older homes, Bombay tree and weeping banyan, Mélanie repeated, as she silently reviewed in her mind scenes from the old century's horrors, Pol Pot's Khmer Rouge soldiers plunging their bayonettes into the bellies of pregnant women tied to trees, the waves of Josef Stalin's killings that she had often imagined, Stalin who so hated the eau de cologne worn by his official murderer, Lavrentry Beria, which did not drown the odour of crime and rape, but let it filter through, almost like an innocent accident, then, as though wanting to nuance her thought, Mère said to Mélanie, I just saw Daniel's father, Joseph, alone in a corner of the boat, crying, I know he loved Jean-Mathieu as much as anybody, and Mélanie wondered, should I feel guilty for not crying too that Jean-Mathieu's time has come? I don't really know, but I can never see Joseph without remembering the Polish cousins, the rabbi kneeling, arms raised before his aggressor as though begging for mercy, Uncle Samuel shot in the winter dawn, and a vain pope compacting with evil, yes, I remember everything, Mélanie, and the ravings of Adolf Eichmann recorded for posterity in his diary, I was part of a team of horses, capable of turning neither left nor right on my own, the coachman's will was the only possible direction, genocide, I look at Daniel's father, and I understand his tears, said Esther, I know it isn't only Jean-Mathieu, this is all still written in his soul and body, the cry for help he carried from Poland for all of them, recently a postcard was found that by some miracle had escaped the censor, *ich liebe dich*, darling, I love you, dated 1943 and written in a warm hand, and the testament Joseph carries in him to epidemic, torture, degradation, gassing, and execution is written in invisible ink, Esther said. But why can't I go with Adrien and Suzanne to visit Jean-Mathieu on his island, Frédéric asked Eduardo and Juan, as they wrapped a dressing-gown around his shoulders, is it because my balance is off, what is Charles doing away in his ashram in India all this time? Why has everyone gone away? Let's go out under the acacia bower, Eduardo suggested, Juan can read the newspapers to you the way he does every morning after your bath, I just want the music reviews, Frédéric said, the rest is sound and fury, thunder and misfortune, that's what Charles used to say when he lived here, reading the papers is like letting a stone monster into your house, why am I wearing this robe, isn't it hot enough to do without clothes? Tonight there's a Cuban musical creation at the theatre and Rachmaninov's First Piano Concerto, Eduardo read, although Frédéric was not listening, when I was sixteen, I could play

all three brilliantly, he interrupted, and there are the new children's
concerts given on a sailboat by Julia Benedicto, Eduardo went on, a
symphonic suite by Prokofiev, I know, said Frédéric wearily, Isaac
organized those benefit concerts, and though he may be a great master
of modern architecture, what does he know about music? Where have
they all gone, where are Adrien, Suzanne, and Jean-Mathieu, he
repeated pitifully, you're not telling me the truth about Jean-Mathieu,
I know it, he said shrugging off the robe, which fell in a heap at his
skeletal feet, my bones have been tormenting me all night long, every
time my legs rubbed together, so what about the legendary Isaac who
hasn't invented a single thing? Why haven't you told me when Jean-
Mathieu's due back, I might as well go back to bed and never get up
again. I'll go get the coffee and cigarettes, Juan said as he picked up
the robe and put it back on Frédéric's shoulders, it's a bit windy, but
it'll be a nice day, Frédéric replied, out on the sea, this same wind
would be quite nasty, has Ari finished his sculpture for the airport
garden out by the ocean, it'll be immense, Juan said, he's shaped it to
suggest waves and dizzying lines between sky and sea to invite us to
rest and reflect, Mère saw Mai with her dress down around her ankles
like an abandoned waif, without a hat and sunburnt in the face, playing by herself on the bridge as though forgotten by her parents, who
on earth had dressed her that morning in an old-fashioned dress with
a broad, white collar, her hair was dishevelled as though it had been
cut crooked, neither Daniel nor Mélanie seemed to be paying any
attention to this unkempt child, Esther thought, each had things to
do, neither looked after the little girl, Mai, named after a little Mar-
tiniquan girl who had disappeared without a trace in Ontario, and
who could you accuse of being negligent, was it Marie-Sylvie, who had
fallen short of her duties, was it Mélanie, or was it Mère who had not
seen her that morning when she woke up, thinking Mélanie was with
her, surely when Mélanie was home, she spent an hour with her

children in the morning before they left for school or kindergarten, the idea that little Mai was somehow cut adrift by everybody troubled Mère, and she reproached herself for having got Mélanie so involved with politics, then Daniel spotted Mai all by herself and hoisted her onto his shoulders, but to Esther, this wavering attention of a father to a little girl he saw so rarely seemed quite disappointing and selfish; Mai's big, round eyes up there on her father's shoulders, overlooking a wind-whipped sea, held an unfathomable sadness behind her blinking eyelids, Poppa, I want to get down, Poppa, she cried inaudibly, as distant as the call of a mourning dove in the troubled air; with a knife in the pocket of his Bermuda jeans and a Davis .32 semiautomatic under his checked sweater like some schoolbook, Jamelle headed toward Trinity Elementary School, where he had just recently been learning to write, not like the other students, who already knew how to write and spent the afternoons getting to know the computer, not for him the rows of stiff backs before the screen, yesterday the teacher had sent him home for stabbing Ingrid Maurice with his pencil, the principal had called him to the office and asked him why he was so aggressive, because he liked Ingrid Maurice, who was only seven, but who didn't like her, Jamelle had replied, and didn't he want to learn to read and write like all the other six-year-olds in his class, and why didn't he bring lunch to school, didn't he have a mother or father to look after him, and Jamelle had just whimpered without saying anything but remembering the semi-automatic his father kept hidden under the cover of the sofa, where Uncle André and his eight-year-old brother, Benjamin, slept huddled together, his mother had often said the gun would be better out of the house, but everyone was afraid Uncle André would burst into a vengeful rage, like when he beat Jamelle and Benjamin and their mother on days when the cocaine shipment arrived, on days like today, when his uncle beat him, Jamelle's head would burst as he walked to school, with the shouts of Uncle André

and his mother arguing till dawn, but what really terrified him was
when they went off and left him at night and he woke up alone on his
dirty mattress, why did they leave him by himself like this, in this
scary place with covered windows where you couldn't even see daylight,
every crack and opening in the windows and walls had been covered
with paper and cardboard, and Jamelle was never ready for school in
time because he could not see in the dark to find his clothes and books
scattered around, that was when his head began to boil as though it
were on fire, where had they all gone, his father, mother, and Uncle
André, tears starting down his cheeks, he called out for them, while
the hen and her chicks clucked their way through the ruined cars and
the broken bottles that quarrelling men had left behind during the
night, what was there to be afraid of now that the sun was up and he
would soon be in the schoolyard at Trinity Elementary School, and
through these windows you could see everything inside, the stars the
students had drawn and stuck to them, Ingrid Maurice reading, and
she was so good at it, but she had told him he was a no-good son of
André and Tara, and they were no good either, Jamelle coming to
school without washing or bringing lunch, standing out there under
the palm tree by the window with the coloured stars stuck on it, he
could see her reading attentively with her nose in her book, petite,
slender, with a firm, determined, unsmiling mouth, she had been
stubborn enough to learn to read before the others, and if by any
chance she had raised her eyes in his direction, there by the palm tree,
she would not even have seen him, or maybe she would have faced
him down, who are you anyway? This time, he was the strong one, he
could watch her unobserved without her saying, go away, you creep
me out with that checkered shirt of yours, you and that shed full of
chickens you live in, she could not say anything, and she never would,
because he was going to stop her first, before she turned her page even,
Ingrid Maurice was going to understand he was as strong and as violent

as Uncle André, even if at home no one cared about him at all and they beat him and twisted his arms and kicked him to the ground every day for no reason, and his mother never did anything to defend him, and if Ingrid Maurice thought she was better than him just because she was White, she was wrong, because Jamelle was stronger than her, even if he wasn't quite six, too bad they'd stopped him from scratching her face with the tip of his pencil, but this morning he was going to get her for saying, who do you think you are, every time she looked up, he had a knife where no one could see it and a gun under the thick cotton shirt, today he was going to be just like Uncle André laying down the law at home, when he said, you just do what I tell you or you're all gonna catch a few of these bullets in your bellies, and you, Jamelle, beat it, you ain't wanted 'round here, can't you see your ma and your pa shootin' up, moron, go on, can't you see no one wants you here, after that, he had kept running for a long time like a hunted animal, till now, at last, he was afraid of nobody, all he had to do was get his gun out of his jeans and it would all be over, the laughing and the meanness, the grade-one Ingrid's neck was bent, delicate and white like the throat of a pigeon, and Jamelle's head was boiling, maybe it was from walking too long in the sun without even a glass of water, or sleeping in filth for four days without washing, caked up with the musty smell of enclosed spaces, windows that let through neither air nor light, and suddenly the shot went off at Ingrid's white neck, and there was nothing Jamelle could do to stop it, what an awful noise, it made Jamelle drop the gun at his feet, in the grade-one room, all the students stopped their reading, what was that, and Jamelle was already running and running, not knowing which way he ought to go, one way was the principal's office, the other was a game room where they would spot him right off, but why, what had he done, nothing except maybe walked too long in the sun, and now he was going to throw up, what he did know was that Ingrid was not going to be saying, you creep, I don't like you, even if she had been first in the class to learn to read, that much was settled, he thought, she'd never ever hurt him again, maybe it was sort of like the point of his pencil, maybe he had just scratched her, and since she was a girl, of course, she'd go and tell the principal, then he'd be punished all over again, and his parents would beat him, he hated them all, Ingrid Maurice too, and he thought how furiously he hated them as he swallowed his tears. Mélanie was disappointed that her mother would interrupt a discussion as important as this one by saying something like, dear, if you want to live longer in this life, you have to learn to forgive, she was depressed by this admission of her mother's, because oppression and cruel humiliation should never be spared punishment, the defilers of the human form should never be absolved, was it really her mother talking like this, at the same instant she heard Mai yelling in her father's arms and ran toward her, thinking how happy she was to have wanted and made a daughter, looking back, it seemed like a more serene time, when she did not protest quite as much, she was more physical then; before Mai's birth, she had spent a lot of time on the water with a master from Puerto Rico who taught her total relaxation of mind and muscles in the silence on the silken buoyancy of water, as though just one arm could have held her up, Mélanie and her daughter had floated, gently undulating, together in warm, effortless liquidness, and thinking that perhaps Mai, so close, could hear her breathing and take comfort in the total absence of bodily movement, Mai would be born with relative ease, stroked by the sea-exercise and her mother's suppleness, while waiting for Mai, Mélanie had learned to breathe differently in the water, she had danced and swum her yoga every morning, Mélanie remembered this routine, more fluid and supple in the expectancy of life, all the more because Vincent's birth had been so difficult, as though she had left him at birth with a hesitancy to live, perhaps because she had been breathing badly and working late into the night then, but

Mai would be the child of flow, and peaceful tides, of breathing guided by meditation, Mai was going to be a force of nature, a marvel of the Coral reef waters, like a dolphin floating and playing in the waves, the vastness of the ocean was her opening onto the world, such that the space where she now found herself seemed awfully small, but how would the world look at her birth, painful and bloody? Then all at once this life of Mai's did not belong to Mélanie any more, except in that cry, Mommy, where is Mommy, yet this flesh, this water, these salt tears in Mai's eyes were still a part of her own flesh, clothed in a love just a little less encompassing, a little more exterior and remote, Mélanie was aware that her love for her daughter was changing, her feelings and sensations cooled slightly by day-to-day living, which no longer felt the same as when she had been expecting, because earlier, before the birth, what a frenzy of love it was that had swept them up, Daniel, Mélanie, and the couple they became whenever, for a few days at least, Vincent's health was stable, it was the fragility of that breath of his, however stubborn, between life and death, that had probably drawn them so tightly together for so long, in a single leap of pleasure suddenly after Mai's birth, they had been dismayed to be no longer as close to each other, how distant those nights seemed when they had slept in each other's arms on the beach, or when they would drink from the same glass on the lit terraces, or danced till dawn, first an orgy of senses and nocturnal outings, then a man and a woman as united as they could be, but distanced by their professions, lovers no longer quite the same as when they had merely been parents ruled by the same obligation; will this boat ever get us there, Suzanne asked Adrien, who was a little annoyed at his wife for being so amiable and smiling on such a tragic day, though, as she had explained to her husband many times, there was no doubt in her mind that death did not exist, life did not actually cease, a departure for a higher sphere perhaps, but no definitive extinction, a theory of hope that was also shared by Jean-Mathieu, she said, and how exactly is that going to bring Jean-Mathieu back here among us, Adrien thought, disdainful of Suzanne's holding ideas different from his own, imperturbable in her serenity, the proof, he said severely to her, that this theory is just a woman's fantasy or a poet's dream is that here we are transporting our friend's ashes in a box on a boat, but that doesn't mean, she replied, that our dear friend's soul may not survive his bodily ruin, Jean-Mathieu is merely waiting for us on the other side, God how long this trip is taking, when are we due to get there? Ah, there's a sweet boy up on the bridge serving drinks, Jean-Mathieu would have liked that, well I don't, Adrien retorted, I suggest you remain sober, Suzanne, we are talking about a dead man, not the bon vivant we once knew, but he's still the same man, always our Jean-Mathieu, she said joyfully, you're such a bore, Adrien, and as the boat jolted her from her torpor, Caroline reached for her camera and took a picture of Mélanie, then Mai, it was the easiest thing to do, use the camera as a screen to shield her from the fact that she was Jean-Mathieu's companion in other people's eyes, they were forever telling her how sorry they were for her, although none of it was true, the two had not even said good-bye to each other, she was not even sure, how could she be, that he was even gone, except of course to Italy, and he would return dazzled, naturally he would, as he did from every trip, cane in hand, elegant as ever, it was more pleasant to photograph the child than the mother, what a wonder of unruly delight, a wild, untamed little creature, come on, smile, Mélanie said to Mai, who offered Caroline her best pout, they never listen at this age, Mélanie said to Caroline, but Caroline noticed above all the child's melancholy expression, almost hostile, she thought, suddenly frozen, as though from the shock of violent pain, at the memory of Jean-Mathieu, wasn't he just about to touch her shoulder and offer his usual good advice, my dear Caroline, mightn't you be wrong about that girl Charlotte, what if she's less honest than you think? But the echo of that dear voice quickly dissipated, and Caroline saw herself as a little girl again, as peevish as Mai in a dress with a white collar, who on earth had dressed her so ridiculously, once again she saw herself torn between her Black nurse and her rich and venerated mother, a mother who, like Caroline herself, had been much loved by men, Caroline thought that if she was badly dressed, it must have been the fault of the servants who got her ready in the morning, then she began to wonder how she had reached this ultimate stage in her life, old age, when young Mai, her moody ghost, could still cause her pain, and what if I was wrong about Charly, she found herself thinking, I'd just be another one of those detestable, senile people who receive neither pity nor respect, but if Charly is not entirely honest, she can still be useful even if she doesn't like me, I'll smother her in presents if I have to, has she called the maid and the secretary to have my pictures sent for the exhibition in New York, you had to admit she wasn't practical, and Charly was a poor companion, thought Caroline, all that she really seemed to give freely and indifferently was pleasure to those who delighted in the elasticity of her feline movements on a beach or by the pool, in a time when it was the fashion to be a little less uncovered, perhaps she would have inspired the photographer Helmut Newton with her worn charm and androgynous grace. But every time she turned her thoughts to the models who had posed for him, the trouble exuding from the lascivious faces of these young women, their eyes masked in black, mouths half open over fierce teeth, Charly's face superimposed itself on Mai's, removing all trace of innocence and seeming ill-natured, inaccessible, dark, and androgynous, dressed in a black smoking jacket, cigarette held in one hand by purple fingernails, the other slipped into her trouser pocket in a pose of studied nonchalance, like Newton's subjects captured in their tender opacity, utterly sensitive, yet impenetrable, Charly's forbidding fixity allowing no foothold, Caroline thought, what was this interrupted ecstasy in her, some effect of her cult of drugs and fetishism that escaped Caroline? In her icy heart, Charly was hatching a passion that was still nameless, dangerous and hidden from Caroline, and Adrien asked again who those boys and girls were tanning themselves on the bridge, and Suzanne replied, readers of Jean-Mathieu, admirers of his work, we're on this boat to hold a wake, what would Jean-Mathieu say if he saw those body-worshippers up there? He'd be delighted, Suzanne, there's nothing on the horizon, not even a fishing boat, but I think we've slowed down, haven't we? See those white clouds over there, Adrien said, we'll be able to spot sea turtles, flying fish, and colonies of birds on the mossy rocks, I know you'll be glad you came, Adrien told his wife, who was always out on the ocean, it's paradise there, you know Isaac chooses only magical spots for gathering his friends, Suzanne's aversion to the water was childish, and Adrien's condescending tone wounded her, but his mind was on other things, he had to think of the speech he would give on the wooden stage in an hour, would he quote Socrates or Bossuet, his gifts as a speaker had earned him tributes at universities and colleges, but all it took was a breeze in the pines and spruces or one face grimacing with boredom in that rarefied audience, for they weren't all as serious or thoughtful on this trip as they ought to be, and it would all turn into the confused ramblings of a teacher before unworthy students, Socrates, Bossuet, or perhaps a poem from his own anthology, no, the young people on the bridge wouldn't appreciate that, these ignorant youngsters didn't seem to realize that Adrien was their national poet and awash in prizes and honours, Suzanne had chosen a flaming red sweater and white pants for him to wear so he would look both impressive and young at the same time, and Suzanne said Caroline with her camera seemed suddenly so frail under her wide hat, what had been going on in her life for someone usually so sociable to refuse to see her friends, Adrien and Suzanne had not seen her for months, yes, Socrates would do it,

Adrien decided, Suzanne, Caroline, and all the other women didn't interest Adrien much, but in Jean-Mathieu he had lost the company of a superior spirit, no, these women are slight, and no one else around him, not even his wife, Suzanne, appeared to understand the magnitude of it, nor the adolescents sunbathing naked on the bridge, not one of them could sense or even guess at how much Adrien would suffer tomorrow and every day of his life for the departure of Jean-Mathieu. Marie-Sylvie told Vincent on the jetty, this is where the big catamaran will dock at sunset, when your parents and their friends get back from The-Island-Nobody-Owns, then looking up at the waving flags and zigzagging gulls in the sky, he asked her if he could go and play now. Under his arm, he had the wonderful present his father had brought back from his trip, it was a super-deluxe metal scooter, so simple and compact that the twentieth century called it The Blade, can I race along the wharf, he asked, and before Marie-Sylvie could answer, she could see he was already off, his foot on the narrow metal step on four wheels, and on his way to the sea, Jenny's letter was in her hand, but she never took her eyes off him, you mustn't be worn out when your Mamma comes back, she called to him over the wind, you know she doesn't like us being this close to the water, I won't tell anyone, he called back exultantly, it'll be our secret, *Southern Light*, I can see Samuel's boat *Southern Light* over there in the marina, we'll have to fold up the scooter and head back to the house soon, she told him, your mother's going to call from the boat later, and I've got to tell her your morning medicine went down properly, *Southern Light, Southern Light*, Vincent yelled, see, I'm not choking anymore, he said, happy at being able to shout into the wind like this, even if the world contained multitudes, this was a civilization devoted to the well-being of a few, Marie-Sylvie thought, and little by little all heaviness and awareness of other people's misfortunes were banished from them, it was a cordless civilization where Marie-Sylvie could always be reached and asked with severity, what have you been doing today, have you taken good care of the kids, by remote control, she could be made to feel guilty of anything at all, the air was saturated with messages that for some carried an easy comfort that could never have been imagined before, while for others it carried the more and more crushing weight of their deprivation, it was a devastating cursedness that ate at Marie-Sylvie's lonesome heart, because Jenny was her only friend, and her letter said she would have to go off and fight a devastating epidemic in the Sahara, she was begging for help, Mélanie, so full of humanity, could perhaps go and join the struggle, thousands of kids were being orphaned in Mère months, Jenny wrote, right here with me are Napiri, Douglas, and Immaculee, a two-year-old girl, there are more than ten million like this, and their numbers are increasing, and when they throw up bile like Napiri did this morning, oh, what can I do with motherless children who will be wiped out by sickness too, nobody wants them, and they are hounded from their villages, a lot of girls under fifteen are already pregnant and have the virus on top of it, there is no help anywhere, and we have so little money to help so many lives, it's a slow death for the proud people of Africa, talk to Mélanie, the only thing that's any good now is active support, real help from individuals, there are newer and newer cases every day here, but Marie-Sylvie wanted them all just to leave her alone, no more letters from Jenny, I'm just Marie-Sylvie de la Toussaint from the City of the Goddamned Sun, me and my crazy brother thrown out to sea like lumps of wood, wreckage in a washed-up boat, and saved by a priest, my brother still wanders around the streets by day, howling and sacrificing birds and animals to his sect at night, I can't take any more of him, none of us can take any more of any of it, epidemics, disasters, floods, and wars, so here we are trying desperately to get away from the rivers of mud, houses burnt or washed away, nowhere to go, climbing trees and hauling up what little we have left for safety, what else is there, even the trees will sink under the mud and muck and rivers and floods, no more cows, no more bridges, no more roads, clinging to the tops of stripped trees, that's us, hanging from the branches with our miserable stuff, a bike, an oar, some melons, waiting for the helicopters and planes to spot us, waiting for someone to throw out a net, manna from heaven, then for hours nothing, nothing at all, but now she felt Vincent's hands on her face and noticed the scooter lying on its side on the stone jetty, you're crying, why are you crying, he asked her, surprised by tears from the one who usually consoled him when something was wrong, he spread his hands over her face, the way his mother did when he was short of breath, and said as she did, it's alright, it's all over, that's what Mamma often says to me, it's alright, it's all over Marie-Sylvie, he gently chided her, how could a child like Vincent lighten her sadness, she thought taking his hand, well, it was time to fold up the scooter and head back to the house, because Mamma would be calling soon, she said, and anyway, they couldn't stay out there on the jetty with the wind rising, now Suzanne could see The-Island-Nobody-Owns and Isaac on the wharf signalling them to close in, then motorboats were sent to pick them up, one by one, and they gathered on the sandy tracks that were all his employees had cleared on the island, an unfinished, rustic-looking structure stood among the sky-pointing pines, what a glorious day, Isaac exclaimed as he kissed Suzanne, and you're all here with me, then he used his cell phone to call up some golf-carts, so the elders, as he called them, would not have to walk at low tide all the way to the end of the island, where the sea made its reappearance, but he was amazed to find that none of his friends wanted to skip the tiring walk, he had to beg them to get into the carts, still Suzanne politely declined, saying she'd walk to the house with the young people, Caroline did relent, though, and admitted to being a little weary, finally a few others followed suit, and off they went in the clear blue day, the younger ones laughing and running behind the carts as though it were some sort of holiday, which prompted an annoyed shout from Adrien, do you think it's funny that Jean-Mathieu has passed on, these young people have no respect, he grumbled to Caroline, and she saw his hands tremble with indignation against the white linen of his pants, they're just young, and they didn't know Jean-Mathieu the way we did, she said, breaking the silence and marvelling at the beauties of the island, for despite its wildness, it all seemed so harmonious and peaceful, Isaac, sitting next to her, slender legs protruding from his khaki shorts and bare feet in old, gaping leather shoes with fine white sand pouring from them, pointed out the beaches and bird colonies of his island, the multicoloured egrets, the ash herons that Jean-Mathieu so loved when he came to write here a few days each month, and Isaac's voice fell, moved and saddened, I thought of him first of all when I bought this island, I thought of the peace and solitude he'd find here, now will it still be the same without him? Caroline noticed that Isaac was still a handsome man, as her gaze wandered over his haggard profile from behind her dark glasses, if they were still saying Jean-Mathieu was not coming back, it must be true, though she still could not believe it, the great egret actually reproduces on this island, and look at the small white herons and their vaporous plumage, they wander along the shore in flocks hunting frogs, the ash herons live in pairs and nest in the trees, he continued, ah, there's my wooden platform, Adrien thought, as they drew closer to the unfinished building and the patios and verandahs where the workers were drinking beer in the sun, Isaac had thought of benches, chairs, everything for the funeral elegy, little wind, a perfect day, I would definitely say Jean-Mathieu was a master of Socratic humour, a wisdom, and a freedom of mind that resembled the philosopher's, you had to love yourself before you were able to love others, as it says in the Delphic precept, "Know thyself," Adrien was thinking, and the warm sea air rose in his nostrils and temples, this youthful streak of Suzanne's can be so annoying, though, just like her daughters when she poked barely noticeable fun at him, it was insidious having all these women around, you had to admit Suzanne wrote as well as he did, she hadn't published much, but some of her poetry was admirable, tonight, when they were alone, he would tell her so, oh, look, here are the white *Plumbago capensis* flowers, Isaac pointed them out to Caroline, it's a tree I had brought from South Africa, and coral vine, the chain of love, it's also called, which I had transplanted fom Mexico, and the passion flower tree, we're awash in trees and flowers from all over the world, *Hibiscus tiliaceus*, China rose hibiscus, and by the time all these graceful plants and flowers are fully developed, where will all of us be, Caroline wondered, in the earth? Put off by the thought, she pulled her camera out of her bag and began photographing the trees Isaac pointed out to her, how agile you are, dear, he said holding onto her elbow as the carts delivered their passengers in front of the building and lush gardens not yet cleared and attended to, Isaac's listless workers were basking in the sun, I wonder where he gets them, they don't impress me, Caroline thought, does he import them from Mexico and Brazil too? They all seem to be of mixed race, and then it was time for Jean-Mathieu's ceremony, everyone seated around her in virtual silence in the cool shade of the palms, and Adrien had climbed the steps to the platform, then she felt the sadness hit her, who had brought her to the edge of this gulf where she would see Jean-Mathieu no more, she wondered, and what was Adrien saying up there about Plato and Socrates, what has a discussion on Socrates got to do with Jean-Mathieu, now was the time to accept that he would never again be with them, she realized, here was Adrien speaking reverently of him in the past tense, he was, he had, he loved, he knew, he understood, he was loved, he loved, he was gone for refuge to the home of non-being, Adrien said, he who so loved the sea in his books, whose soul was rooted in the waters of Halifax, and then later travelling from river to river, as a youngster at first, then the illustrious passenger on liners whose history he wrote, I did love him, Caroline thought as she listened to Adrien's powerful voice, we were different, incompatible, from different social classes, and still I loved him for being more sensitive than I was and loving others when I didn't, and she had the impression she was filming Adrien even while she was listening to him speak, by turns he was solemn, pompous, and touching, one by one, he called them up to the stage, friends, poets, artists, and even a fuzzy-haired girl, and all expressed gratitude to a great poet and defender of feminism, who helped improve the situation of women writers in society, wasn't Caroline responsible for feminizing Jean-Mathieu intellectually, just as she had always worked for women's equality in all the relationships with men she had loved, yes, all the things they had to say, she thought, the self-assurance with which they talked about Jean-Mathieu, sparked flashes of jealousy and sadness in her, as they spoke, she stared at the box on the stage at Adrien's feet, where he could easily bend down and lift it, this seemed to be a sinister ritual they had dreamed up just to rub salt in Caroline's wounds, her eyes came to rest on the box containing a travesty of Jean-Mathieu's body, unimaginable dust, ashes as fine as the sand oozing out of Isaac's shoes just now, some blue or grey substance that was not Jean-Mathieu, nor anyone, and would soon be scattered on an island that seemed to be a refuge for exiles only, a place that symbolized not only the end of Jean-Mathieu's life, but their abominable exile from paradise, every one, and every one was, like Caroline herself, a pagan sensualist who loved the earth too much, she calmed down as Isaac bent his stooped shoulders to take the box respectfully from Adrien and then headed toward the sea, where Daniel was waiting in a fishing boat with oars raised in the low tide, but just then, Isaac's shoes got sucked in by the viscous waters of the mangroves, and soaked to the ankles, he held the box out to a young blond fellow, who skipped out from stone to stone, light as the air that day, Caroline observed, then placed it in the boat, which he had to push several times to get off the sand, then it was done, and a wave lifted the boat, and as it rocked, they all saw Daniel stand up and spread the lavish treasure of ashes that should have belonged to her alone, and that had been taken from her with her soul, and she held this thought, she knew the others would need to laugh and have fun, that they would be thirsty for champagne and wine, and at that instant she would think of Charly for the first time in hours, I hope this time she wasn't lying when she said she would be on the jetty, nothing was less natural than death, it was a shame she was too hurt to cry, and this island of Isaac's really was splendid with those ash herons and silver plovers on the bank, perhaps being heir to a huge fortune, like Isaac, was the only real freedom in this world. Everything else, Caroline thought, was one unavoidable misery, including the desperation of loving and wanting to be loved in return, which so often was the cause of our disillusionment. In a few days, I'll go back to Sri Lanka, Asoka wrote to Ari, and the orphanage at Sri Vajira, there are three hundred children there, all of them war orphans, impossible to bear listening to their songs about losing parents to such atrocities, I'll also go to the girls' orphanage in Ratmalana, and I hope, dear Ari, that you are still meditating every day, you asked me what the word *samsara* means, it's vast, and in the Buddhist dictionary it means "sea," the ocean of life with its ceaseless waves pushing on toward progress and self-improvement, so often it causes us to be born, to die, and to be reborn to reach Nibbana, rebirth is our constant hope, like the alternation of waves, I'm trying to translate the unsayable, that which cannot be sensed except in spiritual terms, still, Ari, here is approximately what *samsara* means, you must be at peace with yourself and not want to advance too far too quickly, it would be unwise, dear Ari, because, after all, you are the being that you are, and lightness is what you must seek, and Ari stepped around *Soldiers' Beach*, his giant steel sculpture attached to his truck as it planted itself

in the sand, an event Ari had planned as a celebration of nature, a
sculpture with magnetic waves, constantly alive, that would integrate
itself completely into sky and water, a marker for refugees and a beacon
to navigators that would light up at night, and he and his sculptor-
painter friends were working on a whole garden of monumental
sculptures by the sea, an artist and an artisan, Ari was nothing if not
that, he thought, and art was a vehement act of protest, his own, but
what would the final need or usefulness of it be when Ari compared
his life with Asoka's, could art be the path of lightness he meant,
Asoka's humility, his pilgrimage on the road to the orphanages in Sri
Vajira and Ratmalana, begging in the villages in his orange robe, and
how could Ari envy him his humility, when he himself was proud, he
had the pride of all artists in isolation, the conflicting tensions of all
his desires, his sculpture would vibrate in air and water, a call like a
gong, all would hear its harmonious music of wind and waves, in the
nineteenth century, the painter Winslow Homer had depicted a man's
heroic struggle with the sea, and today, young sculptors like Ari had
to survive with it, purify its ever-threatened waters, its fauna, the
sculpture, the sea, the sculptor, all were at risk together, and everyone
everywhere knew the invincible fate that confronted humans, and it
was Richard, Rick, that saw him first, as he laughed and turfed him
out of old Williams's boat, what are you doing in the Captain's Viking
Convertible, kid, you know the price they've put on your head, that's
what I noticed, Carlos, that scruffy hair of yours, then like a hunting
trophy, he had shown him off to Venus, saying, look, the hunted murderer, believe me, I'm real sorry he's your brother, because I'm going
to turn him in, hidden there in that Viking Convertible like that and
dying of thirst, here's your brother, Venus, and Venus's shouts tore the
air as she ran toward her brother, but it would not do any good, because
she had always known Rick was a turncoat and an enemy to her race,
he sneered at Venus as she appeared at the bank asking him to let her

terrified brother go, now is it my fault if I found him while I was washing the Captain's boat the way I do every evening, and there he was,
your ugly brother, a killer maybe, I'm the one who caught him, Richard
went right on, he came up late through the mangroves with the oyster-
fishing boats, eh, boy, thirsty and hungry, aren't you, he said, shaking
Carlos by the neck of his shirt, don't you know the police are looking
for you? The sun was going down, piercing the heat-haze over the
ocean, the swimmers and surfers on their sailboards liked this time
of day, when the air was cooling, no one heard Venus yell as she ran
to her brother on the beach, God will look out for us, Perdue Baltimore,
she'll help us, thought Venus, this evening, tonight, and there was the
gun under the pillow of the Captain's bed, hers now that she slept
alone, Rick was a traitor and didn't deserve to live, if she gave in to
him, she'd be able to kill this monster the Captain had let into their
house, Venus's face clouded with impotence and sadness, then her
eyes wandered to the red-lined horizon, Perdue Baltimore, she thought,
she'd help them all, for as Pastor Jeremy said in his sermons, the meek
are beloved of God, and God would protect them. The sun will be
down soon, Marie-Sylvie said, seated side by side with Vincent on a
wooden bench on the jetty, and the great catamaran still isn't in sight,
your parents are going to be late for dinner, hear that, Vincent, it's the
water lapping at the boards on the wharf, the wind's coming up again
tonight, the pelicans and gulls are excited and nervous, don't tell your
parents we came to wait for them here, the two of us, they don't like
you being near the water when the wind is up, don't mention Samuel's
boat, *Southern Light,* either, don't tell them about us at all, it'll be our
secret, and just on the verge of sleeping in Marie-Sylvie de la Toussaint's lap, Vincent could hear Julia Benedicto's concert on the yacht
anchored a little way from shore, her youth orchestra was playing a
symphonic suite by Prokofiev, hear that awful music, Marie-Sylvie
said to him, they have it all in this town, those Cubans, but the rest of

us from the City-of-Hell-Sun, we, but she kept the rest to herself, putting her hand on his warm forehead, they must have gone another way
if they're this late, you seem to have a bit of fever, what would your
mother say if she knew, Vincent was asleep already and did not answer
her. It was time for bed, but where were Mama and Papa, Deandra
and Tiffany asked, nobody had eaten yet, and that brother Carlos
storming through the twins' lives, what had he gone and done now,
Pastor Jeremy said, taking the girls to school, this morning, wearing
their costumes for the Celebration of the Planets, Deandra was the
moon and Tiffany was the sun, weren't these twins ashamed of always
fighting, Mama had sewn the costumes, biting off the thread with her
teeth, but that was before they saw Carlos's picture on TV, then the
fighting stopped and they went outside, stepping on empty cans with
their white Sunday shoes, for Carlos wasn't picking up the recycling
anymore, the holiday ribbons hung freshly pressed from their heads,
usually at about this time, Deandra would be eating quickly, so as to
go out and play in the street until night fell, and Mama would always
end up scolding them for not listening to her, no one in the house did,
not even Pastor Jeremy, and the twins were her cross to bear, she said,
they were sneaky and disobedient, still, when you think about it, Pastor
Jeremy said, God has given us beautiful children, if only they weren't
girls, what are we going to do now? Do you want to play dice or bil-
liards, Deandra asked her sister, and it was Tiffany who saw Polly first,
no, it was me, Deandra said, or we both saw her at the same time, no,
it was me, said Tiffany, I see everything first, I'm the one who fills her
bowl with water every day, Deandra retorted, so I'm the one who saw
her, and there was Polly between the bowl and the cooler, the same
cooler that had sat in the yard for so long that the roosters and hens
lived in it now, Polly was back and sniffing at her empty bowl, then
the full one Deandra gave her, with her humid muzzle she took in the
burnt smell of the yard, she was hungry and thinking of Carlos, his

angry voice and caressing hands; Deandra and Tiffany joined in a joyous clamour, shouting over the flowering thorn bushes at passersby, Polly's back, Polly's back! And the Apostle said to Our Lady of the Bags, go, child, and I shall pray for you, for where I am going you cannot come, it was the evening following a hot day, but the little girl thought night would fall quickly on New York, and she had better go down into the subway's entrails, the mezzanine far from the rails would be a safe place to sleep, because the platforms would be a gathering place for the Lords of Chaos and the Vampire Gargoyles carving their trademark *V* on their victims' foreheads, if the Apostle had been nearby, Our Lady of the Bags would have slept with him in a real bed, and she wouldn't be trembling with fear in the mezzanine of a subway station, the Apostle in a white robe sullied by neither snow nor mud, travelling so far to shine his light on the Shenandoah miners, while she sat all alone on the steps with her Bible upside down on her knee and the pleats of her kilt, from the steps of the passageway she heard steps and voices, these were the Lords of Chaos and the Vampire Gargoyles, had they just finished a mutilation and massacre in an animal shelter, was it the beginning of night when they got ready for their rituals, the chief said that to commune with spirits you had to drink blood and rape a virgin, this was the rite Our Lady of the Bags feared from the vampires loosed in the night, hunched up tight against the wall of the mezzanine, she thought no one would see her here or smell her odour, an odour of wanderings, happy were those like her who were abandoned, who had escaped from institutions and asylums of torment, knowing neither how to read nor how to write, happy they, like her, who would see God, and why hadn't the Apostle, who was a real man, taken her with him, she would have been the drop of rain clinging to his clothes, nothing at all, just as long as he didn't call her retarded and he saw how clean and pretty she was, even if she did live in the street, no, the Lords of Chaos wouldn't be attacking her tonight, for the past few days they had not been attacking anyone with white skin anymore. Charly was able to pull her Ecstasy out of a hole in the back of her doll, though some wore it hidden in one of the many coloured beads around their necks, swallowed it, then sucked on candies in the shape of pacifiers, as they dripped from bathing in the sea or the pool near the dance floor sheltered in a blue tent flapping in the wind, Charly danced, and she was free to get back into her familiar trance until dawn, later would come the down, the blues, the Terrible Tuesday depression, waking up in anxiety and an enfeebled state, the end of a party for everyone, alone, disoriented, hair plastered with sweat, the magic disappeared, out over a raging sea, stars shining to the electronic music of the Atom, the Orchestra of Chemical Sisters, Charly danced in her white jeans embroidered on the sides, the Charly everyone loved, the name they called out every night on the dance floor, and tonight for sure she'd do it again with no rhyme or reason, but they would all be overflowing with exuberance before tomorrow's evil mood and headaches came on, and sometimes in the transcendence and bewitchment of the music, they all formed one body of many races, Charly thought, the trance really came from the rubbing together of all these skins, it was a mediatic trance, you could hear the music sawing apart the hemispheres of the brain with its thumping regularity, you could hear the rushing of blood in everyone's veins, and forgotten was the slavery of Charly's ancestors, who had lived in kennels on the masters' plantations, with Caroline, Charly could get rich, and the two of them would savour fruity evening cocktails and white rum in expensive restaurants and on terraces, pale Lebanese ale at lunch, and although it made no sense at all, Caroline would manage to resign herself to the fact that a little bit of hashish might do her good and rejuvenate her with Charly, who was stunned with voluptuous living, Caroline wasn't the same anymore, just a plaything in my hands, Charly thought, this eight-hour trance was really going to last, a long-lasting pleasure injected along with the music and the dance, this time, she would not be worried during the night about the Terrible Tuesday fear being painful, arms and hands would be intertwined with hers, a face dripping with acrid sweat like hers, skins sharing their secretions at night, a tongue taking a yellow pill from hers, a nose shifting the ring in her left nostril, all these faces and bodies would whip her pleasure into a supreme ecstasy, then suddenly, as a prelude to Terrible Tuesday, someone would start throwing up, a boy would rip off a shirt, but tonight under the stars, Charly was going to party all night long in the wind that whipped the warning flags of danger at sea, Caroline's boat was going to be late, and Charly could dance for a few hours more before its lights showed in the night. Just over there was where the Hudson flowed into the Atlantic, as night wrapped itself tighter and tighter around New York, Renata walked through the streets beside her husband, maybe he was right, she thought, when he reminded her about the judge's objectivity, and tomorrow the meeting on the death penalty would pick up again, it was reassuring, she thought, that they remained two loving creatures able to treat each other with tolerance, sharing their enjoyment at the end of the evening, Renata was always being swept up in some furtive affair with a stranger that her husband did not know about, and it was better he never knew, for the mind of a woman was too complex for him to grasp, strange, she thought, to love with such healthy passion but such unreconcilable love, Franz was here in this city so well suited to his temperament and his tumultuous fervour, as well as his often sublime artistic qualities, he would be conducting an orchestra in the next few days, and there were raves for his musical direction, apparently at a concert in Tel Aviv, he had placed two pianists from warring countries side by side for a Schubert performance, sometimes the diplomacy of art could give birth to a hope of peace, this was how he put it to the journalists, she recognized his unreasonable hope of changing the world that had kept Renata with him for so long, and after so many years apart, how could they be so different, so reserved, Franz no longer his old crazy self, because deprived of his madness and wildness by age, she had ceased loving him, when they met again from time to time, he might say, as he had when he was younger, haven't you got a little bit older, would he be tender and sensual or distant, her husband had warned her about him, he often warned her in advance that things were going to happen to her, yet she went ahead anyway, but the hurt wouldn't come from Franz, Claude had mentioned that too, but from what she was going to witness tomorrow and a few years from now, Nathanaël handcuffed and going to the death chamber between two White officers, eleven years old for now, with eyes begging not to be killed and hair that would catch fire during the execution, he might have been Renata's son, born of her irreconcilable love of life, and despite the rough waters, the great catamaran came into a port that glittered in the night, and Suzanne joyously sprang to life as though returned to the land of the living, where Jean-Mathieu's soul would immediately return to them, it was shameful, she thought, to have abandoned him to the dark waters like that, alone and without friends.

ACKNOWLEDGEMENTS

The original French version of this book was written with support from the Conseil des Arts et des Lettres du Québec, and the English translation with the assistance of the Canada Council for the Arts, both of whom receive my deepest thanks. Thanks are also due to Marisa Zavalloni for her constant support during the writing of the original, as well as to Art Kara, Bhante Wimala, and Bill T. Jones for their inspirational words and thoughts.

— M.-C. B.

MARIE-CLAIRE BLAIS is the internationally revered author of more than thirty books, many of which have been published around the world. In addition to the Governor General's Literary Award for Fiction, which she has won four times, Blais has been awarded the Gilles-Corbeil Prize, the Médicis Prize, the Molson Prize, and Guggenheim Fellowships. She divides her time between Quebec and Florida.

NIGEL SPENCER has won the Governor General's Literary Award for Translation with three novels by Marie-Claire Blais: *Thunder and Light, Augustino and the Choir of Destruction*, and *Mai at the Predators' Ball*, which was also a finalist for the QWF Cole Foundation Prize for Translation. He has translated numerous other works and films by and about Marie-Claire Blais, Poet Laureate Pauline Michel, Évelyne de la Chenelière, and others. He is also a film-subtitler, an editor, and an actor. He lives in Montreal.

LIST

The A List

The Outlander Gil Adamson
The Circle Game Margaret Atwood
Moving Targets Margaret Atwood
Power Politics Margaret Atwood
Second Words Margaret Atwood
Survival Margaret Atwood
These Festive Nights Marie-Claire Blais
La Guerre Trilogy Roch Carrier
The Hockey Sweater and Other Stories Roch Carrier
Hard Core Logo Nick Craine
Great Expectations Edited by Dede Crane and Lisa Moore
Queen Rat Lynn Crosbie
The Honeyman Festival Marian Engel
The Bush Garden Northrop Frye
Eleven Canadian Novelists Interviewed by Graeme Gibson
Five Legs Graeme Gibson
Death Goes Better With Coca Cola Dave Godfrey
Technology and Empire George Grant
Technology and Justice George Grant
De Niro's Game Rawi Hage
Kamouraska Anne Hébert
Ticknor Sheila Heti
Waterloo Express Paulette Jiles
No Pain Like This Body Harold Sonny Ladoo
Red Diaper Baby James Laxer
Civil Elegies Dennis Lee
Mermaids and Ikons Gwendolyn MacEwen
Ana Historic Daphne Marlatt
Like This Leo McKay Jr.
The Selected Short Fiction of Lisa Moore
Furious Erín Moure
Selected Poems Alden Nowlan
Poems for All the Annettes Al Purdy
Manual for Draft Age Immigrants to Canada Mark Satin
Rochdale David Sharpe
The Little Girl Who Was Too Fond of Matches Gaétan Soucy
Stilt Jack John Thompson
Made for Happiness Jean Vanier
Basic Black with Pearls Helen Weinzweig
Passing Ceremony Helen Weinzweig
The Big Why Michael Winter
This All Happened Michael Winter